PRAISE FOR

KHALED AND JAMILA

A NOVEL BY ANAN AMIRI

"*Khaled and Jamila* is a deeply authentic story, an important addition to the canon of Palestinian American literature, and a delightful read. We root for this family as a collective and are wowed by the bravery they each exhibit in the name of love."
—Laila Halaby, author of *The Weight of Ghosts*

"Anan Ameri's Palestinian family saga, *Khaled and Jamila*, is both a vibrant and heart-wrenching look at the challenges of intercultural marriages, and at the same time, it's a testimony to how marriages endure both with and despite lack of family support. A fast read that stays with you."
—Nora Lester Murad, educator and award-winning author of *Ida in the Middle*

"Written by one of Arab America's fiercest advocates and humanitarian leaders, this beautiful novel is a heart-wrenching family saga that travels across many decades and even more memories. A must read."
—Susan Muaddi Darraj, author of *Behind You Is the Sea*

"After writing two memoirs Anan Ameri has given us a gift with her first novel. *Khaled and Jamila* revolves around the lives of Palestinians. The story begins in the West Bank during the fifties, a few years after the Nakba. This book explores family, religion, community, love, war and race. It's a novel in which characters are defined by borders and boundaries that are personal as well as geographical. It's about each new generation finding their own way."
—E. Ethelbert Miller, writer and literary activist, 2023 Grammy Finalist for Spoken Word and Poetry

"*Khaled and Jamila* is a moving story of intergenerational heartache from Palestine to the US. Anan Ameri weaves together dramatic events connecting the personal to the political, highlighting the hypocrisies and crushing disappointments that course through families. A moving reflection on how we repeat the same mistakes across generations."
—Evelyn Alsultany, author of *Broken: The Failed Promise of Muslim Inclusion*

"Spanning decades, *Khaled and Jamila* is a moving and ambitious novel about family loyalties and what one is willing to risk in the name of love. The story opens with Khaled, who leaves his hometown of Al-Bireh, a village in the West Bank of Palestine, in the late 1950s to study at the University of Michigan-Ann Arbor, where he falls in love with a fellow student named Elizabeth. The novel then follows multiple generations as they grapple with the political challenges of their time, all the while exploring the complexities of race and ethnicity."
—Ghassan Zeineddine, author of *Dearborn*

"Anan Ameri's novel, *Khaled and Jamila*, is the heartwarming story of a Palestinian-American family grappling with the challenges of cross-cultural marriage and intergenerational strife against the backdrop of Palestinian dispossession and the constant search for justice. Ameri takes us on a journey that explores the highs and lows of Khaled's search for belonging and meaning in his adopted home, as well as his relationship with his daughter whose life choices put his values and convictions to the test. A great read!"
—Diana Abouali, director, Arab American National Museum

KHALED AND JAMILA

BY ANAN AMERI

Interlink Books

An imprint of Interlink Publishing Group, Inc.
Northampton, Massachusetts

First published in 2025 by

Interlink Books
An imprint of Interlink Publishing Group, Inc.
46 Crosby Street, Northampton, MA 01060
www.interlinkbooks.com

This book is a work of fiction. Any resemblance to individuals is merely coincidental.

Library of Congress Cataloging-in-Publication data:
ISBN-13: 978-1-62371-584-7

Printed and bound in the United States of America

*To the rising generations,
for whom the whole world is family.*

CONTENTS

PART I
KHALED

August 18, 1967

August is always the hottest month in Al-Bireh, not July like it is here in Ann Arbor. But according to my mother, on the day I was born, a few hours before her water broke, the temperature dropped unexpectedly. Not only did it turn out to be the coolest August day in the history of the city, it also became the happiest day of her life. August 19, 1941. I was her first child, and although she had six more after me, she insisted that nothing made her prouder than when people started to call her Um Khaled—the mother of Khaled, and call my dad Abu Khaled, the father of Khaled.

My mother always told me I was the most beautiful newborn she had ever laid her eyes on. Of course, I was more than happy to believe her, although she was only seventeen then, and I'm not sure how many firstborns she'd seen. And being a boy supposedly added to my charm.

My Aunt Zainab gave me a small, twenty-one-karat gold medallion engraved with a verse from the Quran, and the hand of Fatima with a blue bead attached to it, to protect me from the evil eye.

Both were always visibly pinned to my clothes until I was in second grade. After pleading with my mother, she let me pin them on my underclothes. When I got a bit older, she bought me a gold chain to put them on, and insisted I wear it. "You can tuck it under your shirt," she told me. "No one will see." That was do-able in the winter, but definitely not in the summer. Later, my sister told me my parents would argue. "For God's sake, he's a boy. He's too old to wear this," my father would scold my mother. "But they will protect him from evil eyes." "You treat him like a baby. You spoil him." "He's good in school, he's kind and looks after his younger sister and brothers. Everyone loves him. I don't see how I spoil him."

Neighbors would say, Ismallah, he is beautiful, just like his mother. And in many ways, I've always favored my mom. I'm glad that I have. People often comment on the contrast between my parents. They say she is beautiful, gentle, and smart, unlike her husband, who is smart, but not that nice or refined. They'd also say he is at least twenty years older. No one actually knew how old my father was. In fact, he insisted that his birth certificate and passport were not accurate.

So I was my mother's favorite, but she wouldn't admit it. "I love all my children the same," she always insisted. But all my siblings knew it. "You love Khaled more," they'd complain.

"How could you say that? A mother cannot love one child more than the other." Then she would recite an Arab proverb: A mother loves most her sick child until he is healed, her young until he is grown, and the absent one until he returns home.

My father was never someone who showed much affection. In that way, he was no different than other men like him of his generation.

But I heard from many relatives about how happy he was that his firstborn was a boy. If that's true, I never heard it from him, or even felt it when I was growing up. Usually, he just expressed concern that I would turn out to be a sissy or have feminine attributes since I hung around my mother. I also liked my aunts more than my uncles, except for my father's younger brother, my Amo Omar.

My father was a successful businessman, and he wanted me to work with him after I finished college, and to take over his business someday. He'd say, "People like their sons to be doctors or engineers. But there's nothing like owning your own business. If you're good at it, like me, you will make more money and be your own boss."

As I got older, around thirteen, my father expected me to spend my summers working with him or with some of his friends who owned businesses. "Working is good for you, it makes a man out of you," he'd say. "But you must also get a good education, develop a good work ethic, and learn how to run a business. I'm counting on you, my firstborn. If, la samah Allah, something happens to me, you are the one to take care of your siblings and mother. God gave you everything: looks, brains, a good family. And I'm going to send you to the best university in America. There is no reason for you not to succeed."

So I tried my best to live up to my father's expectations and follow the path he set out for me. But there came a time when I needed to start making my own decisions.

And that was when everything started to fall apart.

1
A FATHER'S FURY

Al-Bireh, summer 1956–winter 1957

Um Khaled paced her house back and forth for over half an hour, wishing her son Khaled would get home before his father. She kept asking her son Majed, a year younger than Khaled, about his brother's whereabouts and when he saw him last.

"Yamma, I already told you, I don't know. There were so many people. I did look for him before I left, but I couldn't find him, so I came home alone."

Um Khaled was worried, not only about her son Khaled but also about her husband, who always came home in a foul mood when there was a demonstration, claiming it hurt his business. Abu Khaled did not want any of his children to be involved in politics. He was especially concerned about his eldest son, Khaled, who was fifteen at the time and had been curious about events around him since he was twelve. Recently, as political rallies had skyrocketed, he had been asking his son Khaled not to give in to the temptation or propaganda of "irresponsible" organizers, which included a few of his own nephews.

"Where is that stupid son of yours?" yelled Abu Khaled the moment he walked into the house.

Um Khaled came running to meet him.

"What did he do now?"

"He went to the demonstration. We can't just let him do whatever he wants. We—especially *you*—need to be more strict with him."

"To my knowledge, everyone in town went. They're celebrating Nasser's nationalizing the Suez Canal. It's a big day. He's young. Let him be."

"These days, there's always a reason for some stupid political event interrupting our lives. How many times will I have to close my business, and the kids have to leave school? Don't be so naïve. Do you know who's behind all these events? It's the communists and anarchists. They're always looking for a reason to organize and recruit young people. I want my kids to stay out of politics and focus on their education."

"Abu Khaled, *Salli A'la Al-Nabi*. It's summer, and schools are closed now. Why don't we wait for Khaled to come home and tell us what happened."

"There's no reason to wait. People already saw him. I asked my friend Abu Ahmad to give him a summer job, hoping it would teach him to be responsible. And what does he do? He leaves work to join a demonstration. I already called Abu Ahmad, and he told me that Khaled went. But what pisses me off even more is Abu Ahmad himself. Can you believe it? He told me he had no problem with Khaled leaving work. I don't know who is more stupid, him or Khaled. I should have known better not to send him to work there. I should have had him work with me. That way I could keep an eye on him."

"To be honest with you, I'm glad Khaled is not working with you. You would be fighting all the time. He's a good kid; let him find his way. He is at a sensitive age."

"Stop defending him. I'm sick of you telling me, *Poor Khaled. Let him find his way, He's a young man now*. Well, I don't see him acting like a man. I was the eldest of my siblings, just like him, and I was only ten when I started working at the neighborhood bakery..."

Although she had heard her husband's story a hundred times, she let him vent.

"In the summer, I had to work at the bakery and in the fields to help my father. And I was a very good student, better than your spoiled son. But I had to quit school at thirteen to help support our family. Ten kids, along with my dad's parents, all together in that small house with three rooms. I was seventeen when I left for America. I worked my butt off to help my father raise the rest of my nine siblings. My father was a kind man—he never yelled or hit any of us. But I would never dare to question him or talk back to him..."

By the time he was done, beads of sweat had gathered on his wide forehead and nose. She simply turned on the ceiling fan, got him a fresh handkerchief, and then sat next to him with her hand resting on his.

"Abu Khaled, your health is more important. Getting angry is not good for you. Let me get you something to drink."

Without waiting for his response, she hurried to the kitchen and came back with a small silver tray with coffee and water. As he was about to finish his coffee, she went back to the kitchen and brought him fresh lemonade with mint leaves she just picked from her garden. Abu Khaled swallowed his lemonade in two gulps, closed his eyes, and, within minutes, started to snore. His wife gathered the empty glasses and disappeared into the kitchen. Her gloomy face spoke of worrying about what was to come.

~

When Khaled finally arrived home, his father was still sound asleep. He walked quietly through the living room, not wanting to wake him, went to his room, and softly closed the door.

When Abu Khaled woke up, he called his wife, "Where is he?

Isn't he home yet?"

"Yes, he's here, in his room, studying."

"Layali, go get your brother."

"Habibi Abu Khaled, listen to me. Khaled is a young man now. Please don't yell at him. At this age, they tend to listen much better if we talk to them in a calm way. Trust me, when we yell at them or punish them, they rebel."

"Okay, okay . . . " he said with a gesture of dismissal as he saw his son entering the room.

"Khaled, this time, I'm going to talk to you man to man. But remember, I am the father here, and you need to listen closely to what I say."

Khaled nodded and waited.

"You are not allowed to go to demonstrations or hang out with these communist friends of yours. If you do, not only might you end up in jail, but it could destroy your future. Do you understand?"

"Yes, Yaba."

Khaled's eyes focused on the floor for a few seconds. But then he cautiously looked up at his father.

"I wasn't the only one. All my cousins and the neighbors' kids were there."

"I don't care about them or their future. You are my son, and you'd better do what I tell you. And don't you ever talk back to me. Now get out of here."

~

After that day, every time there was a demonstration (and there were plenty), Khaled's father would warn him not to participate. He also discouraged any discussion of politics in the home, especially when the children were around, which at that time was difficult not to do.

In November of that year 1956, Khaled's eighteen-year-old cousin Basil came to visit. While the two of them were chatting in Khaled's bedroom, Basil asked him, "How come I don't see you at political events anymore?"

"Well, you know how my father is. He doesn't want me to."

"You don't have to listen to him. We are living in a historic moment. Not only did Israel join England and France and attack Egypt for nationalizing the Canal, but they also occupied Gaza, and today, they massacred one hundred and eleven Palestinian civilians. We're planning a big demonstration to protest. You should come."

"I don't think I can. The last time I did, my father was so angry he warned me never to go to any ever again, or else. He even told me to stay away from you and called you a communist."

"That's bullshit. All the high school and middle school kids are coming. Don't be a coward. Come and bring your brother Majed. I better leave before your father comes home. See you tomorrow. Right?"

As Basil was leaving the room, he turned to Khaled.

"Your father should be proud of you. I can't believe that he and my father are brothers."

The two brothers couldn't have been more different. Basil's father, Omar, was very supportive and proud of his children's activism, and often joined them. He was fifteen years younger than Abu Khaled and had had a much gentler upbringing. But that was thanks to his older brother, who had joined many of Al-Bireh's young men who were immigrating to the US in the early nineteen hundreds, and were sending money back to their families.

While Abu Khaled returned to Al-Bireh before the outbreak of the Second World War, many of them stayed in the US and continued to send money. That's how Al-Bireh, along with surrounding villages, prospered; land exchanged hands, and many new homes were built, renovated, or expanded. With his sharp business sense, Abu Khaled invested a good portion of his money in buying and selling land and in construction materials. Abu Khaled also managed to convince a Palestinian from Jerusalem, whom he had befriended in the US, to start up a food import-export business together in Jerusalem, the area's commercial and trade center. They started to supply many of the food merchants and stores and just as he'd done in his construction materials business, it didn't take long for Abu Khaled to expand to many towns and villages surrounding Al-Bireh and Jerusalem.

The night after his conversation with Basil, whom he loved and admired, Khaled couldn't sleep. In spite of his fear, he decided to go to the demonstration. He also asked his younger brother Majed to come along. But in a small town like Al-Bireh, news traveled fast. When their father found out, he came home with rage oozing from his red face.

"Where is he? I am going to kill him this time. And don't you dare tell me how I should handle my children!"

Then he turned to his son Majed.

"I hear that you went, too."

"Khaled asked me to go with him," he responded with a faltering voice.

"How many times do I have to tell you not to go? You listen to me, not to that idiot brother of yours. Where is he?"

"I don't know."

"What do you mean you don't know?" He moved toward his son, his hand lifted, ready to slap him.

Majed stepped back and started to cry.

"Stop whimpering like a woman."

Then he turned to his wife.

"You tell me to take it easy on them. Are you happy now?" But before she had a chance to respond, he instructed her, "Go make me some tea. I'm tired of your sons. Nothing but trouble."

A Father's Fury

As Abu Khaled sat down to drink his tea, Khaled walked into the living room. His father jumped out of his seat, sending the coffee table and teacups flying, crashing on the floor, leaving broken glass and liquid on the walls, furniture, and the expensive Persian rug. Everyone in the room froze in their seats. Before Khaled had a chance to comprehend what was going on, his father had already pulled off his belt and hit him on his back. Khaled's mother jumped up and grabbed his father's arm, screaming.

"What are you doing? For God's sake, stop it!"

Khaled's brother Majed started to cry again, and so did sister Layali, who came running from her room when she heard the yelling.

"Let him try to hit me again and see what happens," Khaled told his mother. "I swear to God, if he touches me, I'll hit him back. I am tired of him trying to control my life."

"Khaled, you can't talk like this to your father."

Abu Khaled moved toward his son, belt in hand.

"What did I hear you say, you'll hit me? As he lifted his arm ready to hit his son again, Khaled ran toward the bathroom. But his father caught up with him and slammed the door behind them.

His father's curses, "May God take you! You are not my son!" mixed with Khaled's cries, rattled the house and all its inhabitants while the mother banged on the door, sobbing.

"Abu Khaled, this is crazy. Stop it! You're going to kill the boy."

Soon all six siblings gathered close by, crying.

"Go to your rooms now," their mother said. Then she asked Majed to take the younger ones away.

Abu Khaled came out, all soaked with sweat and red faced, as if he just took a hot shower. He pushed his wife away.

"Stop crying. You let him do whatever he wants. He's ruining his future. Ruining my business and the whole family. I'd rather kill him than allow him to do that."

He went into their bedroom and slammed the door while his wife went to rescue her son. Tears ran down her face as she helped Khaled to his feet and slowly walked him to his bedroom. Layali stood by her mother crying

"Go get me some ice and a couple towels."

Khaled's arms, legs, and back were all marked with belt welts. He cried from pain and humiliation. His father had hit him and his brother Majed before, but never with the intention to inflict physical harm, as much as to humiliate them and to demonstrate his authority.

His mother and his sister Layali alternately tended to him. For three days, Um Khaled would cut aloe leaves, scrape the gel, and gently soothe her son's welts. Khaled refused to leave his room and hardly ate or drank. His mother would beg her husband to talk to him. But his response was always, "I don't give a shit about how he feels. Actually, I don't care if he lives or dies."

Once Khaled started to feel better, his mother told him not to challenge his father.

"Ya ibni, you should never talk to your father the way you did. To say you would hit him back. Poor man, he has worked so hard all his life. All he wants is to give you and your siblings a good life. You should be more understanding and respectful."

"He is the one who should be respectful of what I want. It can't always be his way."

Um Khaled just shook her head, not wanting to get into a long debate. She was tired of being caught between her husband and her son.

Ten days after the incident, their father came home and asked his wife to bring Khaled and Majed to him.

"You and Majed are going to St. George School in Jerusalem, where they will give you a good education and teach you some manners. None of this bullshit politics. You understand?"

Without waiting for a response, he went on.

"I already hired a taxi to take you in the morning and bring you home after school every day."

His decision to pull his two sons from public school and enroll them in a British private school in Jerusalem infuriated his wife, but she said nothing. Khaled did not say much either, but anger was brewing inside him. He hated his father, and all he really wanted was to run away.

Later that evening, Khaled complained to his mother.

"You just stood there, not saying anything. Why can't you stop him? The school is too far, and I don't know anyone there. I'm in the tenth grade, and he still pushes me around as if I'm just a kid."

Majed, who was in the ninth grade, was also furious, but he directed his anger at his older brother for convincing him to go to the demonstration.

As Khaled started going to St. George School, he became uncomfortable around some of his cousins and the neighbor's kids, most of whom went to the town's public schools. He even tried to avoid them when there was a demonstration or rally, which happened a lot. One time, on his way to see his cousin Basil, he passed by a group of kids hanging out. Before he had a chance to greet them, one of the kids asked him, "How come we don't see you anymore?"

"I've been busy studying."

"Bullshit," another one answered. "He's too important now. He goes to that British school in Jerusalem."

"That's not true. I would have loved to stay at my old school. My father insisted I go there."

"Oh, his Yaba won't let him stay, poor boy..."

"That's a good Yaba's boy," another chimed in. "A real Kit Kat boy from the rich, private school."

The group started laughing.

Khaled wanted to defend himself, to tell them how much he hated his father and his new school. But he couldn't. Their hurtful words added to his already wounded spirit. Little did they know how much he would have liked to join them.

One night, as the family was having dinner, Khaled mentioned that he felt sorry for some students who were dismissed from school for a week because they participated in a rally celebrating the final withdrawal of the British and French forces from the Suez Canal.

"What did I hear you say?" barked Abu Khaled. "Feeling sorry for them? Do they think they can change anything? And they're in a British school. Did they expect the school be happy with what they did?"

His father's lack of sympathy pissed Khaled off, so he decided to take a chance and respond while trying not to get his father any more riled up.

"Yaba, can I ask you a question?"

"What?"

"Do you think that we always have to accept things as they are, or as they are forced on us by Israel or Western powers? How are things ever going to change if people don't try to do something about it?"

"I can't believe my ears. How could my own son be so foolish? Where did you learn to talk like that? And what do you know about 'Western powers?' I am warning you, Khaled, get rid of these stupid ideas. And don't you ever dare participate in any of these demonstrations or protests. You better not let me catch you talking to these stupid communists or so-called leftist cousins and neighbors. I'm not sending you to a private school and paying all this money for nothing."

Over the following days, more demonstrations and rallies rose, lasting a whole week. One day at St George School, there were even rumors that some students were planning not to come back to school after lunch break in order to join demonstrations.

That morning, as the students assembled in lines, ready to enter their classrooms, the British principal brought out a bullhorn to address them.

"I hear that some of you are planning not to come to school after lunch. I am warning you. If you don't come back, you will be dismissed for good. You hear me? Forever. I don't care if you're sick or even dying. No doctors' or parents' reports will be accepted. You are here to learn, and we are providing you with the best education in the world. So, I expect everyone to be back on time after lunch break. You hear me? And I said, *on time*."

Khaled's first-period class was history. A student raised his hand, asking the teacher if they could discuss what was going on and why the people were demonstrating.

"Absolutely not," the teacher answered.

Later, at home, the family was having dinner, and Khaled's Uncle Omar happened to be visiting. When Khaled mentioned what happened at school, his father expressed his support for the principal and the history teacher. But Omar objected.

"I think it would have been better for the history teacher to allow the students to discuss what's going on. After all, what's happening is part of our history."

"I don't think so," said Abu Khaled, "Don't misunderstand me; I am as happy as anyone that that the canal had been returned to Egypt. But that should not mean that students don't go to school. Also, I know that communists are taking advantage of the situation to spread their ideas among students who tend to be naive and vulnerable. I think the principal and teacher did the right thing."

Um Khaled, who often disagreed with her husband but mostly kept her thoughts to herself, surprised everyone.

"Maybe it's better that the history teacher didn't explain. After all, it is a British school, and they would just give the British point of view. To be honest with you, Omar, I didn't want my kids going to that school. It was their father's decision."

"Of course, it was my decision. I'm their father. What's wrong with giving my boys the best education, instead of having them distracted by radical politics."

"I don't know how students can get a good education without knowing or caring about what's happening in their own country," said Uncle Omar.

Khaled was delighted to hear his mother and uncle defy his father. But before a smile had a chance to appear on his face, his father commanded in a loud voice,

"Enough. Can we just have our dinner in peace?!"

Omar stood up, his plate still full of food.

"I should get going," he said as he walked toward the door, not giving anyone a chance to convince him to stay.

2
A SON'S GOODBYE

Al-Bireh, late August 1959

Khaled looked around, wondering how long all these guests were going to stay. They'd been coming day and night for the last few days to say their goodbyes before he traveled to attend college in the US, and would continue to come until he left the country. He wanted time for himself, for his fear to sink in, to think about his decision—although it wasn't really his. Most of all, he wanted to sneak out to see his sweetheart, Wafa. No one knew about her except his cousin Basil and his fifteen-year-old sister Layali, the love messenger who carried their verbal and written notes back and forth. Khaled and Wafa were next-door neighbors and had managed to find ways to secretly spend a few minutes with each other. In their conservative city, love or dating was *haram.*

"You promised me you wouldn't give in to your father's pressure to go to America," said Wafa. "You kept telling me you'd go to the American University in Beirut. You kept saying you'd come home every vacation and during the summers and that you would ask my father for my hand in two years when I graduated from high school. Now I won't get to see you for at least four years. You lied to me."

They were standing at the far corner of the large garden, hidden behind the fig tree. The afternoon August sun had no mercy, but they didn't care. This was the time when they could steal a few minutes, while the adults' watchful eyes were resting.

Khaled's hand gently touched her face to move a strand of hair covering her watery eyes. She pushed his hand away and stepped backward. Tears escaped her. He reached into his pocket and pulled out an ironed, white handkerchief.

"It's clean," he said as more tears slid down her face. "Please don't cry and spoil these beautiful eyes. I am sorry, but you know it's not my decision. It's what my father wants."

He moved closer and wiped her face with his palm and then wrapped his hands around her waist. She was still for a few seconds, avoiding his stare. Then she pulled away.

"You didn't have to listen to your father." Her voice was cracking, but stern and accusatory. "God knows how many arguments I've had with my father, telling him I want to finish high school and be a teacher before I even think about marriage. You can't stand up to your father's pressure, but you expect me to? I can't keep my promise not to get married since you didn't keep yours."

Wafa started to walk away.

"Please, Wafa, don't say that. Please listen to me," he begged, following her. She stopped, leaned her slender body against the trunk of a nearby tree, and hugged herself.

"I know. I shouldn't have listened to him. I'm sorry. But I'm the oldest son, and my father has his own strong expectations of me." Khaled was almost whispering, his eyes fixated on the ground, avoiding her angry stare.

"You never defy your father anymore, do you? You just do whatever he wants. You applied to universities in the US and kept telling me you were doing it to get him off your back. We might as well consider it the end of our relationship since I won't see you for at least four years."

She started to cry again.

"Wafa, please don't say this. You know I love you."

"Four years are too long. How do I know you won't forget me or you won't meet another girl? How do you expect me to stand up to my father's pressure to get married the minute I graduate from high school?"

"Wafa, *Habibati*, I know it's not fair. But I love you, and I will be faithful to you. I promise to take classes every summer and hopefully graduate in three years. You have to trust me."

"How do I know you won't break your promise as you did now?"

"I said I'm sorry, Wafa, please." Blood rushed to his face, and he kept blinking to hold back his tears.

"I love you too. But four years seems like forever."

"I told you. It's not going to be four years. Please give me a chance, and I won't disappoint you. I need your support. I need to know that you will wait for me. I can't leave without knowing that."

~

That evening, after all the guests had gone, Um Khaled went to the salon, the largest and best-furnished room in the house, reserved for special occasions and formal guests. She took her high heels off and the pins out of her hair, letting it flow like a dark river reaching her mid-back. With a heavy heart, she sat on the couch, closed her eyes, and placed her hands on her stomach. A cool breeze came through the open window. The silence of the late night, except for the crickets chirping, soothed her.

"Oh, here you are," said Khaled turning on the lights. The intense glare of the elaborate chandelier was too bright.

"Khaled, please, keep the lights off."

Khaled did as he was told. He walked over and laid down on the couch, resting his head on his mother's lap. She kissed her hand and she planted the kiss on his forehead, then gently caressed his hair.

Khaled stared at her. The moonlight penetrating the large window, gave her face a gentle glow. They were peacefully quiet for a few minutes, but then her trembling voice betrayed her.

"I am going to miss you," she said.

"I'm going to miss you, too."

Khaled had been seeking this private moment with his mother for a few days, itching to tell her about Wafa. He had never kept a secret from her, but he didn't know how to share this one. He tried to be as casual as he could.

"Wafa is a nice girl. I think she's beautiful, too, but not as beautiful as you."

Silence followed. He waited for her response, while his mother seemed to be assessing what she had just heard. Khaled broke the awkward moment.

"Yamma, do you like Wafa? Do you think she will wait for me until I come back?"

"Wait for you? For what? You don't have anything going between you two. Do you? You better think twice before you do anything damaging to her reputation. She is a decent girl, and her family has been our neighbors for many years."

A trace of panic spread over her round face.

"No Yamma, there's nothing going on between us. I was just wondering if you like her."

"I do like her. She's very nice. But I'm not sure about her family. They think they're better than us."

"Why? What makes them better?"

"That's the way they think. But if you ask me, I believe a person who works hard and makes their own money, like your father, is no less, if not better, than those who inherit their wealth. But don't worry, when you come back, we'll find you the best bride. Any young woman here would want you, with your university degree from America, coming from a good wealthy family, and you're so kind and handsome. What more is there to want?"

Deep down, Um Khaled wondered if maybe she should approve of the idea that her son liked Wafa. Maybe this would ensure his return. So many had gone to America with the intention of coming back but never did.

Um Khaled was almost twenty-three years younger than her husband and was more loving and attentive, especially to her children. Although Khaled felt much closer to her than to his father, he couldn't bring himself to tell her about his love for the neighbor's daughter, a love that had never gone beyond passing notes through his sister Layali, meeting secretly for a few minutes now and then, and lately, moments of touching hands and a few brief embraces.

The guests kept coming for a few days to say goodbye to Khaled and wish him luck in his new adventure. They took over every corner of the house. While the adults sat in the large salons and the living room, their children invaded the rest of the space, including most of the bedrooms, the three verandas, and the large garden. In the morning, women started to arrive around ten and spent a few hours gossiping and laughing. Their host, Um Khaled, assisted by her daughter Layali, moved from one room to another, checking to see if the guests had enough drinks, fruit, and cookies. She would smile politely and occasionally wipe an escaping tear.

"Um Khaled, stop worrying. He's going to be fine," said Um Basil.

"I know, but he is *bikry*, my firstborn, and I am having a hard time seeing him go all the way to America. This is what his father wants, and you know Abu Khaled, it has to be his way. What if he never comes back, like so many other young people?" she said through her tears.

"Of course he will come back. Most of those who don't return are from poor families or don't make it in America and are embarrassed to come back. Not like Khaled. Just look at this house. Why would he give up this kind of wealth and status? Also, his father won't allow it. Khaled wouldn't dare defy him."

And so went the conversations every morning until one of the women would suddenly say, "Oh my God, it's almost one. I better go home and get lunch ready for my husband." The women would get up, only to spend another ten or fifteen minutes talking at the front door or looking for their children, who were scattered all over the house or running in the garden or even the street, chasing each other. After their naps, some—especially close relatives—would come back with their husbands and children and stay until midnight. The tea, coffee, and lemonade served would have quenched the thirst of an army. And the food Abu Khaled catered, along with large trays of the delicious, sweet *kinafeh*, must have cost a fortune, but he did not care. The more people came, the happier he was.

Khaled, who was the center of attention, did not mind the morning crowd. They were mostly women who kept his mother company and lifted her spirits. Their presence also allowed him to sleep late, spend some time with his friends and siblings, and hopefully sneak a few minutes with Wafa.

What he hated was the late afternoons and evening crowds. Despite the oppressive heat, his father insisted that he wear a nice suit, a white shirt, and a tie. These guests stayed late, and their loud conversations, endless advice, and his mother's tearful eyes exhausted him.

After three days of this marathon of oppressive love, Khaled asked his parents, while the family was having lunch, how much longer it was going to last.

Abu Khaled interrupted his son before he had a chance to say more.

"For God's sake, what are you complaining about now? You should be happy we have such a large family and so many friends who care about you."

"But I also want to spend some time with my friends and cousins. I won't be seeing them for years."

Anger took over Abu Khaled's face. His two thick eyebrows became one and his eyes seemed ready to launch out of their sockets.

"You won't be seeing any of us either. You know how many people wish they had what you have or were going to America to study?" he said, almost yelling.

"Take it easy on him," Um Khaled said.

"He should be grateful I'm doing this for him. Does he understand how much money this is going to cost?"

Abu Khaled was strict with his children, especially the boys. He insisted that his two eldest sons, Khaled and Majed, work during the summers at his business, or for other merchants, as soon as each turned thirteen.

"Work is good for them. A man's place is not at home," he would say.

Khaled put his fork down and stared at his plate. After a few seconds, he took a deep breath, trying to disguise his growing frustration.

"You're right. I'm sorry, Yaba."

His body moved to the edge of his seat, wanting to leave, but he didn't dare.

"I wish he weren't going so far away. He's too young." said Um Khaled, her eyes swelling with tears.

"You made your mother cry. Are you happy now?"

Abu Khaled pushed his chair back and dashed out of the room.

Dead silence followed.

With their eyes on their plates, they finished their lunch and dispersed, each to a different corner of the house.

Khaled knew most of the people who came to bid him farewell. But there was also a large number of guests who were his father's business acquaintances. Many of them brought him expensive gifts that he couldn't possibly take with him. Once in a while, he managed to escape to his room, claiming he needed to finish his packing, only to have one of his younger siblings come saying, "Yaba is looking for you."

The day before Khaled's departure, the house was more packed than any of the previous days. But thanks to the Mediterranean tradition of afternoon naps, Khaled managed to see Wafa again.

He promised to write often and have his letter mailed to his cousin Basil, who would find a way to get the letter to her. Sending letters to her directly might alert her parents. She seemed much less upset—they had declared their commitment and eternal love to each other.

This made it much easier for him to handle the evening crowd, as men occupied the huge salon and the women the adjacent smaller one. Khaled had no choice but to sit with the men who felt compelled to give him advice, especially what he should or should not do.

"Stay away from *willad al-haram.* May God protect you from sinful people."

"Stay away from those loose American girls. Don't let them seduce you."

"Don't drink, don't gamble. Pay attention to your studies."

"My son Mohammad is in America, too. Tell him to write to us."

Khaled's grandmother, who was sitting quietly in the adjacent room, walked over to him.

"Be a man, like your father. Look at him. He went to America, worked hard, made lots of money, and came back to open his business. Now he is one of the most influential men not only in Al-Bireh, but in the whole area. People seek his friendship and want to be seen with him. You are so lucky he is sending you to America."

Khaled was the envy of other recent graduates. Not only had he gotten accepted to the University of Michigan in Ann Arbor, but his father was going to pay for it. Many of his peers were going to nearby universities, like Damascus, Baghdad, Beirut or Cairo. Some were going to Europe, but none to the US. To him, they were the lucky ones. At least they would be able to come home for the holidays and summers.

Exhausted and overwhelmed by his own thoughts and emotions, he lay on his bed staring out the window at the bright stars. No matter how much he told himself, "I have a long trip ahead of me. I should get some sleep," sleep didn't come until the sun shed its first rays.

3
TAKING OFF

Khaled woke with a start. The twins, Yasmine and Yazan, were tickling his nose with a feather, "Get up. Mother said breakfast is ready."

He wished he could sleep more. *I am too tired,* he thought to himself. Then it dawned on him: *Oh, my God, I leave today*. He wanted to cover his face again and never get out of bed.

"Everyone is waiting for you. Our aunts and uncles are already here," said Yazan.

"Come here, you two."

Khaled moved over to make room for the two six-year-olds, the youngest of his six siblings. They jumped into his bed and climbed over him. As he hugged them, his mind drifted to the day they were born, feeling sad to leave them for three or four years, fearful they might not recognize him by the time he came back. He held them tighter.

"I love you . . . "

A lump in his throat stopped him from saying more.

His sister Layali came in.

"You're still in bed? Everyone's waiting for you."

"I really don't want to go."

Layali sat on the edge of the bed.

"Me too, I wish you wouldn't go. Well, the time will go by fast and you'll be back before you know it."

But then she started to cry.

"Why are you crying now," said Yasmine.

"She's just being silly," said Khaled. "Let me get up and get ready. I'll be downstairs in a few minutes."

~

By the time Khaled had washed himself and gotten dressed, more of his relatives were already there. Wafa was there too, claiming to have forgotten one of her books in Layali's room. Her brown curly hair was pulled back with a ribbon. "I like your hair this way. It shows your beautiful eyes," Khaled had told her more than once. She also had her red dress on, Khaled's favorite. His mother noticed Wafa's hairstyle and dress. It seemed too fancy for picking up a book from a neighbor early in the morning.

Wafa went with Layali to fetch the book and came back a few minutes later. Slowly, she approached Khaled with a faint smile, shook his hand, and whispered, trying to steady her voice, "*Ma'a El-Salameh,* and Good Luck." Her hands were moist and slippery. Khaled's heart skipped a beat, and blood rushed to his neck and face. Even his ears turned red. His body moved closer, craving to hold her, to touch her face. Hesitantly, she withdrew her hand and rushed out the door.

Um Khaled looked at her son's stern face, recalling their recent conversation. He looked away, avoiding her penetrating gaze, then patted his pockets. "I forgot my pen," he said as he rushed out.

In his room, he leaned against the closed door and took a couple deep breaths to quiet his fears.

~

After breakfast, it was time to leave. The family car, along with a few others packed with grandparents, aunts, uncles, and cousins, formed a caravan to accompany Khaled to the airport. The drive from Al-Bireh to Qalandia Airport in Jerusalem took about twenty five minutes. When it was time to say their final goodbyes, Khaled shook hands with and kissed the cheeks of the army that had accompanied him, and politely listened to more advice and good wishes, all pleading one more time with Allah to protect him, especially from American women, sex, and liquor. His parents stood aside until all had said their farewells.

Abu Khaled moved closer to his son and shook his hand while placing one kiss on each cheek.

"Be careful my son. Keep your passport and money in your pockets. Write to us once a week. Don't forget to send us a telegram as soon as you arrive. And, most important of all, stay away from politics." He put his hand on his son's shoulder, forcing a wide smile, "*Allah Ma'ak ya ibni,* may God be with you my son."

Um Khaled held him tight, wishing he would stay. She felt as if a piece of her was being ripped away. How did he get to be eighteen so fast?

"*Allah yehmeek,* and may He give me the patience to wait for your return . . ."

She started sobbing and couldn't say any more. Layali gently pulled her away.

"Yamma, please stop. You're making us all cry."

Khaled walked slowly toward the Passengers Only area. All the words of advice and wishes followed him. Without looking back, he kept walking, noticing their voices gradually fading away. With an expensive briefcase in his right hand, a growing lump in his throat, and a surge of tears he struggled to repress, Khaled stepped into the unknown. For the first time in his life, he was immensely alone.

Taking Off

Khaled sat in a window seat staring at the world beneath him getting smaller and smaller. Suddenly, despite the bright blue sky, the airplane bounced. With a trembling hand, Khaled grabbed the arm of his seat. His fear surprised him. True, he had never been on an airplane before, but he always watched planes with fascination and often dreamt about being a pilot. But even the mention of it set both of his parents on edge. His mother feared for her son's life doing what she saw as a dangerous job. His father had already decided where and what Khaled should study, as well as where he was going to work after graduation.

For Khaled, the idea of working with his father terrified him, but he didn't argue. He kept the dream of being a pilot to himself and ultimately buried it, as he had buried many other dreams. Khaled wondered if he was in fact scared of the plane ride, or if he was actually afraid of what awaited him on the other side of the planet, where he never wanted to be. He had never been away from his family except for a one-month summer camp in Lebanon. Even then, he was with couple of his cousins. As he reflected on his life, his father's grip over him, his love for Wafa, and the way he disappointed her, tears started pushing their way to the surface, and the tie his father insisted he wear seemed to get tighter.

Hot and sweaty, he unbuckled the top button of his white shirt, took off his tie, folded it, and carefully placed it in his brief case. A few minutes later he looked around and slowly peeled off his jacket. He was careful not to touch the man sitting next to him, fearing he would notice his red eyes. Since childhood, he had been taught that, unlike women, men don't cry.

Khaled spent the next thirty-six hours in planes and airports. His trip took him to Cairo, London, New York, and finally Detroit.

When he fell asleep, which he managed to do on every flight, he dreamt of Wafa. Unlike in real life, in his dreams he could hold her, caress her face, and even kiss her. He wondered if she would wait for him. *She's smart and beautiful, many men will be after her. What if she falls in love with one of them?* His own thoughts terrified him. His resentment toward his father—and toward himself for not having the courage to challenge him—was brewing in his guts. Khaled escaped these tormenting thoughts by going back to sleep, hoping Wafa would visit him one more time.

~

At Detroit airport, Khaled headed first to the bathroom. After meticulously brushing his teeth and rinsing his face, he pulled out his tie and wrinkled jacket and put them on, ready to meet Mr. Whitlock. He cursed under his breath at his reflection in the mirror. Not only did he look exhausted with puffy eyes and a pale face, but his suit was badly wrinkled, and his pants had a couple of dark stains. He wetted his handkerchief and tried to wipe the stains off his pants and massage the wrinkles out, but that made his clothes look even worse.

A loud announcement about a departing plane snapped Khaled back to the task at hand. As he hurried to get his luggage, he tried to recall the instructions he had received from the University, which he read several times during his long flight.

"Mr. Whitlock from the office of Foreign Student's Affairs will meet you at the airport Baggage Pickup area. He will have a sign with your name."

~

Khaled picked up his luggage and looked around. He saw two people with signs, and he ran toward them, but neither had his name. He waited, staring at everyone coming into the luggage area, but no one carried a sign. People who arrived with him were meeting their loved ones, hugging and kissing. Khaled started to panic. *How am I going to find Mr. Whitlock in this big airport? I don't even know what he looks like. What if he doesn't come? What would I do? Where would I go?*

Khaled was exhausted and felt like he'd been traveling forever. Most people who arrived on his plane had already left. Khaled dragged his two bags to a nearby seat, trying to recall if there was a phone number in all the papers he received from the University. He held his head in his two hands and looked at the floor, trying to figure out what he should do next.

"Oh, here you are . . . you must be Khaled! Right? Sorry, we're late . . ."

Mr. Whitlock, short and stocky, was walking toward him, followed by a student. He wore a light khaki suit with a pale blue shirt that matched the color of his small, sunken eyes, and a strawberry-red tie matching his face. Although Mr. Whitlock's pants were wrinkled between his heavy thighs, his shirt and jacket were crisp, which made Khaled more aware of his clothes.

"Hello, Mr. Whitlock. I'm Khaled Nasser," he said, stretching out his hand. "Thanks for meeting me. I was worried you wouldn't show up."

"Of course, we'd come. Happy to meet you. How was your flight?"

Mr. Whitlock didn't wait for Khaled to respond.

"I know it's a long trip. You must be tired. Hungry, too. Welcome. Let me introduce you to Kanji Hirano. He is a second-year engineering student. He will be helping you for the next few days to get settled and find your way around campus . . ."

Khaled had a hard time understanding Mr. Whitlock's rapid English and drifted away while he continued his monologue. Khaled noticed that Kanji wore casual clothes: khaki pants, short-sleeved yellow shirt, and no tie, which made Khaled self-conscious of about how formally he was dressed.

"Welcome to Ann Arbor and U-Michigan. You're going to like it here."

"Thanks, Kanji."

Unlike Mr. Whitlock, Kanji was slim, with an athletic body, dark eyes, and shiny, pitch-black hair. Khaled was curious about his flawless accent. He wondered how long it would take for him to speak that way.

~

The ride from the airport took about half an hour, and the afternoon heat was stifling. Mr. Whitlock talked for most of the way, asking Khaled questions and telling him about the school. He gave Khaled no chance to respond or talk with Kanji. Meanwhile, Khaled stared out the window, amazed by the wide multi-lane roads, the speed and size of the cars, the lush green, and the enormous trees on either side of the road.

"You must be hungry," said Mr. Whitlock, interrupting Khaled's daydreaming. Without waiting for a response, he pulled into the small R.Squeeze Inn restaurant in Ypsilanti, adjacent to Ann Arbor.

The three of them went in and sat in a booth.

"Let me help you order," said Mr. Whitlock. "This small place is famous for its hamburgers. How about a burger, fries and a Coke? A real American meal! I'm sure you're going to like it."

Khaled wanted to think about what to order or ask Kanji, but he was embarrassed to object to Mr. Whitlock's suggestion. To his relief, both Kanji and Mr. Whitlock ordered the same.

Khaled was eager to learn more about Kanji. Where did he come from, how long had he been in the US, and did he miss his family? But Mr. Whitlock took over again. He reminded Khaled of his father. In spite of their differences in appearance, both dominated conversations and asked a bunch of questions without ever waiting for an answer. They just went ahead and decided for you. When their order arrived, Khaled was overwhelmed by the size of his Coke and the amount of food, enough for at least three people.

He stared at the thick burger, not sure how to wrap his mouth around it. So, he waited until his hosts bit into theirs to follow what they did. He was also surprised to see both of them squeezing waves of ketchup on their fries.

"Try it, I bet you you'll like it," said Kanji, nimbly putting a few fries on Khaled's plate.

"Thank you, it's good," said Khaled after he ate what Kanji had given him. "But I prefer it just with salt and pepper."

Khaled actually loved the fries and Coke and inhaled both, but he didn't care that much for the burger. The bread was soft and doughy, and the meat too greasy, but he ate it anyway. At home, despite his family being well-off, they had to eat all the food on their plates. It was *haram*, a sin, to throw food away.

"It was good, you liked it, right? Would you like dessert?" said Mr. Whitlock.

"I did like the food, but I'm too full. Can I skip the dessert?"

Khaled, as well as Kanji, were surprised when Mr. Whitlock replied.

"As you like."

Kanji kicked Khaled's leg under the table, and they both smiled.

4
SETTLING IN

"Here we are," said Mr. Whitlock as he parked his Buick in front of a red brick building on Thompson Street. He turned off the engine and got out. Slowly, he walked to the back of the car and opened the trunk. "Let's help Khaled with his luggage," he said, looking at Kanji while walking back toward the front of the car, making it clear he did not intend to lift a finger.

Once the trunk was emptied, Mr. Whitlock opened the driver's door. Before getting into the car, he looked at Khaled. "Well... welcome to our university. I've got to go now. Kanji will take you to your room and help you find your way for the next couple of days. If you need anything, you know where to find me."

He got into his car and drove away.

Standing at the West Quadrangle dormitory entrance, Khaled's attention was stuck on Mr. Whitlock's words. He had no idea how to find the man, nor what he would do when Kanji disappeared in two days. It was only Wednesday, and school wouldn't start until Monday. The thought of being alone for five days sent shudders through his body.

"Are you okay?" asked Kanji.

"Yes. I'm just tired."

"Let's get you settled so you can get some sleep."

Kanji grabbed one of the two large suitcases while Khaled carried the other and followed him into the elevator. Jet-lagged and disoriented, Khaled stared at the lit number 3 button.

They walked the long corridor of the third floor in silence. Khaled wanted to talk to Kanji but couldn't think of anything to say. At room 319, Kanji took a key from his pocket and opened the door while Khaled looked both ways, searching for a trace of life.

"Finally, you're here. This is your room."

Kanji stepped backward to allow Khaled to enter first. Khaled stood by the door, examining the bare space.

"Go on in. Don't you like it?"

Khaled didn't respond. He moved his legs stiffly, one at a time, as if they were made of lead. Standing inside, he scanned the walls and furniture. The two windowless walls facing each other were painted dirty white and had no pictures. Each was lined up with a single bed with a bare mattress, a small desk, a tiny dresser, and a wall closet. The only pleasant feature was a large window overlooking the lush green campus with flowering bushes and huge trees. He never knew that trees could grow so large.

After a couple minutes just standing there, Kanji asked, "What's wrong?"

"Everything I've seen so far is so huge—the streets, the cars, the trees, even the food portions are so large. How come this room is so small and bare? It's ugly."

"This is one of the nicest dorms. Once you unpack and have your own books and pictures, it will look much nicer. Trust me, after a hot shower and a good night's sleep, everything will look better."

"I don't have any sheets or towels."

"You don't? How about shampoo and soap?"

"No. My dad said that it would be cheaper to buy them here."

"Don't worry about it. I'll bring some from the dorm's supply room. Tomorrow we'll go shopping and buy what you need."

Waiting for Kanji, Khaled scanned the room again. It was half the size of the one he shared with his brother Majed. The closet and set of drawers were too small to hold his belongings. He looked outside his door and walked to the bathroom area, but saw no one. The thought of being alone in this huge building terrified him. As soon as Kanji came back, he asked, "Am I the only one in this dorm building?"

"There are a few foreign students already here. You'll meet them tomorrow at the cafeteria. It's on the lower floor of this building. Your roommate will arrive this weekend. His name is Richard Johnson. He's from Cincinnati, Ohio. Don't worry. By Sunday night, this place will be so packed and so noisy, you'll miss the quiet," Kanji said, laughing. Khaled didn't know what was so funny, but he managed to force a smile.

"You must be exhausted. Let me help you with your bed. Then I'll leave, and you can get some rest."

It was only then that it dawned on Khaled that he had never made his own bed.

Khaled wished Kanji would stay with him until his roommate arrived, but he was too embarrassed to ask. As if Kanji had read his mind, he said, "I sleep upstairs in the resident's assistant room, number 411. There's a sign on the door. You can't miss it. If you need anything, just let me know."

"You live here?"

Khaled couldn't contain his excitement. He wasn't sure if he really liked Kanji or if it was the anxiety of being alone in the deserted building.

"Yes. I stayed in this dorm last year, and this year, I got a job as a student supervisor assistant. So, I'm here if you need anything."

"Oh, that's a relief. Now that I know, I'll sleep much better."

"I'm sure you're going to sleep like a log. If you want, I can pick you up tomorrow at eleven. We can go for a late breakfast, then shopping. How about it?"

"Thanks a million. Sure, that would be great."

Kanji handed Khaled a keychain with two keys. "This is your room key, and this one is for the building's front door. Good night."

~

Without lifting the cover or taking a shower, Khaled laid on the bed, trying to figure out what Kanji meant by sleeping like a log. *Tomorrow, I'll look it up in my dictionary. Or did he say sleeping like a dog?* Before closing his eyes, he looked around and examined the room again. *This is the most depressing place I've ever been in. It's so small, and I have to share it with a stranger, Richard Jo... Jo... whatever his last name is. I wonder what kind of a person he is. I should have asked Kanji about him.* Tears escaped his eyes. He wiped his face and runny nose with the back of his hand. Within minutes, he was out. In his sleep, Kanji was there along with his mother and his sweetheart, Wafa.

~

A hard knock on the door propelled Khaled out of his dreams and out of bed. It took him a few moments to realize where he was.

"Did I wake you up?" Kanji asked, with a bright smile spreading across his face. His straight black hair covered his forehead.

"I'm sorry. What time is it?"

"It's after eleven. I've been knocking at the door for a while. I thought you might be out."

"Where would I go?"

"I don't know, outside, looking around? Anyway, why don't I leave you to get dressed and come back in half an hour?"

A while later, they walked out of the building, chatting like old friends. It was much cooler than the day before. The soft sun and fresh air gently massaged Khaled's face and relaxed his shoulders.

"My God, what a beautiful day. My dad told me that Michigan is cold, unlike California, where the weather is similar to Palestine's. But it's very nice here. It's much greener than I ever expected."

"I told you everything would be better after a good night's sleep."

Khaled suddenly recalled how he had fallen asleep crying. He wondered if Kanji also cried on his first night in the dorm, but he was too ashamed to ask.

At Loy's Restaurant on Huron Street, Khaled decided to order the special: coffee, eggs, and pancakes. Kanji ordered coffee, two eggs, and toast.

"This is a lot of food. I didn't expect to get this much," said Khaled, pointing to the stack of pancakes. Even so, he kept stuffing his face, saying, "Oh my God . . . this is good . . . real good," while pouring more maple syrup on everything.

"If you eat like this, before you know it, you'll gain lots of weight. Most foreign students do, especially in their first year."

"What about you? You don't seem to have gained any."

"I'm talking about foreign students."

"What do you mean foreign students, aren't you one?"

"No, I'm not. I'm American."

Oblivious to Kanji's tense response, Khaled said, "You don't look American to me."

"I was born here. So were my parents. Americans don't all look alike."

Khaled was taken aback by Kanji's sharp tone. He couldn't

figure out why he seemed to be so upset. The silence that followed unnerved him.

After staring out the window for what seemed like forever, Kanji abruptly said, "Let's go to the store to get your stuff. I have to go back to work. Give me your list."

"I didn't make a list, but I can tell you what I need: sheets, towels, soap, shampoo, and shaving cream. I also need snacks and drinks to keep in my room."

"The cafeteria is open. It serves three meals a day. Also, there's a small store not far from the dorm. For now, let's go to Sears and get the basics."

They walked to Main Street in silence. Khaled was perplexed by the sudden change in Kanji from kind and eager to help to withdrawn for no apparent reason.

At Sears, Kanji went quickly to the bedding department, and Khaled trailed behind.

"Here are the sheets and towels. Pick up what you need."

Khaled looked at the endless number of sheets, the different sizes. Reluctantly, he asked Kanji, "I'm not sure what size sheets I should get."

"Twin."

Khaled picked up sheets and towels. He wanted to wander into the store and look around. He had never been to such a large store with so much merchandise. He thought of stopping at the women's section, which they had passed through, to buy a gift for Wafa and mail it to her later. But Kanji's restlessness made it clear that he wanted to leave.

At the entrance to the dorm, Kanji said, "Orientation is Monday. Be sure not to miss it. There are instructions about it on the dorm bulletin board."

"Am I not going to see you until Monday?" Khaled asked, almost panicking.

"We'll see."

Khaled watched Kanji walk away. He felt betrayed and fought back the tears pushing their way to the corner of his eyes. Carrying his stuff, he walked alone to his room, where he dropped what he had bought on the second bed and lay down, feeling tired, lonely, and sad. *I shouldn't have come here. This country is too far away. I won't get to see Wafa or my family for years. And this place is confusing. I could have gotten lost in Sears. I like Kanji and thought we could become friends, but he became agitated and in a hurry for no reason. Did I say or do something that upset him? Even if I did, he should tell me what it was.*

Lying on the bed, he kept trying to recall the conversation he'd had with Kanji. He decided to go to him later to find out what happened. He wished Wafa was there to talk with him about it and help figure it out. In his head, he drafted a letter to her, starting from the minute he left home, the long plane rides, the ride from the airport and the wide highways with multiple lanes, the huge plates of food, and Sears, a store that had everything and bigger than all the Al-Bireh stores put together. And, of course, he'd tell her about Kanji, how eager he was to understand what he might have done that would upset him that much.

When Khaled opened his eyes again, it was dark.

5
A ROOMMATE

Khaled spent most of the following two days between the cafeteria and his room. He ventured out twice, trying to discover his surroundings. Bewildered by the campus's size and its many huge buildings, he never ventured too far from his dorm for fear of getting lost. At the cafeteria, he met a few students and exchanged greetings and names, but mostly he kept to himself. Although eager to meet people and make friends, he felt homesick and unusually tired. Why was he waking up in the middle of the night, and sleeping during the day? Jet lag was an unknown to him.

On Saturday morning, Khaled was surprised by an unexpected visit. He jumped from his bed to greet Kanji.

"Nice to see you. I hope you're feeling better."

"I am fine, thank you," Kanji answered quickly. "I just came to let you know that Richard, your roommate, will be arriving this afternoon."

"That's great," said Khaled, although he wasn't sure he was ready to share his room with a stranger.

"Come in, have a seat," Khaled offered, hurrying to clear a pile of clothes from the extra bed.

"I have to go," said Kanji. He started to walk out, then turned and instructed, "Could you please clear that bed by the time Richard arrives?"

Before Khaled had a chance to respond, Kanji was gone. Khaled started to walk after him. But he wasn't sure what he would say to him, so he stopped and went back to his room.

~

A couple of hours later, Kanji came back, along with Richard and his parents.

"Let me introduce you all," he said. "This is Khaled Nasser, and this is Richard and his parents, Mr. and Mrs. Johnson. Khaled arrived only three days ago, and he is probably still jet-lagged. I'll leave you to get acquainted. I'm sure you're going to get along just fine."

He chatted a bit more with the Johnsons before handing the key to Richard.

"If you need anything, let me know. I'm on the fourth floor, Room 411."

Khaled watched in silence, noticing how cheerful and friendly Kanji was, just like when he first met him, which only added to his confusion. He also wondered what Kanji meant by saying Khaled was still jet-lagged. Was he saying something bad about him?

When Kanji left the room, Khaled went after him.

"Why, all of a sudden, don't you want to talk to me? I don't understand. If I said or did anything wrong, you should tell me."

"It's nothing. And you don't have to be loud."

"Sorry. I didn't mean to be loud."

"I can't talk now."

"Then when?"

"Maybe next week." Kanji's voice softened. "Too many students are arriving this weekend. I'm really busy right now. But if you need anything, let me know."

Khaled hunched over against the hallway wall. His chest

felt tight. When he finally walked back to his room, he found Richard's mother helping her son make the bed. Khaled watched with envy.

"I'll leave you to finish unpacking," Richard's dad said. "I'll come back in half an hour, and we can all have a bite. Then we can go buy you whatever you need."

Khaled was relieved to learn they would be leaving soon. He grabbed his towel and escaped. *I don't know what's wrong with me. This has never happened to me before. I feel like sleeping or crying.* He took a long shower, letting the soothing hot water wash away his agitation.

~

When Khaled returned to his room, Richard and his mother were sitting next to each other on the made bed. Richard was looking over his mother's shoulder at a sheet of paper she was holding. Khaled stood by the door, trying not to interrupt, while his mind drifted back to Al-Bireh. It was only a few days ago that he had been at home lying on the couch with his head on his mother's lap. Richard's mother seemed affectionate, like his mom, but she was not as beautiful, though her fresh hairdo, makeup, and clothes were more stylish. He couldn't help but notice her short skirt and her thigh showing as she sat cross-legged. Struggling not to stare, he turned his attention to Richard's short-sleeve, checkered shirt that hugged his wide shoulders. His childish face, smiling blue eyes, rosy plump cheeks, and smooth forehead covered with golden strands of hair didn't seem to match his body. Khaled wondered if Richard was as happy as his face seemed.

His thoughts were interrupted when Richard's father abruptly returned to the room. He stared at Khaled as if he was surprised to see him there.

"Hello . . . I'm sorry, I forgot your name."

"Khaled."

"I'm counting on you and Richard getting along. Why don't you join us for an early dinner?"

"Thank you, Mr. Johnson. I very much appreciate the invitation, but I'm very tired."

"Well, we'll leave you to rest," said Mrs. Johnson. She put her hand on Khaled's shoulder, "Hopefully, you can join us tomorrow for late breakfast before we leave."

Khaled sat on his bed for a while, trying to keep his heavy eyelids open. He got up, stretched, and then walked to the window. The sun was still bright, and the tree branches danced gently with the breeze. After a few minutes, Khaled decided to go for a walk. But while waiting for the elevator, he realized how tired he was, so he walked back to his room. He looked around at what looked like a pathetic place. Not knowing what to do, he stepped toward Richard's closet, curious to find out what he brought with him. Reluctantly, he reached for the handle without opening it. But regretting his curiosity, he stepped back and laid down on his bed.

Khaled wasn't sure if he liked sharing the room with Richard, or any other stranger, although he did yearn for company. After all, he grew up in a house full of people: six siblings, parents, and a grandmother, along with lots of aunts, uncles, neighbors, and friends coming and going all the time. As he remembered, he closed his eyes to stop the tears.

When Richard came back, Khaled was sound asleep.

At the Chatter Box restaurant on South Main, Khaled stared at the menu for a long time. When the waitress came for the second time to ask if they were ready to order, Khaled said, "I'm not sure what to order."

"Can I help you?" asked Mrs. Johnson.

"Yes, thanks. I've been to restaurants twice. But both times, I got too much food."

"It's the American way, we love to eat. What kind of food do you like?"

"I'd like either pancakes or eggs, but not both."

Once the waitress had taken their order, Richard's mother said, "Now tell us a little about yourself. Where did you come from? How far did you have to travel?"

Khaled was surprised that no one knew where Al-Bireh was, and they were surprised that he had to travel so far.

"No wonder you were tired yesterday," she sympathized. "That's a long way to travel to go to college, but I suppose many foreign students come here to study. We have some of the best universities, and this one is definitely among the best of the best. You must have been very good at school, no? And your English is amazing. Where did you learn to speak so well?"

"I went to a private school in Jerusalem."

"Oh my gosh, Jerusalem. That must be very exciting. I would love to go there someday," said Mrs. Johnson.

"That's costly," said Mr. Johnson, "a private school and the University of Michigan. Your father must be doing well."

"I guess so," said Khaled, getting a bit uncomfortable. He did not really want to think or talk about his father.

"What kind of a job does he have?"

"Let's let him eat his breakfast," interrupted Mrs. Johnson, touching her husband's hand, trying to make him stop talking. She turned to Khaled. "Please don't mind my husband. He's just a curious man."

"It's okay. I don't mind."

"I agree," said Richard. "Let the poor guy eat."

"I really don't mind," said Khaled.

Once they were done eating, Mrs. Johnson asked Khaled what he planned to study.

"I'm really not sure. I would love to be an airplane pilot, but my dad wants me to study business administration, hoping I will go back and work with him. He even has plans for me to take over his business once he retires. But since both of my parents don't want me to be a pilot, I would prefer to study electrical or mechanical engineering."

"You don't sound that excited about studying what your dad wants for you," said Mrs. Johnson.

"Mom, it's funny you say that," said Richard, "You know that I want to study journalism, but Dad wants me to study engineering. Khaled prefers engineering, but his dad wants him to study something else."

"That's because I care about you," said Mr. Johnson. "I want to be sure you can get a good job and earn enough to support yourself and—"

"Oh my gosh, I didn't realize it was that late," Richard's mother said, interrupting her husband, winking at her son, not to respond to his father. "I guess it's time to go. We have a long ride home."

As they were saying their goodbyes, Mrs. Johnson hugged and kissed her son, then turned and did the same to Khaled. "If you need anything, please let me know. You sound like a nice young man. I'm confident you and Richard will be best friends."

Then she turned to Richard. "Try to help him. Being in a new country can be difficult."

Khaled was moved by Mrs. Johnson's warmth and kindness. And while initially he wasn't sure if he wanted to have a roommate or join the Johnsons for brunch, he was happy he did.

~

Not having a chance to chat freely at breakfast, Richard and Khaled spent their evening talking about school, sports, and girls. They went to the cafeteria and orientation together. Richard made it a point to meet and introduce Khaled to most of the students who lived on the same floor. Within a week of Richard's arrival, Khaled felt the weight of loneliness melting away. He even felt comfortable enough to tell Richard about Wafa and about his encounter with Kanji.

"Kanji? I can't believe it. He's such a nice guy. All the students here seem to like him."

"I know. But I'm just telling you what happened. He flipped on me for no apparent reason."

"Why don't you go talk to him?"

"I tried, but he doesn't seem to want to talk."

"Well, try again."

For two days, Khaled contemplated about what Richard had told him. Then reluctantly, he knocked on Kanji's ajar door.

"Can I come in?"

"Of course," said Kanji. "Come on in."

Khaled settled into a chair, while Kanji sat on his bed. His eyes moved around the room. It was the same size as his, but it looked larger and more cheerful. It had only one bed and two chairs. The walls were lined with bright posters. The nightstand had simple but elegant framed pictures of people Khaled assumed to be his parents and sister.

After what seemed like a very long, awkward silence, Khaled spoke.

"When I first arrived, you were very friendly and helpful. Then all of a sudden, you seemed upset and didn't want to talk to me. Have I said or done anything to upset you?"

"To be honest with you, you did."

"What did I do?"

"How could you ask me if I was a real American? I assumed you would know better."

"I don't understand, know better about what?"

"This is hard for me to talk about. But since you don't seem to know much about this country, I should explain a few things before you say stuff to other people that could get you into trouble. People here come in different colors and have different backgrounds. Not all Americans have blond hair and blue eyes, and they don't all think alike, either."

Kanji paused, as if weighing how much to say.

Khaled's forehead tightened, and his eyes narrowed as he tried to concentrate. He couldn't quite comprehend what Kanji had just told him. He took a breath and waited.

"When you said I don't look like a real American, I remembered when I was growing up. You know, during World War II, the US government put all Japanese in America, including American citizens and legal residents, in internment camps. I was a kid then, but I still think about those years. My mother crying and my father screaming at her, telling her to stop. When I left you that day, I felt conflicted. I wanted to tell you why what you said bothered me, but I couldn't. No one in my family or our community ever talked about the camps. Every time my sister or I brought it up, my parents always changed the subject. When we insisted, my parents would say, 'Talking about it won't change a thing. It will only bring us more pain. It's better if you forget and move on.' I don't like to remember or talk about it either. But how could we forget or pretend it never happened? How would people know about the injustice inflicted upon us if we keep silent? That's why I decided to tell you."

"I'm really sorry. I wish you'd told me then."

"I wasn't sure how to handle it."

"Well, thank you for telling me now. I've been worrying about it since that day."

Khaled walked away, not completely understanding what had happened to Kanji and his family. But he decided not to ask, concerned he would say the wrong thing and upset Kanji again. He went outside and sat on a bench in the University quad, trying to sort out his conversation with Kanji. After an hour, he went back to his room, tired and confused.

"What are you doing? I hope you're not writing another letter to your girlfriend," said Richard as he walked into the room.

"I took your advice and talked to Kanji."

"And . . . ?"

"I think it went well. He doesn't seem upset with me anymore. At least, I hope so. He told me about being with his family in some camp during World War II. To be honest, I'd never heard about it before."

Richard laid down on his bed, babbling about wanting to study journalism so he could write the real stories about American history.

"Do you know anything about the internment camps, what happened?" Khaled asked.

"A little. But I want to learn more about it and other stuff."

"Can you explain it to me?"

"I will. But not now. I'm a bit tired."

Khaled went back to finishing his letter to Wafa.

> *I've never heard about internment camps. I wonder if they were like the Palestinian refugee camps. My father warned me to stay away from politics, but if I have to live here for a few more years, I need to know more about this country's history.*

6
LIFE IN THE STATES

Winter 1959

With their good-natured personalities, Khaled and Richard soon became best friends. Khaled also made other friends much faster than he anticipated, and yet hardly a day went by without him missing Wafa. Richard often teased him when he talked about his distant girlfriend or caught him writing her a letter. Once in a while, he'd try to snatch the letter from Khaled's hand. Or he might stand next to him, loudly dictating a love letter or acting one out as if in a melodramatic romance on stage. Then he would drop dead on his bed with his palm on his heart.

"Actually, I'm the one who is going to kill you," Khaled might respond, grabbing Richard's neck and pretending to choke him.

"I don't understand you, Khaled," said Richard. "There are lots of beautiful girls on campus who would love to date you. I even hear some talking about you. 'Look how handsome he is . . . Oh my God, I love those big dark eyes and long eyelashes!' They even rave about your thick lips. Why don't you try and date one of *them*, or even *two*?"

"I love Wafa, and I won't cheat on her. I plan to marry her as soon as I graduate."

"I bet you'll forget about her once you start dating other women."

"I'm not planning to date anyone. No woman is as beautiful or smart."

"Maybe she'll forget you and find another guy."

"Shut up," Khaled said, throwing a pillow at him.

~

School was easy for Khaled. In high school, he was a straight-A student. He was so used to the British lilt of his teachers in school that, at the University, his biggest challenge was understanding his professors' American accents. But once he got the hang of it, thanks to his roommate and to the small radio they listened to the daily news from, he sailed through.

To celebrate the end of their first semester and getting all A's, Richard invited Khaled to join him at a friend's house.

"David is twenty-one and promised to bring us all the beer and drinks we want as long as we pay for it."

"We have to pay? What kind of invitation is that?" objected Khaled, "You know I don't drink. And isn't it illegal? What if we get busted?"

"We won't. All the students do it. Come on, it'll be fun. We don't have to worry about coming back early to study. Besides, we both deserve to celebrate for getting good grades."

"How many times do I have to tell you? Drinking is against my religion."

"What kind of a religion is that? God will understand. He'll forgive you."

"Okay, I'll come. But I won't drink any alcohol."

~

David's large house, which he shared with other three students, was packed. Everyone was drinking and laughing. Khaled went into the kitchen and found himself a bottle of Coca-Cola.

"Don't be a jerk. Have a drink," Richard urged him, and the other students cheered in agreement.

"I promised my parents not to."

"What a nice guy," one of their friends kidded him.

"My mom would love to have you as her son instead of me," another chimed in.

"We all promise our parents all kinds of things," said Richard. "For God's sake, have a beer. It won't kill you. I'll even get it for you." He walked to the kitchen and came back with two beers.

"Here, my treat! Let's drink to the best roommate ever," he toasted, lifting his beer.

After being teased by all their friends, Khaled accepted Richard's offer. He convinced himself that he just wanted to try it and didn't want to be impolite by rejecting Richard's generosity.

Although Khaled's family was not a strictly observant religious household, they never had alcohol at home. But Khaled knew that some men in Al-Bireh, including his father, did drink discreetly, either at someone's house or at restaurants and bars in the adjacent town of Ramallah, whose inhabitants were mostly Christians.

Khaled sipped his beer. He wasn't sure he liked the taste, but he was curious about alcohol and why people enjoyed it so much. Soon, he felt lightheaded, but he liked the sensation, so he went to the kitchen for another one. Richard asked him to slow down and have some food, but he ignored him.

"You've been pushing me to drink, and now you want me to stop. Make up your mind."

Khaled not only enjoyed the buzz, but also the freedom his drink gave to flirt with the girls around. After he went to grab his third beer, he came back and sat between Mary and Elizabeth, joking with them about his parents and siblings. Soon, his jokes became bolder. By the time he finished his fifth beer, he felt dizzy and sick. He excused himself and staggered slowly, finding his way to the bathroom. When he didn't come back, Richard went looking for him.

"My God, what did you do to yourself? Are you okay?"

Richard knelt next to Khaled, who was sitting on the floor leaning back against the wall, his clothes covered with vomit and his face wet with tears.

"I feel so sick... You made me drink that stupid beer."

"I gave you *one* and told you to slow down and eat something, but you wouldn't listen. What was I supposed to do?"

Richard walked back to his friends and told them he had to take Khaled home. Although the dorm was not that far, Khaled could hardly stand, so Richard had to order a taxi. Once at the dorm, Richard helped Khaled clean up and get settled in bed.

Khaled woke up late with a throbbing headache. His mouth was drier than a desert and his tongue felt like sandpaper. He tried to recall the evening and felt ashamed as he remembered how drunk he was. He also remembered Elizabeth, along with a tinge of both pleasure and guilt. *I'm such a jerk. I shouldn't have given in to the temptation of alcohol.* He wondered if getting sick was God's punishment. Khaled promised *Allah* and himself that he would never drink again. Although he couldn't remember the last time he had prayed, he decided to pray and fast for one day to repent for his sins.

Not knowing what else he could do to gain God's forgiveness, he kept reciting a verse from the Quran, *Inna Allaha Ghafoorun Raheem;* God is merciful and forgiving. Khaled envied his Christian friends whose religion allowed them to drink. They could even go to confession and admit wrongdoing, and God would erase their sins. So, he decided to talk directly to God and promise not to drink again.

A few days after the drinking party, Richard invited Khaled to go with him to spend Christmas with his family in Cincinnati.

"My mother must have liked you a lot. She asks about you every time we talk and wants me to bring you with me to celebrate with us—my parents and sister. Most of the kids on campus will be gone and it will be too lonely to spend Christmas by yourself."

"That would be wonderful. Are you sure?"

"No, I'm lying. I think you should stay here alone."

"How long are you going to be there?"

"A week at most. We could go there on Christmas Eve and come back the day after New Year's Day."

On Christmas day, Richard's paternal grandparents and his uncle's family of four arrived in the afternoon. As the family gathered around the fire to share gifts, Richard's father brought the adults drinks, whiskey for the men and gin and tonics for the women. Richard whispered to Khaled that they could sneak some beer later, but Khaled wouldn't hear of it. The memory of his drinking night was still fresh in his mind, and he wasn't about to embarrass himself at Richard's parents' home.

After the drinks were served came the gift opening. Khaled was fascinated by the size of the Christmas tree with its elaborate decorations, and the number of wrapped gifts under it. He was so surprised when Richard's mother handed him a box, with a sweater similar to the one she gave Richard, that he couldn't hold back his tears.

"Thank you very much. I've never received a Christmas gift before," he said as he wiped his tears with the back of his hand.

"How come?" asked the grandfather. "Richard told me you came from the Holy Land and went to school in Jerusalem. Don't you celebrate Christmas there?"

"Christians do. I come from Al-Bireh. It's a Muslim town not far from Jerusalem. But next to our town is Ramallah, a Christian town, and I have been to my Christian friend's homes at Christmas, but no one ever gave me a gift."

Richard's grandfather, as well as his whole family, were surprised to learn from Khaled that some Palestinian Christians celebrated Christmas on the seventh of January, that gifts were given only to the children, and that the most important religious holiday for Palestinian Christians wasn't Christmas, but Easter.

They sat around the long dining table that was packed with all kinds of food, some Khaled had never eaten or seen before, including a whole roasted turkey, stuffing, cranberry sauce, and honey-baked ham. This was the first home-cooked meal he'd had since he left his home over four months ago. Out of curiosity, as well as politeness, Khaled ate everything he was offered including the ham, which, as a Muslim, he wasn't supposed to eat, but he really liked it a lot. *It's my friend's holiday,* he reasoned, *and I am a guest here. I should be polite and eat what I'm offered. Allah will understand.*

~

Khaled enjoyed spending the holiday week with Richard's family. On New Year's Eve, Richard's father popped a bottle of champagne. The noise made Khaled jump out of his seat, setting off everyone laughing. Once the laughter subsided, Richard's father poured and distributed the champagne, including to Khaled and Richard.

"Here, happy New Year. Enjoy, but don't get the idea that you can drink before you're twenty-one."

"Don't worry about it, Dad. I won't."

As his father turned his head, Richard winked at his friend and they both smiled. Khaled loved the hospitality, affection, and kindness he received, especially from Richard's mother. It made him miss his own mother and holidays in Palestine.

He reflected on the festivities of the month of Ramadan and the *Eids.* The Muslim holidays were times when extended families and friends gathered to celebrate; when kids got new clothes and were given gifts of cash from their elder relatives; when they were allowed to run the streets with their friends and to spend their holiday cash as they pleased; when certain rules that governed their young lives were eased, and the most delicious foods and desserts were in abundance.

~

Since the beer incident at David's house over two weeks before, Khaled had been unable to write to Wafa. It was the first time that he hadn't written to her weekly. He kept telling himself that tomorrow he would. His previous letters to her were almost like a diary, reporting details from pretty much every aspect of his life. Sometimes, he would send her two or three letters in the same envelope. When he finally sat down to write, he told her about getting straight-As, going with Richard to celebrate the end of the semester, and his trip to Cincinnati. But he couldn't bring himself to mention his drinking night or eating ham. He managed to convince himself that omitting certain facts was not really lying.

~

At the end of their first year, Richard asked Khaled if he would like to go with him to David's to celebrate the graduation of one of David's roommates.

"I'd love to. But I'm not going to drink, and you and your friends can't make fun of me for not drinking."

"What if we tease you about drinking Coke."

"Richard, I'm serious."

"Me too," said Richard as both of them laughed.

At David's, Khaled got himself a Coke. As he watched his friends having a good time drinking, he reminded himself how sick and sorry he was when he drank before. But soon, he couldn't resist the temptation and went to the kitchen and got a beer, convincing himself that this time he wouldn't drink more than one.

When he got his second, Richard told him, "You need to slow down and eat something before having another one."

"I don't see you doing that."

"Well, I already ate. And I've been drinking beer for a couple years, which you haven't. Take it slow until your body gets used to it."

"Don't worry about me. I'll be fine."

"Well, I'm telling you, if you get sick, don't count on me to take care of you."

Totally ignoring Richard's advice, Khaled felt dizzy and sick after his fourth beer. Without telling anyone, he left quietly and managed to walk to his dorm. The next morning, when he woke up with a bad headache, he felt regretful and promised Allah he would never drink again or join Richard or other friends at drinking parties.

Despite all the promises he made to God and to himself, Khaled could not resist the temptation of drinking. Soon, thanks to Richard, he learned how to enjoy his beers. *Drinking helps me relax and puts me at ease flirting with my female friends. It's not like I am cheating on Wafa. Plus, I get straight-A's, so what's the harm?*

Khaled also started to enjoy being away from his father's oppressive attitudes, nosy relatives and neighbors, and the confinement of his small town where everyone knows what you're doing and feels free to tell you what you should or should not do.

As time went by, he became more accustomed to his new life. His yearning for Wafa and for his family diminished. His letters to both gradually became shorter and less frequent, and most of the details about his life—other than school and weather—began to disappear.

This change did not go unnoticed. Wafa gently urged him to write more: "I enjoyed your detailed letters. They helped me visualize your life in America and made me feel closer to you." His mother expressed her concerns about her son more directly, asking him questions and wanting answers. So Khaled sought out Richard's advice.

"I don't know how to respond to this letter from my mother. She is asking me why I don't write as much as I used to. She wants to be sure I haven't surrendered to the seductive American life, which to her means women, sex, and drinking."

"Mothers always worry, especially about their sons. If I were you, I wouldn't think much of it. When my dad starts asking questions, that's when I usually worry," Richard said.

"As long as I'm doing well in school, none of the other stuff matters to my father. After all, he lived in the States for many years, where he drank, smoked, and had friendships with women. But after a time, he came back, started a successful business, and married my mother. I'm sure he assumes I'm going to do the same."

"Are you?" asked Richard.

7
THE GIRL IN THE YELLOW DRESS

Summer 1960

Khaled sipped his cold beer served in a ceramic coffee mug while chatting with Joe, the bartender. He had met the twenty-five-year-old anarchist, activist and university dropout through his roommate Richard. The two quickly became friends. Khaled found refuge in the Old German Restaurant, especially in the late afternoon when it was almost empty and he could enjoy Joe's company and the day's special offering.

Joe found Khaled to be someone with whom he could freely share his political views about the Civil Rights Movement, the Cuban Revolution, or US imperialism. Khaled enjoyed listening to and talking with Joe. He felt comfortable opening up with him about things like his experience with Kanji when he first arrived and questions he had about the Japanese internment camps or Native American reservations and the annihilation of their culture, as well as his love to Wafa.

It was an unusually hot week. The sun beat down on the earth and all those who dared to be outdoors. But the restaurant stayed cool and dim as the sun struggled to shed light on the dark bricks, walls, and ceiling beams. Upscale, though not far from campus, it was not often frequented by students. It was also not far from Khaled's apartment, which he'd shared with Richard since the end of their freshman year.

Most of the students were away, spending the summer with their families. For Khaled, home was too far and too costly. He was taking summer classes, hoping to finish one semester—or even one year—early and return to his sweetheart, Wafa. Richard also stayed. He had landed a summer job working evenings at the daily newspaper, the *Ann Arbor News*. With their conflicting schedules, they hadn't been able to spend much time together. Befriending Joe and hanging out at the Old German broke the monotony of long summer days and eased Khaled's loneliness.

A bright light suddenly illuminated the place as the door swung open, interrupting Khaled's thoughts. As he turned his head, he noticed three young women, but the brightness made it too hard to see more. It took a few seconds for his eyes to adjust.

The women looked around, deciding where to sit, then spotted and settled into a brown leather booth not far from him. They ordered hamburgers, fries, and Cokes. Khaled watched them. He was particularly drawn to the woman in the bright yellow dress that exposed her shoulders and hugged her slim figure. She looked familiar. Searching his memory, he remembered meeting her twice. The first time was when he had his initial experience with alcohol and got totally wasted. He even remembered flirting with her and thinking about her the next morning. The second time, a couple of months later, he saw her at the library; embarrassed by his drinking experience, he tried to avoid her by hiding behind a bookshelf, but she was quick to approach him.

"Hi. Sorry, I forgot your name. You're Richard's friend, right?"

"Yes, I am. My name is Khaled."

"I'm Elizabeth. We met not too long ago. I believe it was just before Christmas. We were celebrating the end of the fall semester. I'm sure you won't remember. You were so drunk, Richard had to take you home."

"I'm still ashamed of what happened that night. It was my first drink ever. I was hoping you wouldn't remember."

"Don't be silly. We all get drunk at one time or another. Anyway, nice to see you again, sober," she teased. "I have to get to class. Have a nice day."

As Khaled watched her walk away, he thought it was interesting that a woman would not only drink but admit that she'd gotten drunk.

But now, sitting at the bar a few months later, Khaled wondered if she still even remembered him. He was tempted to go over and talk to her.

"Do you know these women? Do they come here often?" Khaled asked Joe, breaking the silence that had invaded their space with the women's arrival.

"No, I don't. I've never seen them here before. Why are you asking?"

"I remember meeting the one in the yellow dress. I think her name is Elizabeth, but I haven't seen her in a while."

Khaled became totally absorbed in watching the three women, fascinated by the sudden changes in their demeanor. At times, they would lean their heads together and whisper. Then, all of a sudden, they would get flamboyant and loud, laughing hysterically. He was curious to know what was so funny.

"Hey man, what's going on?" asked Joe. "I'm talking to you."

"What?"

"You've been staring at these girls since they walked in. I thought you had a girl waiting for you in your country."

"I do, I do. I'm just watching. Not much else to do in this place."

Thinking of Wafa, Khaled felt a little guilty. *Of course, I am still in love with Wafa. But I am lonely and want to meet and talk to people. There's nothing wrong with that. I just wish Elizabeth would recognize me and invite me to sit with her and her friends.*

When Elizabeth finally noticed him, he gestured to her to come and sit with him. She smiled. Two deep dimples indented her rosy cheeks while she shook her head. "No."

He smiled back and then asked Joe to check and see if they wanted anything else.

"My treat."

"I will," Joe said as he handed him a piece of gum. "To refresh your breath. Just in case."

"Don't worry about it. The one I like already knows I drink."

"I'm not worried about you, shithead. I'm worried about losing my job if the boss finds out."

Joe walked to the women's table and asked them if they needed anything else.

After ordering desserts and coffee, Elizabeth looked at Khaled and mouthed, "Thank you." Before he had a chance to reply, she turned to her friends and said something. Like little kids, they giggled.

When she looked at him again, he was still staring. He waved his hand, inviting her to come over and sit with him. Once again, she shook her head no. He pointed to himself then to her, moving his fingers as if asking, "Can I come over?" She laughed aloud, threw her head back, extending her long neck, and her straight blond hair reached her shoulders.

Slowly, he got off his stool. Mustering his most charming smile and with deliberate, almost comically confident steps, he walked up to her.

"Hello. My name is Khaled. May I join you?"

"Hi. I'm Elizabeth," she said, smiling. "These are my friends, Emily and Elaine."

"Nice to meet you. The three Es. May I call you E1, E2, and E3? That way, I won't forget your names."

The women all laughed. Proud of his wit, Khaled cocked his head, and his wide grin almost touched his ears.

"Have a seat. Join us, we're celebrating Elaine's birthday," Elizabeth said, moving to make room for him to sit next to her.

Khaled wondered if Elizabeth recognized him. He looked at Elaine.

"Happy Birthday, Elaine!"

"Thank you."

"I noticed that you've been looking at us with your big dark eyes since we entered the restaurant," Elizabeth said.

"And your blue eyes have been answering back."

"You do look familiar. Did we ever meet before?"

"No, never," he said, blushing.

"I'm sure we did . . . Oh, now I remember. We met—"

"Please don't . . . Have you had enough to eat and drink?" he offered quickly.

Luckily, the desserts and coffee arrived.

"Nice to run into you again," Khaled said, trying not to give her a chance to talk about the first time they met. "Are you taking summer classes?"

"No. Actually, I've been working full time."

"How come?"

"I don't have a choice. I had only a one-year scholarship. I need to save money for next year."

"How about your parents? Won't they help pay for your education?"

"They claim they can't afford it, though they manage to pay for my brother. My dad doesn't believe in education for women. To him, a woman's place is at home, cooking, cleaning, and raising kids."

"Sounds like most people back home."

"I noticed you have an accent. It's cute. I like it. But where is back home for you?"

"I'm Palestinian, from Al-Bireh."

Elizabeth wasn't sure exactly where that was, but she didn't ask. Instead, she asked him what he planned to study.

"Business administration. But I'm seriously thinking about changing my major to engineering. How about you?"

"Psychology. Although my mother, who doesn't object as much as my dad about me going to school, keeps telling me I am wasting my money and time studying psychology. She thinks I should study to become either a secretary or a teacher."

"I would rather not study business administration. But that's what my father wants. I'm the oldest of my six siblings, and he expects me go back and work with him."

"I can't believe it," Elizabeth responded. "That sounds just like my family. I come from a big family like yours, even bigger. We are ten, six boys and four girls. I'm number two. My youngest sister is only three. I could be her mother. As the oldest daughter I am expected to do a lot around the house. My brothers don't lift a finger. I'm so glad I don't live at home."

"I'm not sure I can say that. I have mixed feelings about being so far from my family. Sometimes it does get lonely, especially around the holidays, and the summers, but it's also liberating. Back home, everyone knows you. People are in your business all the time. But they're hospitable, warm, loving. As the saying goes, too much love can kill you."

For the next hour, Khaled and Elizabeth talked and cracked jokes. Once in a while they would remember including Emily and Elaine. Khaled talked to Elizabeth with ease and openness about his hometown, his mother and his siblings. But he avoided talking about his father and never mentioned Wafa.

"It's time to go," Elizabeth finally announced.

Khaled looked at her. "Please stay," he asked softly.

"I can't."

"Why not?"

"Because . . . "

Before they separated, they agreed to meet the next week—same time, same place—and they exchanged phone numbers.

"Come alone? No other Es," he whispered.

Hands in his pockets and head down, Khaled walked aimlessly for a long time. The sun had softened, and a light breeze cooled the air. He went to the arboretum and walked, going over his conversation with Elizabeth, recalling every word and gesture. He tried to convince himself that nothing he said or did fell into the category of being unfaithful to Wafa. *We just talked, nothing happened,* he kept telling himself. He recalled what Joe had told him about having a girl in his country waiting for him. He tried to imagine how he would feel if Wafa did the same, but quickly dismissed the idea. *She wouldn't do that. And it's not the same.*

By the time he got to his apartment, he was dragging his feet and rubbing his temples. The apartment was dark and quiet. He checked Richard'sbedroom and found that it was empty. He was relieved as he had no desire to talk. In the bathroom, he reached into the medicine cabinet for two aspirin, swallowed them, then walked to his room and collapsed on the bed.

But sleep refused to come. His conversation with Elizabeth was still haunting him, like a song that invades your brain and refuses to leave. Though it was past midnight, he decided to get up. In the shower, he let the hot water caress his body for a long time. He massaged his head and shoulders, but his tight chest and hurting soul were unforgiving. He wondered if what he was experiencing was love at first sight.

Khaled grabbed a box of fine stationery and an expensive pen, a high-school graduation gift from his Uncle Omar. At the small dining table, he started writing a letter to Wafa. By his sixth attempt, Richard walked in.

"You're still up? Writing to that girl again?"

The wastebasket under the table caught Richard's attention.

"What's going on? Look at all these crumpled drafts. You're wasting all your fancy stationery. What a shame." Richard said as he reached into the waste basket.

"Stop it. This is not funny," Khaled said, pushing Richard away harder than he intended.

"Wow. This sounds serious. What happened?"

"Nothing. I'm tired. I'm going to sleep."

"Who's stopping you? It's not like you were asleep, and I woke you up."

Richard walked to the refrigerator to look for something to eat.

Khaled collected all the crumpled paper, walked into his bedroom, and stuck them under his pillow. It was dawn before sleep relieved him. When he woke up, it was almost 1:00 PM. Richard was having a bowl of cereal.

"Hi Richard. I'm sorry about last night. I was tired."

"Don't worry about it. You seemed more upset than tired. I'd love to hear what's going on, but I have to shower and go to work."

~

When Richard came home at around eleven PM, he found Khaled sitting at the kitchen table with paper and pen.

"You're not writing to her? Again? I thought you were taking summer classes. Don't you ever study? It seems all you do is write letters."

"I'm trying to write, but I can't."

Khaled looked away, embarrassed.

"What's going on, my friend? Is everything okay between you and your girl?" Richard grabbed two cold beers and sat next to him.

"It's not Wafa."

"I don't understand... What is it then? Anything wrong with school or your family?"

"Well..."

"Well, what?"

"Yesterday at the Old German, I met three women. One of them was Elizabeth."

"I'm not sure what you're talking about."

"Don't you remember Elizabeth? She was with us when we went to celebrate the end of our first semester."

"You mean when you got really drunk?"

"Why does everyone remember that? I'm asking you if you remember her, not what I did that night."

"Yes, I do. What about her?"

"I really like her. I think she likes me too. We agreed to meet again next week. I'm not sure if it's a good idea, but I can't get her out of my head. I don't understand what's happening to me. I love Wafa. I don't want to be unfaithful."

"What are you complaining about? You have two women who like you, and I can't even find one. Am I supposed to feel sorry for you?"

For the rest of the week, Khaled had the same conversation with Richard every time they talked.

"I don't know what to do. I like Elizabeth and want to see her again, but I feel guilty. What would you do if you were in my place?"

"I wish I had your problem. But when it comes to women, my mother always told me to be careful not to get a woman pregnant or make a commitment until I graduate and have a job good enough to support a family. So what if you see Elizabeth again? Just follow my mom's advice. I don't think it's realistic not to date anyone during all your school years. In the end, you'll go back home and marry your girl, and that's what really matters."

Khaled couldn't even imagine sharing his quandary with his mother. As close as he felt to her, he was unable to tell her about his love for and promise to Wafa, let alone being with an American girl.

"I'm not sure about your mother's advice. My mother would disown me if she knew."

"For God's sake, stop torturing yourself. You only talked to her. If it's bothering you that much, just call and cancel. It's not like you owe her anything."

"You're right. I should cancel. I will do that," he said, not sure if he really meant it.

8
STANDING ELIZABETH UP

Khaled spent the week after meeting Elizabeth swinging between excitement and guilt. Being unfaithful or deceptive was not who he thought he was, but the desire to see Elizabeth was unstoppable. Sleep was hard to come by. When it did, Wafa or his mother were always there awakening him. He tossed and turned until his bones ached, forever comparing Wafa and Elizabeth. He knew his dad had befriended women when he lived in the US, then returned home and married his mother. But he was not his father, nor did he want to be. In their culture, which Wafa resented and mocked, it was acceptable for men to do that, but women who dared to do the same would be shunned and shamed. He recalled Wafa once telling him, "I don't believe in this double standard culture that favors men and allows them to do what women can't."

"I agree with you," he said, not sure if he honestly did. But they had promised to be faithful and honest with each other. He had already lied to her about drinking and was unable to imagine her in a bar or talking to men in the same way he talked to Elizabeth. Nor could Khaled imagine her wanting to be with a man other than himself, the same way he wanted to be with Elizabeth.

Since childhood, he'd had a way with women. He found their companionship more interesting, and in turn, they liked his kindness and innocent flirtation. In the past, talking and joking with women, including classmates, came naturally and was harmless. But he had never felt as much at ease with another woman as he did with Elizabeth, not even with Wafa. True, Elizabeth was not as beautiful, but her inviting laugh, piercing blue eyes, and her soft, almost transparent skin were calling him to embrace her. He wanted to touch and count the brown freckles on her nose and arms and bury his face in her hair. He felt conflicted about seeing her again and planned to call and cance, but every time he grabbed the phone and was about to dial, his fingers refused to cooperate. *Let me think first. What am I going to tell her without hurting her feelings?* he kept asking himself.

When the crucial day finally arrived and the dreadful hour got nearer, Khaled felt exhausted. He decided to lie down before taking a shower. The sleep that refused to visit him all these nights became a dark wave that took him under.

The phone . . . the phone . . . it's ringing . . . why won't it stop . . . where is Richard . . . who could this be? Slowly, he got up and dragged his body to the phone. His heavy hand lifted the receiver.

"You stood me up," she yelled. "I'm not the one who asked for a date. You did."

"Oh . . . what time is it? I'm so sorry, Elizabeth. I had a headache and fell asleep."

"You could have called."

"But— "

"I don't want to hear some bullshit excuse."

A thud pierced his ears. The deadly silence that followed sent shivers through his spine.

It took him a few minutes to overcome his shock. While he felt a sense of relief for not going, he regretted the way it happened. *I shouldn't have asked her for a date. But the least I could have done was to call and cancel. I must call her back and apologize.*

He made himself a cup of coffee and sat at the kitchen table, thinking about his options. Recalling how upset she was made it hard to call, but he knew he had to. He dialed her number. But there was no answer. He tried again several times without luck. He wished he knew where she lived. He wanted to go there and apologize in person.

The following day, he called again, and Emily answered the phone.

"No, she's not here."

"Can you please tell her that I called? Tell her that I'm really sorry about what happened yesterday. Ask her to call me back. Will you?"

~

But Elizabeth did not call. As much as he wanted to call her again, he decided not to. Her message was clear: she did not want to talk or see him again, and he should not harass her. *Maybe it's better this way,* he thought.

He kept reminding himself about Wafa. But his desire to see Elizabeth would not leave him alone. For the next few weeks, he couldn't stop thinking about her. He kept asking his friend Joe if she had come back to the Old German Restaurant. His answer was always no.

"You seem obsessed with her. What about your girl in the old country? I bet she would dump you if she found out."

"I am not obsessed. I just want to apologize. What I did was horrible, and she was really upset."

"Don't be so dramatic. You're not the first man to stand a girl up. Get over it."

"I did not stand her up. I had a headache and fell asleep. That's the truth."

"Okay, okay. Have another beer," said Joe as he refilled Khaled's coffee mug.

On a crispy October afternoon, Khaled was about ready to enter the Student Union to meet some friends when he found himself face to face with Elizabeth as she was leaving the building.

"Hello, Elizabeth! It's wonderful to see you."

"Really? Khaled, correct? The man who stood me up is now happy to see me." Her voice was sharp but shaky.

"Please, Elizabeth, I'm really sorry about what happened."

"It's a bit too late to be sorry, isn't it?"

"Elizabeth, please listen to me. I know you're upset, and I don't blame you. I really am sorry. I tried to call and apologize, but you didn't want to talk to me."

"Should I?

"All I'm asking for is a chance to explain."

"There's not much to explain."

"Just give me a chance. Honestly, Elizabeth, I did have a bad headache. I laid down to take a quick nap to get rid of it before meeting you, but I fell asleep until you called. You have to believe me. I would never intentionally stand you up. I would never do this to you or anyone else. I hope you'll believe me and accept my apology."

To his surprise, tears were gathering in his eyes. Elizabeth looked at him, perplexed by his sadness. She looked softly at him for a few seconds.

"Apology accepted," she finally said.

"Can I buy you a cup of coffee as a peace offering?"

"Not today. I have to go to work."

"How about the weekend?"

"Not this weekend. I have to go home."

"Does that mean you'll accept my invitation some other day?"

"We'll see."

"Will you call me?"

"I need to think about it." Her voice was soft and kind. She looked at her watch."I'm running late. I have to go."

Before he had a chance to respond, she turned around and started to walk fast, almost running, her ponytail bouncing and her shirt almost reaching the edge of her short skirt. Khaled stood there watching her until she turned the corner and disappeared.

As he walked slowly, reflecting on their short encounter, he couldn't figure out if she was interested in seeing him again. But he was relieved that he finally had a chance to apologize. While his ego was a bit wounded that she didn't accept his invitation, he was thankful that she at least forgave him and possibly forced him to stay faithful to Wafa.

9
JFK IN ANN ARBOR

October 14, 1960

"Here you are! You look like shit. What happened to you?" Khaled asked his roommate. "And where have you been? You— "

"Where have I been?" Richard interrupted. "I've been to heaven and back while you were home just sleeping, drinking coffee. My roommate is an idiot. La . . . la . . . la . . . " He moved his body in a silly dance.

Khaled was still in his pajamas, drinking his morning coffee. He gestured to his friend to sit down, but Richard continued his dance.

"Richard, what's going on? Are you drunk or what?"

"What happened last night is a million times better than all the beer and whiskey ever invented. You're an idiot . . . You missed the most exciting historical event that ever happened here. Right here in Ann Arbor, at *our* university."

"Stop calling me an idiot and stop going round and round about how great it was. Either settle down and spit it out, or go take a shower. You actually stink."

"Honestly, Khaled, I don't even know where to start or how to describe it. It's the best thing that ever happened to me. You just missed a once-in-a-lifetime experience. Thousands of students were there, singing, chanting, and laughing. We waited until two in the morning before John Kennedy showed up and spoke."

Regret and resentment washed over Khaled as he saw how excited and happy his friend was. He swallowed hard, trying to push sad memories away and bring himself back to Richard.

"Wait a minute . . . Are you trying to tell me that John Kennedy, the one running for president, came and spoke that late?"

"Yes, Khaled. That is exactly what I'm trying to tell you. He arrived at two AM."

"It's ten now, so where have you been since then? You must have found yourself a warmer bed to spend the night."

"I'm serious, Khaled. Tell me, when would I ever have another chance to see Kennedy in person? And on top of that, be the only one from my newspaper to write about him? I'm sorry you didn't come. It was a historical moment. I am sure he's going to win the election. It'll be so cool to have a young, handsome president for a change. Some students got tired of waiting and left. Even some journalists left after midnight, thinking he wasn't going to show up. I'm glad I stayed. I took pictures and notes and then rushed to the office and wrote about it. I was in the office until now. My article is going to be included in the special issue that's coming out this afternoon. It's like a dream. What more could I ask for?"

"That's amazing. I'm really happy for you," Khaled said genuinely. "You haven't slept at all. No wonder you look so miserable."

"Who cares? To be there and listen to Kennedy announce this new program called the Peace Corps was worth it. He asked how many of us are willing, after we graduate, to serve our country and world peace by living and working abroad. Thousands of students were cheering and yelling, 'We'll go, we'll go!' What a cool idea. It's a way to live and learn about other countries. I think I'll sign up."

"Sounds like a great program. Who knows, maybe I'll join you."

"I think it's only for American citizens. I'm not sure if you can."

"Then you could come to Palestine and serve there. It would be fun to be together after we graduate."

"Sounds good to me. Right now, I'm going to take a shower and have a nap. Then we can go out to get a few copies of the newspaper. Can't wait to see it. I'll get a bunch and send a couple to my parents. They'll be so proud."

"I am sure they will," Khaled said as his mind drifted back to Al-Bireh and his father. He felt hate building up inside him. He shook his head, dismissing his troubling thoughts.

"What's wrong, Khaled? Are you all right?"

"I feel stupid and cowardly for not going with you last night, that's all."

A few weeks later, Richard came home at around midnight.

"Hi, Khaled. Are you up?" he called excitedly.

"Yes. I'm here, studying. What's up? You sound so happy."

"I'll tell you in a minute. Let me grab a Coke first."

"Get two and the chips. I just bought some."

Richard walked into Khaled's bedroom, handed him a Coke, and sat at the foot of the bed, placing a bag of chips between them.

"Your newspaper job suits you," Khaled said. "You always come home excited about one thing or another."

"It's great work. There's always something exciting happening. Actually, I'm thinking of changing my major to journalism."

"Really? What's happening now?"

"My boss was so happy with what I did when Kennedy came, now he wants me to cover a meeting of a new organization called Students for a Democratic Society, SDS. When I called my dad to tell him, he said, 'What the hell for? America is already a democratic society.'"

"That's funny. My dad would've said the same. But I don't agree with him or with your dad. Do you?"

"Of course not. Otherwise, I wouldn't have joined the organization. I'm so excited. He wants me to interview some of the founders. It's a public meeting. You should come."

"When is it?"

"Tomorrow at three in the Student Union."

"I wish I could," Khaled said, shaking his head. Deep lines appeared on his forehead, and a sad look came over his face.

"What's wrong? It's a student meeting, not a funeral."

"I know, but I can't."

"Why not? There are so many exciting things happening on campus, and you always find an excuse not to go. It's not like you're not interested or so busy. You don't even have a job. I see you spending a lot of time reading newspapers and listening to the news. You're curious about what's going on here and in the world, but you never want to participate or do anything. You're like these rich intellectual kids. What's the point of learning about the world if you're not going to do something about it?"

"Of course, I care. You act like you're the only one who does."

"Honestly, Khaled, I'm puzzled by you. We're best friends, but I have to admit, sometimes I don't understand you."

"It's my dad. He would probably disown me if he knew I went to any of these events. Sometimes, I feel like I hate the SOB. Ever since I was a teenager, he warned me not to get involved in politics. Actually, the last thing he said to me before getting on the plane was to focus on my studies and stay away from politics."

"My dad doesn't want me to be involved in politics either. Do you really think all these politically active students ask their parents for permission?"

"Probably not. And to be honest with you, I'd love to be able to say, 'Fuck you, Dad. I can make my own decisions.' But it's a long, complicated story."

"It's because of the money, isn't it? Are you afraid he would cut you off, and you wouldn't be able to find a job like many of us?"

"It's more complicated than that."

"I'm all ears."

"Of course, I'm interested in politics," said Khaled, taking a deep breath to steady his voice. "How could I not be? I come from a place where politics are ingrained in everything. Ever since my childhood and the loss of half of our country in 1948, along with the displacement of so many Palestinians, politics and the news are always in everybody's conversations. But my father stayed away from politics. He was more concerned about protecting and expanding his business. His favorite response was always, 'What happened to our people is a tragedy. But we can't spend our lives dwelling on the past. We have to move on.'"

Khaled's voice started to shake. His throat was closing on him. He started to get up.

"Where are you going?" asked Richard.

"I need to get some water."

"Stay, I'll get it."

Richard came back with a glass of water, handed it to Khaled, and sat back down on the bed.

"You seem so upset. There must be more you're not telling me about you and your father. So, what is it?"

"Unlike my dad, I became interested in politics when I was in middle school. My favorite teacher, *Ustath* Omar, came from the Al-Am'ari refugee camp, not too far from Al-Bireh. He took the time to join his students at recess or afterschool activities to tell us about different local, national, and international events going on. I also liked hanging with some of the neighbor's kids and a few of my older cousins, who were also interested in politics. Whenever there was a demonstration or a political rally, which happened a lot at the time, my father would come home furious, cursing the protesters and the communists behind them, who hurt his business or, even worse, forced him to close. Once in a while, I would sneak into a demonstration without telling him. But in our small town, nothing stayed secret."

Khaled choked and couldn't say more, and turned his face away from Richard. He remembered his father's reaction when he disobeyed him and went to a demonstration. He was not only beaten badly but he was sent against his will to a private English school in Jerusalem, which he hated. He was fifteen years old. He never talked about it to anyone. And the terror of that incident never left him.

"Oh my God, Khaled. I'm sorry. So, what happened?"

"Nothing."

"Well, something did. You were telling me about participating in a demonstration without telling your dad. Then, you stopped as if you saw a ghost. What is it? I'm your friend. You can tell me."

"I can't. It's too hard to talk about. I'd rather pretend it never happened. But with all that's taking place on campus and your involvement, it's coming back to me.."

"What is, Khaled? Let it out. The more you hold it in, the worse it gets. Trust me, you'll feel better if you talk about it."

"Not today, maybe later. Maybe never . . . I think I need some fresh air."

10
STUDENTS FOR A DEMOCRATIC SOCIETY

Khaled dragged his feet up the stairs of the Student Union. With every step, he could hear his heartbeats getting louder. He took a few deep breaths and cautiously stepped into the unknown. Not venturing far from the entrance, he scanned the large room packed with people, looking for a familiar face, but found none. He was torn between his desire to be there at the meeting and his fear of being seen by any of the Arab students, especially the few Palestinians he had met in his freshman year. They had asked him to join the Organization of Arab Students and kept inviting him to political and cultural events, many of which centered around Palestine, but he kept declining. *What if one of them sees me now? And what if the news ends up reaching my father?* Resentment swelled inside him as he wondered if he would ever be able to free himself from his father's grip. He tried to dismiss his fear as unreasonable and refocused his attention on what was happening in the noisy room he'd just entered.

He looked for a seat, but every single one was taken. A large number of students sat on the floor or lined the walls. He was pleased to find an empty wall space near an entrance, not far from where he was standing. *This is a perfect spot, just in case I decide to leave,* he thought.

Sudden cheering and chanting by the students brought his attention to what was happening around him. A young man with a guitar hanging across his chest had just appeared on the stage and walked toward the microphone. A large Students for a Democratic Society banner, almost the width of the room, stretched above him. As the musician started singing "We Shall Overcome," the crowd got even rowdier, and some students started to sing along. The place exploded again as the singer finished the song.

When the cheering quieted a bit, a young woman with long curly hair, wearing a colorful skirt and a bright red shirt, walked to the stage, adjusted the microphone, and with much enthusiasm yelled, "Please help me welcome the founder of Students for a Democratic Society— " Before she had a chance to finish her sentence, the students started clapping and chanting, "Allen... Allen... Allen... " The young woman smiled and clapped along, and then she gestured to them to sit down, which no one did. She tried again, this time almost screaming, hoping to override the chanting.

"Please, sit down. Please, sit down... Do you want to hear Allen or not?"

A loud scream, "Yes, we do. Yes, we do."

"Then let's do that." She searched the room, then continued. "Thank you. My name is Karen, and I am so happy and honored to introduce to you the one and only Mr. Robert Allen Haber."

The room exploded again. All the students stood up, waving hundreds of signs, mostly handwritten. The young Allen, dressed in a white shirt and dark blue pants, walked to the microphone amid more yelling and screaming. In his speech, he called on the students to organize and stand up for a genuinely democratic society, criticizing the US political system that favors wars over world peace, that had failed to address the social ills that had divided and infested society—exploitation, materialism, racism, and poverty. Upon finishing his speech, he thanked the crowd and walked away amid screams of the euphoric young people ready to take on the world.

Khaled was overwhelmed by the size of the audience and their passion. He hadn't attended a student meeting or political event since he was in the tenth grade. The energy of the crowd took him back to demonstrations and rallies in Palestine. He remembered his father blaming the leftists and communists for what he called lawless activities led by a bunch of immoral, lazy atheists. He wondered if his father would call these American students the same.

As the meeting came to a close, people began to move toward the exits. Khaled's heart skipped a beat as his eyes caught on to a girl with blonde hair. *Am I imagining things? That can't be her... My eyes must be playing tricks on me.* He looked again, closing and opening his eyes a few times just in case. *It's her... it's Elizabeth ... She's heading toward the exit, coming closer to me ... Oh my God, she doesn't seem to be alone. Who is that young man putting his arm around her shoulder?... Could he be her boyfriend?* He watched with envy. Then Elizabeth turned her head and talked to a woman walking closely behind her, and he relaxed a bit. But he kept his eyes on her, fearing she would escape his vision.

He followed her and her friends while keeping his distance, not sure if he should approach her. She was with three men and one woman, all young enough to be students. They walked across the street to the Diag, the heart of the school's main campus, and stood there talking, waving, and sometimes hugging other students as they passed by. Elizabeth looked happy, laughing the same laugh that drew him into her. Finally, she hugged her friends and walked away. A sigh of relief escaped him. He decided to follow her. He walked faster as he saw her cross State Street and walk into the Arcade, a covered passageway with shops.

"Hi. How wonderful to run into you. I hope you still remember me."

"How could I forget you?"

"Can I walk with you?"

"It's a public street. I can't stop you," she said playfully.

Hands stuffed in his pockets, he walked the short Arcade next to her, not sure how to break the silence. Finally, he asked,

"How did you like the meeting?"

"It was okay."

"You don't sound excited."

"My friends asked me to come, so I thought I'd check it out."

"Me too. My friend Richard convinced me. I'm glad we both listened to our friends. I am so happy to see you. I hope you are, too."

"What difference does it make how I feel?"

"You're not still mad at me, are you? I thought you accepted my apology."

"Doesn't mean I accepted your bullshit excuse."

"Honestly, it was the truth. And if I remember correctly, you agreed we could get together for coffee or a drink, but you said you were very busy. I hope you have time today. Please, let's go someplace quiet where I can apologize and explain again in style. I know a small restaurant on Main and Huron. Not many students go there. It's usually empty this time of the day."

"I'm not that hungry."

"We don't have to eat. We can just have something warm to drink."

The small place with no more than ten tables was almost empty. At one table was an elderly couple. At the other was a man in his early forties, dressed in a business suit, having a sandwich while going through a stack of files. The aroma of coffee and the fall afternoon sun added much-needed warmth to the nondescript place.

"Let's sit there at the sunny table," said Khaled, pointing to a corner table by a large window.

"Please allow me," he said as she tried to take off her jacket. Then he pulled a chair out to help her sit down. Her hair's subtle, clean scent took him to when they first met, to when he fell in love.

"Thank you. I guess you can be a gentleman if you want."

"I hope I'm always a gentleman who sometimes makes stupid mistakes." Not wanting to dwell on the topic, he quickly added, "I'm starving. I want to order a sandwich and coffee. Try their grilled sandwich. It's really good. My treat."

"Do you always treat people? You must have a lot of money."

"I only treat people I like, especially women," he said, wanting to break the ice, but he regretted the minute the words escaped his mouth. He knew couldn't take it back.

"I see," she said with a sarcastic smile.

A young waiter came to get their order. Both ordered grilled cheese sandwiches and coffee.

"Elizabeth, I'm really sorry about what happened. I hope you did find it in your heart to forgive me."

Elizabeth was quiet for a minute, rolling and unrolling the sleeve of her sweater. "I hope I have a forgiving heart," she finally said. "But I'm not stupid. You did not fall asleep. You changed your mind about seeing me but didn't have the courage, or shall I say, the decency to call."

"You can say I lacked both. But honestly, Elizabeth, I did fall asleep."

"That's even worse. Falling asleep in the middle of the day, before your first date. Sounds like you weren't that interested."

"I was . . . I was."

"Khaled, would you please stop trying to bullshit me?"

"All right. To tell you the truth, I was conflicted. I wanted to see you, but I knew I shouldn't. I spent the week thinking about calling to cancel. But I couldn't bring myself to do it. When the time came, I laid down to take a quick nap but fell into deep sleep. Your phone call woke me up. That's the truth."

"You said you were conflicted? Conflicted about what?"

"I hope I can explain it to you someday."

Khaled looked outside the window, trying to avoid saying more. He was delighted when the waiter came to pick up their empty plates and ask if they would care for dessert.

"Thank you. We would love some dessert and more coffee," he said. He looked at Elizabeth. "What would you like? I love their cheesecake. It's my favorite. Actually, all their desserts are delicious. They have carrot cake, brownies, pies . . ."

"I'd like another coffee and carrot cake."

"I was surprised to see you at the meeting," Khaled said, trying to avoid returning to the same conversation. "Are you involved in this organization?"

Elizabeth looked down, staring at the table, as if not sure how to respond.

"Are you with me?"

"Yes, yes. I am. Between my classes and job, I really don't have time for politics. Also, my parents, especially my father, would be very angry if he found out I went to a meeting like this."

"My father is the same. I'm glad he's so far away. Since I was young, I have been interested in politics and participated in demonstrations and rallies. My father, who hates politics, found a way to put an end to it. Now I just follow the news. But as I watched Richard coming home happy after going to events like this, I decided to give it a try."

As the sun shed its last rays on the city, more people started to come into the restaurant. Elizabeth looked at her watch and told Khaled that it was time for her to go home.

"Where do you live?"

"On campus. Not far from here."

"May I walk you home?"

"You don't have to."

"I want to."

When they walked outside, the cold air hit Khaled's face. Growing up in Palestine, he wasn't used to such cold weather. In spite of the uncomfortable cold that seeped into his bones, he wanted their walk to last, to have more time to think, to make up his mind if he wanted to or should ask her out again.

"You seem to be deep into your thoughts," Elizabeth commented as they reached her apartment.

"Not really, I'm just cold. I can't get used to this weather. Then quickly, he asked, "Am I forgiven, or do I need to apologize again?"

"Yes. You are forgiven. Apology accepted. Though you haven't told me why you were conflicted about seeing me."

"Maybe I can tell you later. Hopefully you want to see me again."

"Well, I need to think about it."

"How long will that take?"

"I don't know."

"Okay, take your time. But would you let me give you a kiss on the cheek as a thank you for forgiving me?"

"I have to think about that too," she said while getting closer, stretching her neck to be kissed.

11
FALLING FOR ELIZABETH

Khaled could not evict Elizabeth from his brain.

Unfamiliar yet pleasant sensations went through his body as he remembered his lips touching Elizabeth's face. It both surprised and disarmed him. And he wanted more. *Fate keeps bringing us together, I am sure of it . . . it's fate.* Even so, he did not want to depend on fate alone or look too eager to meet her. But after one week, he couldn't wait anymore. He dialed her number.

"It's time to keep your promise to have coffee with me."

"I didn't promise. I said I would think about it."

"And? Did you?"

"Not really."

Her flirtatious laugh was music to his ears.

"How about Saturday? We can go to dinner and then have coffee. What do you say about that?"

"This weekend I have to go to Grand Rapids to see my family." She paused for a few seconds. "But the following weekend, I'm willing to go to the Old German for another burger."

"Forget about the Old German and their burgers. Let's go to a different place, a fresh start."

"You are so funny. But I liked it there, and I'd only been there once."

Khaled was worried that going to the Old German would subject him to Joe's comments about his girlfriend in the old country. But he quickly realized that at dinnertime, Joe would be busy at the bar and wouldn't have time to talk, so he decided to go along with Elizabeth's choice.

Khaled arrived at the restaurant early, wanting to be there before Elizabeth. He tried very hard not to think of Wafa or the advice he was given before coming to the US. So, he focused on watching the entrance. This was his first date ever, and he wasn't sure how to handle himself. *What do I do when she gets here? How do I greet her? Shaking hands doesn't sound right. Should I hug her? Kiss her? Would she kiss me back?*

He waited. At a few minutes before eight, he checked the time, straightened his shirt and ran his fingers through his thick hair. 8:05 . . . 8:10 . . . 8:15. *Where is she?* He kept looking back and forth between his watch and the door. 8:20 . . . 8:25 . . . no Elizabeth. It felt like he'd been waiting an eternity. He was embarrassed by the way the waiter kept checking on him, so he ordered a Coke and chips. At around 8:45, it dawned on him. *Is it possible she never intended to come? Could this be her revenge? Was she trying to give him a taste of rejection?* For the next ten minutes, Khaled fought the urge to just leave.

Then, as he asked for the bill, Elizabeth entered.

She rushed toward him, joyful and colorful. Her bright red coat, loud, multicolored scarf, bouncy hair, and lipstick that matched the color of her coat drew not only his attention but turned many heads.

"Hi, Khaled. Sorry I'm late."

She hugged him and gave him a long, warm embrace, enough to make him dizzy.

"This place looks much nicer and fancier at night."

"Nothing but the best for you."

Elizabeth settled in and looked at the menu.

"Their dinner menu is much more expensive than I thought."

"Don't worry about it. Please just order what you like."

"You don't even have a job. Is your family that rich?"

"Forget about me and my family. How come you were so late? I was ready to leave. I thought you weren't coming."

"You mean you were afraid I was going to stand you up the way you did."

"Elizabeth, when are you going to forget that?"

"All depends on your future behavior."

"Does that mean this isn't a one-time date?"

"As I told you before, it all depends on your future behavior, which includes tonight."

"Tonight? It's not me who was late."

"Don't try to outsmart me. Remember, when I saw you last you told me you stood me up because you were conflicted about seeing me. When I asked why, you promised to tell me later. Are you going to tell me tonight?

"No . . . not tonight. Not after you made me wait for almost an hour." He smiled trying to make light of it.

"Then when?"

"Well, it all depends on your future behavior."

"I am serious Khaled, are you going to tell me or not?"

Khaled regretted telling her that he was conflicted. He could see she wasn't going to let it go.

"My family won't be happy if they know I'm dating an American woman."

She laughed.

"Is that it? My dad would be ready to kill me if he found out about many things I do."

"Like what?"

"Like dating a Muslim Palestinian."

"That's it?"

"No, there's more. But I'm really conflicted about letting you know. Maybe I will tell you later."

For almost a year and a half, Khaled and Elizabeth dated on and off. Both worried about where this relationship could take them. He was torn between surrendering to his desire to be with Elizabeth and staying faithful to Wafa. He was totally confused, not knowing what to do or whom he really loved. Wafa sensed him drifting away, so she would ask him about it. *"Your letters are becoming so redundant and far and in-between. What's going on?"* Whenever Khaled received a letter from her, he would decide not to see Elizabeth again. But that never lasted for long.

Likewise, Elizabeth had told him more than once that she was not sure if they should continue to see each other. "If my family found out, they would be so upset they might be ready to disown me. They expect me to date a Catholic, church-going conservative guy. Also, you're planning to go back home when you graduate. I often tell myself to just enjoy it and worry when the time comes. But other times, like you, I worry that both of us are going to get hurt."

Despite their anxiety and fears, neither one was able to let go.

During the long Michigan cold weather, they would see each other in the Student Union, coffee shops, and restaurants. Once in a while, Elizabeth would join Khaled at a political meeting or lecture, mostly about the Students for a Democratic Society or the Civil Rights Movement. In the summer, they went on picnics and long walks, mostly alone but sometimes with a few close friends. But their favorite activity was going to the movie theater, where the darkness engulfed them.

Khaled often wanted to be with Elizabeth in a more private place. He had invited her to his apartment and asked her if he could visit her, but she always found excuses: "I can't. I'm working," or "I'm studying," or "I am going to my family's this weekend."

Coming from a small, conservative town where dating was not acceptable and sex before marriage was taboo, Khaled understood Elizabeth and respected her restraint. So he was taken by surprise when she invited him to her apartment.

"Elaine and Emily are throwing me a birthday party, and I would like you to come. Also, please tell Richard. I'd like him to come, too."

At the party, Khaled was surprised by the number of people jammed into the small apartment. It was noisy, and he didn't have much opportunity to talk to Elizabeth, but he was happy to be there.

~

Elizabeth surprised Khaled again when she told him, "We've been to every restaurant and coffee shop in town at least half a dozen times. Don't you get tired of eating out? It's also very expensive."

"What do you want me to do? I don't know how to cook. Not even fry an egg."

"Lucky you. Being the first-born girl with so many younger siblings, I was cooking at the age of ten or eleven. How about you come over, and I cook you a nice dinner? I will even bake a carrot cake."

The idea of being with Elizabeth at her apartment was both tantalizing and terrifying. His imagination gave him a chill, and he started to feel warmth spreading through his groin.

"Khaled, I am talking to you."

"I know . . . I'm just . . . just . . . thinking."

"About what? I'm asking you to come to dinner at my place. That's all."

"Are you sure you want to do that? You always complain about not having enough time."

Khaled regretted the words that came out, fearing she would change her mind.

"Don't worry about me. I learned to juggle many things at the same time before I was even a teenager. Unlike you, I wasn't born with a silver spoon in my mouth."

"Why do you have to spoil things by bringing this up all the time? I'm not responsible for my father's wealth. Just like you, I have no control over who my father is, or my family, or my religion."

He toned down his voice and forced a smile.

"Elizabeth, would you please stop bringing this up?"

"Sorry. I was kidding. I didn't mean to hurt you. I would really like to have you over for dinner. This weekend I'm working Friday and Sunday. How about Saturday?"

Khaled wondered if Elaine and Emily, Elizabeth's roommates, were going to be there. Not wanting to ask directly, he said, "How about your girlfriends? Are you going to cook for all of us? That's a lot of cooking."

"They are going out of town, back Sunday. I'm lucky I was able to change my schedule and work Sunday instead of Saturday."

Not having enough money, Elizabeth went to school part-time and worked part-time at the Ann Arbor Public Library. Sometimes, she also worked weekends at Angelo's restaurant.

"Thank you. Of course, I will come. Am I allowed to bring some beer?"

"How are you going to get it?"

"Don't worry, I'll manage. I can't wait to be twenty-one. I'm going to have a great celebration at the Pretzel Bell Bar, and I am going to honor the tradition of drinking twenty-one beers. It's a tradition here, isn't it?"

"You get drunk from four beers, or was it five? remember?"

"Elizabeth, I'm kidding. You really don't know how to forget, do you?"

With a huge bouquet of flowers in one hand and a six-pack of beer in the other, the freshly showered and shaved Khaled knocked at her door.

"Oh my God, Khaled, no one ever gave me flowers. They're gorgeous! Let's empty your hands so I can give you a worthy thank you."

Elizabeth helped Khaled place the flowers and beer on the kitchen counter and gave him the promised welcome.

After they let go of each other's embrace, Elizabeth said, "You smell delicious."

"So do you."

He was surprised at how relaxed and forthcoming Elizabeth was and wondered what the night had in store for them.

Khaled looked around the apartment. He had been there once on her birthday, but the place was so crowded that he didn't notice how simple and elegant the place was. The small dining table was covered with an embroidered tablecloth, with matching napkins. The living room was bright. On each side of a large window were two bookshelves. The couch and two chairs were old but clean. A medium-sized center table had a large potato chip bowl. A few posters covered the walls. His mind drifted to the bedrooms. He wondered if Elizabeth had her own and if she would let him see it. His own thoughts frightened him.

"These chips look good. Can we have a beer and some chips before dinner?"

"Of course we can. Actually, dinner isn't ready yet. I have a roast in the oven and will need at least another twenty minutes. But first, let me find a vase for the flowers.

They sat on the couch, not too close at first. But slowly, they inched their way toward each other. He stretched out his hand to hold hers, assessing what might come next. They had never been alone this way. The most physical intimacy they'd had was at the movies, holding hands, kissing, and touching. But whenever Khaled's hands tried to explore more, Elizabeth found a way to stop him. Not sure how she was going to react and not wanting to ask, Khaled held Elizabeth in his arms and showered her with kisses, starting on her forehead and moving down to her eyes, nose, lips, chin, and neck. He caressed her gently and noticed her reaction; she seemed to surrender. While holding her with one hand, he rested his second hand on her knee, then he placed it under her skirt and started to move gently up, hardly touching. But once he got almost there, she held his hand in place without moving it away. Then his other hand touched her breast, resting there for a minute or so. She looked at him, joyful tears flooding her eyes.

"Khaled, that's too much. Please, let's stop. We should not be doing this."

"As you like. No upper thighs and no breast. Right? But the rest is allowed?"

"Shut up," Elizabeth said as she hugged him and kissed his full lips.

They managed to make it to the kitchen to get two more beers and continued their kissing, hugging, and fondling until the apartment smelled of smoke.

"Oh my God, I forgot the meat. We better stop before we burn up the apartment."

She rushed to the kitchen and took the roast out. They cut it in the middle, hoping to find some edible part, but there was hardly anything worth eating.

They sat at the dining table, having a salad, cold bean casserole, and huge portions of carrot cake. She even gave him two generous slices to take home.

"Don't forget to give Richard his share."

"I won't. But you owe me another home-cooked meal. This one doesn't count. Hopefully, next time, you won't burn the food."

"Go to hell, Khaled. If you hadn't seduced me, we would've had a perfect roast."

A few weeks after the roasted dinner, Richard asked Khaled if he wanted to go with him to Cincinnati for the weekend.

"Thanks for the invite, but not this weekend."

"Now that Elizabeth invites you to her home, you don't want to leave town? I thought you loved spending time with my family."

"I do, but I have an exam on Monday. I have to study."

"Liar. It's Elizabeth. And in case you invite her over, be sure not to fuck on the couch or in my bed."

"Shut up. Just shut up. We do not do that!"

"Oh right, you are so pure. 'We don't do sex.' There is a sexual revolution happening, in case you haven't heard."

"I've heard about it, but neither I nor Elizabeth are part of it."

"You have no idea what you're missing."

As soon as Richard left town, Khaled invited Elizabeth to come over. A couple of hours later, he called to cancel, claiming he had to study.

"Why are you playing these games? Don't be a coward. If you don't want to have a relationship, just say it."

Khaled panicked. "Elizabeth, how could you say that? Of course I do."

"What is it then?"

"I'm afraid both of us are going to get hurt. I have to go home after I graduate."

"You have told me that a million times. I'm afraid, too. I thought we agreed we would worry about that when the time comes. And don't take me for granted. I'm tired of it. At this rate, there might not be a next time."

Despite Khaled's genuine intention to end his relationship with Elizabeth, or at least tell her about Wafa, or tell Wafa about her, he was never able to bring himself to do any of it, and that sat heavily on his conscious. *I hate myself. I am such a coward.* He thought of Wafa's last letter that arrived three weeks before. She was obviously unhappy and suspicious.

> *Khaled, I'm not that stupid. I am getting these cold letters from you mostly about your school and the weather. They lack the excitement and warmth of the Khaled I know. I feel like there are things you are not telling me. If you don't love me anymore, or you don't want us to continue this relationship, or if you have another woman in your life, you need to tell me.*

Wafa's letters, combined with Khaled's own conflicting thoughts, continued to trouble him.

My father would disown me if he knew I was dating an American girl. I will go back home and marry Wafa, my true love. But I like Elizabeth, and she likes me, too. There's nothing wrong with us having a close, intimate relationship while we're going to school...

12
ROMANCE IN A RED CAR

Summer 1961

Despite Khaled's resentment toward his father, he asked him for money to buy a car.

> *This will be my last year here. I have been studying hard and would love to see parts of this country before I leave. Would you please send me money to buy a used car? It will only cost about $500. I will have it for one year and then sell it. I think I can get most of the money back. I will give it to you when I return. I promise.*

Not lacking for money, Abu Khaled replied to his son's letter, saying,

> *I am going to send you $1,000 so you can get a safe, dependable one. I also want you to be very careful when you drive. I don't want to hear about you getting tickets or, even worse, getting in an accident.*

"Guess what," Khaled burst out to Elizabeth as he lifted her off the floor and started spinning. She kissed the top of his head and yelled, "Let me down, tell me . . . tell me!"

"I'm getting a car! Best gift ever. I'm going to be your private driver. We'll drive all over this summer. I'll take you wherever you want."

"You really are spoiled, aren't you? Did your dad send you the money? I wish I had a dad like yours."

"No, you don't."

"Your dad doesn't seem to be as mean as you say. All you had to do was ask."

"Trust me, he's more than mean."

"At least he's rich. Mine's mean and poor. Awful combination."

They went together to a used car dealer in Dearborn and drove back in a red convertible Chevy Impala.

~

Khaled and Elizabeth began taking rides all around Michigan and going to drive-in movies. Along the way, they continued to explore each other's bodies in the front and back seats of the car. "Let's go for a ride" became their private joke. But Elizabeth told him more than once, "Please, Khaled, be careful. I really don't want to go all the way."

~

Despite their best intentions, willpower was no match for their youthful, kicking hormones. And when Khaled held Elizabeth's naked body and lost his virginity, he thought he was having a heart attack and soon would leave this earth and meet his *Allah*. His heartbeat was deafening, and his muscles tightened as a loud scream escaped him. A flood of sweat drenched his body. But ecstasy overpowered his fear. *This is a sweet death. Please, God, let me live so I can die again.* He rolled over, wrapped Elizabeth with his four limbs and drifted away.

"I want to make love to you forever. I don't want to stop," he said, moving one hand between her thighs.

"Me too. We've wasted too much time. We need to make up for it," Elizabeth said, squeezing his hand.

She placed a gentle kiss on his lips. He kissed back, first her ear, then his mouth worked its way down her collarbone. Wafa's eyes appeared. He froze.

"Not now . . . please . . . not now," he whispered.

He closed his eyes and shook his head, trying to get rid of the appearance of Wafa. Slowly he moved his body away from Elizabeth, resting his head on the pillow, and placed his arm over his eyes.

"What's wrong? Are you ok?" Elizabeth asked. "Khaled, talk to me?" she said again, louder.

He wrapped his arms around her. "Nothing. I just died and went to heaven."

Khaled stayed still for a while. Elizabeth laid next to him, resting her head on his shoulder.

"It's time. I have to shower and make it to class on time. Can I take a shower here?" Khaled asked.

"Of course you can. But I don't want you to go. Please stay."

"I can't miss this class. We have a midterm exam next week."

"I can't believe it. You are the only one I know who takes classes every summer. It's your last summer here, and you don't even need the credit."

"Of course I do. Remember, I am getting a double major in four years. Also, being busy keeps me out of trouble."

"You're already in trouble. Come back after class. I'll be home . . . Let me get you a clean towel."

In the bathroom, he stood naked in front of the mirror, admiring his olive skin and muscular, tall body. He marveled at the black hair strands resting on his forehead, the glow in his face and the glitter of his dark eyes. *Not bad,* he said to himself. *I look even more handsome after sex.*

When Khaled entered the classroom, he was a bit taller, and his body more upright. He felt light as if walking on air. A smile stretched from one ear to the other. He was almost laughing. He looked at his classmates, wondering if any of them could tell that he'd just had sex. He searched their faces, trying to see if he could tell who had sex the previous night or that day.

But then, Wafa appeared again. For a second, he saw her sitting in one of the chairs in the classroom, staring at him like a ghost who came back to haunt him. He closed his eyes and shook his head again, trying to dismiss her image. *May God forgive you, Wafa... Why can't you leave me alone... Maybe I should ask God to forgive me. I'm the one cheating on her... She did not do anything wrong.* Khaled remembered the last time he saw her and his promise to come back to marry her. *I will, I will,* he told himself, while wondering if sex with her, or any other woman, would be as delicious.

After class, he called Elizabeth to tell her that he'd gone to his own apartment.

"Please come over. It's not always that I have the apartment to myself."

"I can't."

"Why not?"

"I'm tired, and I have to study."

"You are not going to play this game with me again. Not now... not after what happened today."

"I will call you later. I promise."

"I'm not ready to hear any more of these stupid promises. Are you coming over or not?"

"Yes... yes, I am. Let me study for a couple hours. Then I promise I'll call you."

"I think you take these extra classes to give yourself excuses. But I can't take your bullshit anymore."

Elizabeth hung up.

Khaled walked over to his small desk, drawn to Wafa's last letter sitting there. It had been there for almost a month, and he had read it a few times, feeling sad. She was obviously ready to give up on him. He couldn't blame her or bring himself to write back. Making love with Elizabeth was all he could think about. *Tomorrow, I will give it another try,* he vowed. But the promises he made to write Wafa were as good as the promises he'd made not to see or have sex with Elizabeth again. Promises, deep in his heart, he knew he would not keep.

~

When the mailman delivered Khaled a fat envelope, he took it to his room and closed the door. As he opened it, a bunch of his own letters dropped out, along with a short note.

> Look at these letters. They're all the same except for a few words here and there. If this is the best you can do, you might as well stop writing. These are not the letters I expect from you. This is not from Khaled, who is honest and open and who says what's on his mind. The man I love and I assume also loves me. You either write me an honest letter telling me what is going on or stop writing. I do not need one more of your boring, dishonest letters.

Khaled was sad but relieved. Now he could enjoy dating Elizabeth without any feelings of guilt toward Wafa. But he also knew than once he graduated, he and Elizabeth would have to say their goodbyes. He would return home as his father expected, and his family dearly wished.

13
MEETING THE FAMILY

A couple of weeks before school started, Elizabeth told Khaled that she had to go home for the weekend. It was her sister Mary Ann's seventeenth birthday.

"How about we take a long ride all the way to Grand Rapids? You get to meet my parents and the army of siblings."

"Are you serious? I thought your parents wouldn't like you dating a non-Catholic, let alone a Muslim."

"Wait a minute. They can't know we're dating. We have to pretend we're just friends. We took a few classes together, and you were willing to drive me home. That's it. I'll ask them if you could stay for dinner. One more person won't make a difference."

"You mean I have to drive you all the way to Grand Rapids and back to Ann Arbor so I can have dinner?"

"I can take the bus. Would you prefer that?" Elizabeth said in her flirtatious voice, obviously not meaning it.

"No, no, I want to drive you! I want to meet your parents and the army of siblings. And I want to see where you grew up. But, if you don't mind, I'd like to ask Richard to come along, especially if I have to drive back the same day."

"That won't be as much fun."

"I know, but I need some company to keep me awake."

"As long as neither of you mentions anything about us dating. Also, they can't know that I drink and don't go to church."

"That's a long list. I'll try my best to remember. But if I were you, I wouldn't trust Richard."

"I'm serious, Khaled."

"Okay, relax. We'll behave."

~

Despite his appearance of confidence, Khaled was anxious about meeting Elizabeth's parents. He came from a culture where dating was not acceptable, let alone meeting the parents of one's girlfriend. On the day of the trip, he took his time showering, shaving, and getting dressed—a crisp ironed shirt, dress slacks, and black shoes.

"Khaled, you look way too formal," Elizabeth said the moment she saw him. "We're going to a backyard barbeque for my sister's birthday."

"I have to impress your parents, don't I?"

"No, you don't. Remember, they don't know we are dating."

"What kind of an American family is that? It sounds worse than mine. I thought dating was kind of normal in this country."

"Not all Americans are like what you see in Ann Arbor."

~

The three-hour drive from Ann Arbor to Grand Rapids took them almost five hours. They stopped for late breakfast, then for gas. And then coffee. They took their sweet time driving, listening to the radio, and singing along. Elizabeth sat close to Khaled, their bodies almost touching, while Khaled's hand kept sliding up her thigh.

"Khaled, stop it," Elizabeth would scold, obviously not that seriously.

"Yes, Khaled, stop it," Richard piped in, imitating Elizabeth, or "Hey guys, remember me? I'm still here."

As they approached Grand Rapids, Elizabeth instructed Khaled and Richard not to expect much. Her family was not as fancy and didn't have the same kind of money as theirs. "Maybe I should have taken the bus. I don't want you to be disappointed."

"How many times do I have to tell you? I love you for who you are. I don't care what kind of a job your father has or how much money. That's nonsense."

"Well, dear Elizabeth, I have good news for you," Richard said. "The world is changing. Long live the proletariat! You should be proud you come from a working-class family."

"I am. But I would be prouder if your proletariat had a bit more money."

As they got close to her house, Elizabeth asked Khaled to stop the car when he could.

"Why?"

"I want to switch seats with Richard. I don't want my parents to see me sitting next to you."

They stopped, and before she got in the back seat, Elizabeth straightened her clothes and combed her hair.

"How do I look?"

"As good as a nun," Richard responded.

They pulled into the cracked driveway of a small house. It was around three in the afternoon. The smoke and the smell of grilled meat and grease attacked their eyes and nostrils, and the bright sun exposed the outside walls and the roof, both pleading for attention. The fenced backyard, with brownish grass, was packed with people of all sizes and ages. A hoard of kids ran toward the car, screaming, "Elizabeth is here... Elizabeth is here!" A middle-aged woman whose harsh life left its marks on her face and body trailed behind. Her colorful print dress, with big patches of underarm sweat, was layered with a stained apron. Khaled stood by the car watching. The warm motherly welcome, the kids' excitement, and the distant father all reminded him of his own family. He realized how much he missed his mother and siblings. But he also was relieved to be so far from his father.

Elizabeth slowly walked toward her dad, who was standing by the grill watching. "Hi, Dad. How are you?"

"I'm fine. Too much grilling to feed this crowd."

Khaled's chest tightened. *I guess this is not exactly like my* family, he observed . . . *My father's always happy to feed people. The more, the merrier, maybe because he's never had to grill or even lift a finger.* He stepped back, closer to his car, not sure if Richard and he should just leave. Then he heard Elizabeth saying, "Khaled, Richard, come on in," waving her hands. Then she turned to her parents, "Mom, Dad, let me introduce you to my classmates. This is Khaled, and this is Richard."

As the father sized them up, looking back and forth at each of them, Elizabeth's mother welcomed them.

"Nice meeting you. Thank you for driving Elizabeth. Please feel at home. Dinner will be ready soon. What would you like to drink? We have lemonade and Coca-Cola."

Before Khaled had a chance to respond, she turned to one of her daughters.

"Diane, go get a few Cokes from the icebox."

"Thank you. We will have something to drink and then leave," Khaled said politely. "We have a long drive home."

"You can't leave now. You drove all the way to bring Elizabeth home. The least we can do is to have you join us for dinner. And you must stay for dessert. Not much, just a birthday cake and ice cream."

Khaled smiled at Richard, thinking, *I guess no beer will be served here.* After getting their Cokes, they walked to Elizabeth's father, who was busy grilling hot dogs and burgers. They tried to strike up a conversation with him—out of politeness rather than interest. His clothes were not much better than his wife's. He had on a dirty old pair of denim overalls and an old checkered yellow-and-white shirt with his sleeves rolled up to his elbows. A baseball cap covered his head, and a small mustache rested on top of his thin lip. His face and arms were covered with freckles, and a dirty washcloth hung on his shoulder.

Khaled couldn't help but compare Elizabeth's parents to his own. His mother had help around the house, and she was always dressed nicely, especially when they had company. He never saw his father do one domestic chore. On the contrary, he always expected to be served. Khaled had been to Richard's parents' home in Cincinnati, but in spite of many cultural differences, the gap did not strike him as much as it did with Elizabeth's family.

After exchanging a few pleasantries, the father served up a few rapid-fire questions. "How did you meet Elizabeth?" "What are you studying?" "When are you graduating?" After their overly courteous replies, he turned to Khaled.

"You don't speak like an American. Where are you from?"

His tone wasn't hostile, but not exactly friendly either.

"I'm from Al-Bireh, in Palestine?" Khaled answered uncertainly.

"And where is that?"

"Palestine, the country of Jesus?"

"I'm not sure I follow. What did you say about Jesus?"

"My town, Al-Bireh, is very close to Jerusalem, where Jesus was crucified, and not far from Bethlehem, where Jesus was born."

"Oh, that Palestine. You came all the way from there just to go to school here?"

"Yes, I did. You have the best universities in the world."

"That must cost a fortune."

"Yes, it does. But when I go back home, I'll get a good job that pays well, so it's worth it."

"I guess so."

Elizabeth's father turned his attention back to flipping his burgers while Khaled and Richard stood by, watching him awkwardly. They were relieved when Elizabeth came to their rescue.

"Let me introduce you to my siblings. I'll do it by age. Here you go, Michael, twenty-three, he's the oldest. Then me, I am number two, then comes Mary Ann, seventeen, the birthday girl, she will graduate from school next summer. She wants to be a secretary."

Elizabeth looked at her dad and whispered out loud. "She's very smart. I'm trying to convince her to study something else."

She continued.

"This is Diane. She is fifteen. Then, five boys in a row—Ray, fourteen; Patrick, thirteen; Donald, ten; Richard, eight; and John, six. And finally, another girl, Janet, the baby. She is only four—I could be her mother!"

Elizabeth looked sternly at Khaled and Richard.

"I'm going to test you after dinner to see how many names you remember."

Khaled noticed how poorly everyone was dressed except for Elizabeth and Mary Ann. All the boys were in similar clothes: khaki or jean shorts, checkered or plain t-shirts, and brown sandals. Despite their ages, they all also resembled one another, with their blond hair, fair complexion, and blue eyes. Even if he could remember all the names, it was still hard to tell them apart, except for the oldest brother.

Elizabeth's mother started calling on her girls to bring the potato salad and the corn from the kitchen and set the two picnic tables. Elizabeth and her two older sisters went inside and brought the food, along with paper plates, salt and pepper, mustard, and ketchup, while the older son helped his dad bring the food. The father sat at the same table with his wife, Khaled, Richard, and

Elizabeth, along with a few of the older siblings. While the father didn't show much interest in having conversations with Khaled or Richard, he didn't stop watching them, especially when they interacted with Elizabeth.

After dinner, Khaled and Richard said their goodbyes, thanked Elizabeth's parents for their hospitality, and left.

~

"Diane, Mary Ann, you go ahead and pick up and wash the dishes. And don't forget to make coffee for your father," the mother ordered. Then she grabbed Elizabeth by the wrist, saying, "Come with me." Without a word, Elizabeth followed. Her mother wouldn't let go of her until they got into her bedroom, and she closed the door.

"This friend of yours—not Richard, the other one—whatever his name is, he's not just your classmate, is he?"

"I don't know what you're talking about. He and Richard are my classmates and my friends."

"Elizabeth, don't lie to me. I could tell from the way you were looking at each other. You're not just friends."

"No, Mom, you have to believe me. We're just friends. He's helping me with my math classes. When I told him I was going home to visit, he offered to drive me. I asked if it was okay with you and Dad, and you both said it's fine."

"And why would he offer to drive you all the way here and then drive back the same day?"

"He likes to drive and hasn't seen much of Michigan, that's all."

"You're lying. I raised you to be a good Christian. What would your dad say if he found out?"

"Mom, there's nothing to find out," Elizabeth said as she left the room fuming.

For the next two days, she and her mother didn't say much to each other, and she became eager to just leave.

When Elizabeth got back to Ann Arbor, she told Khaled, "My mother wasn't fooled. She figured it out."

"Figured out what?"

"She figured out that we're dating. After you left, she asked me, but I denied it. I had to assure her again and again that there was nothing between us, just to put her mind to rest. I don't think she believed me. She did say that you look like a nice young gentleman, but not the right one for me. She also said that she and my father would be heartbroken if I even thought about dating or marrying a Muslim or an Arab man."

"How did she know I'm Muslim?"

"She asked me if you were a Christian, and I said no, he's a Muslim. I'm not sure she knows what that is."

"And what did you say when she told you can't marry a Muslim?"

"What did expect me to say? I told her, of course not."

"You mean you wouldn't marry me?"

"I'm not ready to get married anytime soon—to you or anyone else. You've been telling me all along you don't want to stay after you graduate and that your family would never approve of you marrying an American girl. Well, mine would never approve of me marrying you."

The thought of marrying Elizabeth hadn't really crossed his mind. But hearing her say those words to him, that she wouldn't marry him, was painful.

14
OVERWHELMING NEWS

Winter 1962

Muted sobs escaped Elizabeth's bedroom. Emily tiptoed and stuck her ear to the door. What could it be? They had been friends and roommates for a few years. At their tender womanhood age, they shared whatever life offered them—the good and the bad, the happy and the sad. Reluctantly, Emily knocked at the door. The sobbing suddenly stopped. The prolonged silence unnerved her. Tightness found its way to her chest. She knocked again. No response.

"Elizabeth, are you okay?"

More silence.

"Elizabeth, can I come in?"

When the silence prevailed, Emily pushed the door open and rushed in, only to stop in her tracks. Elizabeth was lying in her bed, fully dressed. Her face was puffy and red, her nose swollen, and her eyes bloodshot. Strands of wet hair clung to her face.

"My God, Elizabeth, what happened? Did someone die?"

Elizabeth shook her head no and started to sob again.

"Is it Khaled? Is he okay? Did you break up?" Emily asked as she sat down at the foot of the bed.

Elizabeth finally looked at her friend. Streams of tears marked their way to her chin and the sheets.

"What is it, Elizabeth? Please talk to me," Emily begged.

"I'm so ashamed. I can't believe this is happening to me. I did everything I could not to get pregnant," Elizabeth finally said.

Realizing the enormity of the situation and the trouble Elizabeth was in, Emily moved from the foot of the bed and sat close to her. She gave her friend a long, warm hug.

"Oh, Emily, I don't know what to do," Elizabeth finally said. "I am in a big mess. My parents are going kill me. How stupid could I be? I don't know how to deal with this."

Elizabeth started sobbing again.

"I'd rather be dead than face this."

Emily was quiet for a while, searching for what to say.

"I'm sorry, my friend. But you're not the first or the last woman to get pregnant. We'll deal with it. It's Khaled's, right?"

"Of course, it's Khaled's. When have you ever seen me with another man?"

"I apologize. I didn't mean it that way," Emily explained as she gently brushed Elizabeth's hair off her face. "Have you told him?"

"I'm not sure I can or even want to."

"What do you mean?" Emily asked, a bit surprised. "You have to tell him. It's his child. He has to know." It pained Emily to see her friend so trapped. "Stop torturing yourself. If you don't want to have a child out of wedlock and don't want your family or Khaled to know, the only option is to have an abortion. Is that what you want?"

"I don't want to hear any talk about abortion," Elizabeth snapped, "You know it's illegal, and dangerous, I'm not going to have one. And leave Khaled out of it."

"Many women find a way to do it. I can help you get a trusted doctor. And I can borrow money from my mother."

"I told you Emily. I don't want to talk about abortion. It's not an option."

"Elizabeth, please," Emily said in a comforting but firmer tone. "There's no way to keep the news from Khaled or from your family. And if you do want to keep the baby, you need to take better care of yourself, start eating and sleeping."

"Please stop telling me what I should or shouldn't do."

She started crying again.

On a Saturday afternoon, Khaled unexpectedly appeared at Elizabeth's door. She threw her arms around his neck, held him tight, and wept like she never had before.

"What is it? I haven't heard from you for two weeks. Are your parents and family all right?"

He walked her slowly to the couch, gently helped her sit down and then sat down next to her. "Elizabeth, what is it?"

He waited, for what seemed like forever, watching her cry. Almost begging for an answer, Khaled finally asked, "Are you going to talk to me, or should I leave?"

"I don't know how to tell you."

"Tell me what?"

"I am . . . I'm . . . pregnant," she mumbled quietly.

"I can't hear you."

"I'm pregnant."

"What?" he asked again, hesitantly. "How did this happen?"

Khaled regretted asking such a dumb question. Now what? He wished he could turn back the clock. Poor Elizabeth, what would her parents say? Why didn't he listen to his mother about dating and sex? *Please, God, what are we supposed to do?* he found himself asking. No one could know about this. In a few months he'd be graduating and going home. His father would kill him . . .

Elizabeth's stream of tears stopped and her sharp response interrupted Khaled's stream, of thought.

"Did you just ask me *how* this happened? Is that all you have to say? You mean to tell me you don't know how a woman gets pregnant?"

She got up and started to walk away, but he reached for her arm.

"Please, sit down. I was just trying to take in what you told me. I wasn't expecting this."

Elizabeth sat back down and he held her. She nestled in his arms and buried her face in his chest. Shivers shook her small body and he held her more tightly. It broke his heart to see her cry like this. He wished he could take her pain away. Khaled knew all along that he truly loved her, no matter how much he'd tried to convince himself otherwise.

He gently touched her chin with his fingertips, lifted her head, and kissed her forehead.

"We'll figure something out."

"You don't have to do anything. You really don't."

"Of course I do. I just need some time to think. Can I get you anything?"

"Just some water. Thanks."

Khaled went into the kitchen, his heart racing a mile a minute. He felt dizzy. He leaned against the kitchen counter to steady himself, trying to digest the news. How stupid could he be? How was it that the thought of getting her pregnant never crossed his mind? What about her? She must have thought about it. *Could she have done something to prevent it from happening,* he wondered. They were so attracted to each other. *I don't know how to comfort her. And I don't know what to tell her... Think, Khaled, think. Don't do or say anything you might regret.*

But Khaled was already buried in regret. Finally, he went back to the living room, handed Elizabeth a glass of water, sat next to her, and sipped his in silence.

"For God's sake, Khaled, say something," Elizabeth said after a while.

"How long have you known this?" he asked.

"A little over two weeks."

"Two weeks? Two weeks, and you said nothing?" He felt anger creeping into his shaky voice. "Is that why you've been avoiding me?"

"I didn't know what or how to tell you. I wasn't sure how you might react. All along you've been telling me you were leaving the US as soon as you graduated, which is in less than six months."

"You mean if I didn't come by today, you wouldn't have told me?" His voice was sharp, but he stopped himself, thought for a few seconds, then said, "I'm sorry, Elizabeth. I didn't mean to sound that way."

"I don't blame you for being upset."

He sat there for a long time, not knowing what else to say beyond asking her if she had told anyone. Clouds shrouded his brain, and his body felt numb. He needed to leave, to be alone to clear his head. He looked at his watch and stood up.

"I'm sorry Elizabeth. I have to leave soon. Can I get you anything before I go?"

"Leave now? Where to?" she asked in surprise, looking almost hurt by his words.

"I'm supposed to meet two classmates at the library. We're working on a project. It's due on Monday. If we finish before it gets late, I'll come back."

"You will?"

She gave him a doubtful, faint smile. He had disappeared on her before.

"Of course I will."

~

But Khaled could not bring himself to meet his classmates at the library. Instead, he wandered around Ann Arbor's snowy streets, kicking at balls of dirty snow until his face and feet were numb.

He was angry at himself, angry at Elizabeth, angry that such thing could happen to them. Feeling exhausted, he decided to go home, hoping Richard would be there. He needed to talk to him.

"What's up, Khaled?" his roommate greeted him. "You look like you just saw a ghost."

"It's worse."

"What happened?"

"Let me get a drink first."

Khaled returned from the kitchen with a beer and stood by the window, looking away from Richard.

"I thought you were going to tell me something."

"I just found out Elizabeth is pregnant."

Rarely at a loss for words, Richard stared at the floor, totally silent. After a time, he looked up at his roommate.

"What are you going to do?"

"I really don't know."

"How about Elizabeth? What does she want to do."

"I don't know. I just found out. She's so upset, all I could do was comfort her."

"If neither one of you want to have a child now, Elizabeth could consider having an abortion. Many women do that."

Khaled was already overwhelmed by the news about Elizabeth pregnancy. Abortion hadn't crossed his mind, until Richard mentioned it. He didn't really know much about it either and had never even given it any thought before. *Is abortion legal, is it safe, is it haram?* he wondered.

15
FIRST FRUIT OF LOVE

"Elizabeth, we've been discussing this for over two months now. You don't want your parents to know. Neither do I. And you don't want to have an abortion. But what other options do we have? Soon, we won't even have this one."

Khaled voice was harsh, his frustration boiling over despite his attempt to keep his cool.

"If you're going to start yelling you might as well leave," she replied. "I don't need you or your help, How many times do I have to tell you? I'm not going to have an abortion. It's against my religion."

"It's possibly against my religion, too. But since when has religion been first on our list? We use religion when it suits us?"

"You're acting as if it's all my fault. That's why I didn't want to tell you. I wish I hadn't."

"Don't I have the right to be upset? You're angry too, aren't you? We have a big problem on our hands, and I don't see another solution. And every time we talk about it, all you tell me it's against your religion."

Elizabeth was quiet for a while. Khaled was right. She had told him more than once how much she resented her strict Catholic upbringing.

"Since I was a toddler, church values were so drilled into my brain that now I can't even imagine myself having an abortion. I'm also scared. I've heard so many horror stories about women having severe complications, even dying. It's easy for you and Emily to tell me to have an abortion. But I'm the one who has to go through with it, not you."

Khaled and Elizabeth spent every day discussing what to do, often arguing and storming off, only to come back to talk more about it, without reaching a solution. Khaled could not think of another way out, and Elizabeth refused to consider an abortion.

He was discovering a side of her he never had before. All along, she'd put down her family's strict religious values. She hadn't gone to church since she left home for college. So why now? He hated seeing her hurt and scared. But he wasn't ready to be a father, to get married, or stay in the US after graduation. The thought of his parents finding out, especially his father, terrified him.

One day Khaled decided to try his luck again convincing Elizabeth to have an abortion. He promised himself to stay calm no matter where the conversation took them. He was tired of arguing, and it pained him to see her suffer.

"Habibti Elizabeth, please listen to me. You know I love you and want what's best for you. But the longer you wait, the harder it will be to have it done. Do you really want to have a child? What about your family? What will they think? What about my family?"

"I am tired of you telling me what to do. Honestly, Khaled, I don't care what my family—or yours—thinks!"

"Well, I do," he said exasperated.

The more they talked, the further apart they felt, unable to see eye to eye.

"That's fine Khaled. You go ahead with your grandiose plans, get your degree, and go home. I don't want anything from you.

This is my baby you're talking about. I'd rather die than kill my own child."

Elizabeth's words, *kill my own child,* jarred him.

"Listen Elizabeth, this is my child, too!" he answered back.

He was taken by surprised to hear himself say it, let alone feel it.

Khaled left, and again wandered streets of Ann Arbor, thinking. He and Elizabeth had been arguing about what to do for over two months now. But when Elizabeth talked about abortion as killing her own child, it hit him differently. His strong emotions and even tears, overwhelmed him. For the first time, he felt that this was his child too, and Elizabeth, whom he loved dearly was the mother of his child, and the only right thing for them to do was to get married.

He truly loved her.

The idea of killing this baby sent shivers through his body. He also felt love for this child and started imagining what it would look like. Would it be a boy or a girl? He was sure his family wouldn't be happy, especially his father. But he wasn't the first one there to marry a foreigner. He decided he would still return to Palestine with Elizabeth after graduation, or maybe after the baby was born.

Despite his worries about his family's reactions, Khaled finally felt at peace with himself. He was tempted to go back and propose to Elizabeth right then. But he thought again and decided not to rush things. *I'll sleep on it and talk to Richard first. Then tomorrow, I will go and see Elizabeth.*

The moment he stepped into Elizabeth's apartment, Khaled went up to her, embraced her, held her hand, and got down on one knee.

"Elizabeth, will you marry me?"

"Get up, silly man. This is no time to be kidding," she said holding back a laugh.

"I'm serious," he said standing up. "We should get married."

"Khaled, you don't have to feel pressured to marry me." His heart ached at how Elizabeth's voice ringed a mixture of hope and sadness.

"Trust me. I've given this a lot of thought. True, I was not ready to settle down so soon. But I love you, Elizabeth. And I love our baby, too."

"Seriously? What made you change your mind overnight."

"All I know is what I want," he said sincerely, meaning every word.

"You didn't answer. Will you marry me?" He asked again.

Elizabeth was at a complete loss for words. She could not believe her ears, especially when Khaled said, "our baby." A different kind of tears filled her eyes, and she hugged him.

"Of course I will."

Then she let go of him and asked somberly, "But what about your family?"

"Of course, at first, my parents—especially my dad—are going to be very upset. But I am their son, and ultimately they'll accept it. I'm sure once my mother gets to know you, she will fall in love with you, just as I did."

~

As the days passed, they started discussing how to tell their parents. He still had a few months before graduation and needed his father's financial assistance, especially now. Khaled decided not to say anything, at least not yet.

"Let's figure it out one step at a time," Khaled suggested. "What about yours?"

"Of course I'll tell them we're getting married. But they can't know I'm pregnant."

She pressed her dress against her belly.

"No one could tell yet, right?"

Khaled wanted to go to Grand Rapids to ask Elizabeth's parents for their permission. He was sure they'd say yes. After all, he was about to graduate from one of the best schools in the country. They had already met him before and learned that he came from the Holy Land, and that his parents worked hard and provided well for their family. So what was there to object to?

Elizabeth was not so optimistic.

When she called her parents to tell them that Khaled would be coming over to ask for their permission to marry, her father wouldn't hear of it.

"I shouldn't have allowed you to go to college. That's what happens when women are given a bit of freedom. They think they can marry whoever they want. He's not even a Christian," he yelled and hung up the phone.

Elizabeth tried to talk to her mother, but that didn't go well, either. Faced with their strong objections, she decided to tell her mother about the pregnancy, hoping that if her parents knew, it would change their minds.

"You're going to tell them? Are you sure?" Khaled asked.

"I don't know how else to convince them."

When she finally mustered the courage to call, her mother screamed.

"You're pregnant? What kind of a girl did I raise?"

She started to cry and hung up the phone.

Elizabeth kept calling and begging.

"Please, Mom, just listen to me. Khaled is a decent man. He wants to come see you and Dad to ask for my hand. We need your blessing."

"Don't you ever dare come here," her mother said. "I don't

want your brothers and sisters or the neighbors to see you pregnant. What am I going to tell them? Your father would never talk to Khaled or walk a pregnant daughter down the aisle. I don't blame him. You've disgraced our family. I knew you were dating this jerk from the moment I saw him."

"Please, Mom, I need your support. Talk to Dad. You can convince him."

"Neither I nor your father will ever approve of what you're doing. We'll have nothing to do with you or with your out-of-wedlock child. You should go far away, disappear. Find someplace where you can hide until you give birth. Then give the child up for adoption."

"You want me to give away my own child, your first grandchild?"

"No grandchild of mine is going to be born from this sin."

~

On a cold Thursday in early March, Elizabeth and Khaled, accompanied by Emily and Richard, their two witnesses, went to the city hall and tied the knot. A quiet dinner followed. Within a couple of weeks, Elizabeth moved into Khaled's apartment, and Richard, who was planning to stay in Ann Arbor after graduation, moved to live with a couple of his activist friends.

~

Khaled kept postponing the inevitable. He had no doubt that his mother, whom he loved dearly, would be disappointed that her firstborn had gotten married to an American woman. In her last letter, she had written to him,

> *I cannot wait to see you coming home.* Inshallah, *soon after, we will find you a nice, lovely wife from a good family and have the most beautiful wedding for you. I will dance until I cannot stand on my feet.*

Her words pained him, but he kept assuring himself that once his mother met Elizabeth and his baby, she would be fine. She had always been loving and forgiving. His biggest dread was his father, whose fury usually came as a hurricane. He could envision him cursing, screaming, and smashing things around the house. Khaled was relieved that he would be far away when his father got the news, but he felt bad for his mother and siblings.

Only a few days after being married, Khaled received a letter from his father.

> *My son, I am so proud of you. I decided to come, along with your mother and brother Majed, for your graduation. We plan to spend a month traveling together in the US. Then the four of us can all come back home together.*

Khaled panicked. He wrote to his sister Layali.

> *You must convince them not to come. Also, I am not planning to come immediately after graduation. It's a long story. I will tell you about it later.*

Layali wrote back.

> *I'm curious why you don't want them to come. And how can I convince them? They are so proud of you and want to be with you at your graduation. I never saw Father so happy. When he talks about you, his face lights up. But I'm so mad at him and Mother that I don't even want to talk to them. They want to bring Majed with them but won't let me come. They say someone has to stay home to take care of the young ones. It's not fair! They are already planning your graduation party. Our aunts and uncles say it looks more like a wedding, and our father says that will be coming soon after.*

Khaled had no choice but to send his family a telegram:

> Please do not buy your plane tickets. A letter that explains is coming soon.

Khaled sat to write the most difficult letter he'd ever written.

> *I don't want you to be surprised when you come. I just got married to an American girl. Her name is Elizabeth. She is very nice and comes from a good family. You will love her when you meet her. I am also going to be a father soon.*

Two weeks later, he received a telegram from his father.

> *You are not my son, and I don't want to ever see or hear from you again.*

16
A SHORT HONEYMOON

Summer 1962

With a double major in engineering and business, good grades, and rave recommendations, Khaled was able to land a job at Ford Motor Company in Dearborn, thirty-five miles east of Ann Arbor. Elizabeth, who had been working and going to school part-time, decided to quit her job and go to school full time. She wanted to earn as many credits as she could before their child arrived. Khaled and Elizabeth had a lot to celebrate—a new life together, Khaled's graduation and his job, and a child on the way. Not having their families' blessing was a dark cloud, but it wasn't the end of the world.

"I'm not really surprised by my father's reaction," Khaled told Elizabeth. "I have mixed feelings about it, but I'm not sure that I feel that bad."

"How could you say that? I know you don't like your father that much, but he was good to you. He paid for your education, and he sent you money to buy a car. Not many dads do that."

"Yes, he did provide me with a good education, and the car. But he's not a kind or a loving father. He's a control freak. You have to obey him blindly to deserve his love. His reaction to our marriage and the baby has made it so difficult for me to visit home—alone or with you. I also know that he would make it impossible for my mother or any of my siblings to visit us. I do feel bad about his reaction, but honestly, I also feel free. It's like a big weight I've been carrying since I was a teenager has been lifted off my shoulders."

"Well, look at my parents," said Elizabeth. "They don't want anything to do with me, and they won't even let any of my siblings contact me. I wonder what kind of bullshit they tell them about me. I miss my brothers and sisters, especially Mary Ann and the youngest ones. They're like my own children!"

Elizabeth got choked up and couldn't say more.

"I'm sorry, Elizabeth. They'll come around, and so will my dad. I'm sure of it," said Khaled, hugging his wife.

"Don't be so sure. I know my father. Your father might be a control freak, but mine thinks he's God on earth and can judge and punish as he pleases. Look at these letters I sent to them. All returned unopened."

"To hell with these fathers. Let's forget about them and go for a walk. It's a beautiful day."

"Remember Khaled. You're going to be a father soon."

"I would never be like either of them. I promise."

~

Thanks to his mother and to his sister Layali, Khaled was able to stay in touch with his family. With each of his letters, he would send pictures—his graduation ceremony, standing in front of the Ford Motor Company's blue glass building, in his office, dressed in a suit and tie, or with Elizabeth at home, in a restaurant, or at different spots in Ann Arbor. In each letter, he asked about his father, wondering if he was still upset. Layali was forthcoming and wrote back frequently and freely.

He does not want us to talk about you. Not when he is around. He often yells at Mother whenever she tries to talk to him about you. He would scream telling her "I don't want to hear his name. That son of yours, after all that I did for him, all the money I spent on his education. Like a fool I even sent him extra money to buy a car, and what did he do? He marries an American girl. God knows what kind of family she comes from. Getting pregnant before marriage, she must be a whore." My mother cried whenever he talked badly about you. But finally, she'd had it and stood up to him.

"This is Khaled you are talking about. How could you say that about your own son? Don't you ever say it again, especially when his brothers and sisters are around. You know he is a good man, and I am sure his wife is a good woman, too. Just remember, Khaled never wanted to go to America. He begged you to let him go to school in Beirut. I begged you, too. But you insisted. Like always, it had to be your way. He was so young and didn't know a single soul where you sent him, away from his family and friends for four years. So what did you expect? You talk like he is the only one to marry a foreigner. Look at Abu Hisham El-Khatib. He is married to a German Jewish woman, and she is a great wife and a great mother. She loves Palestine as her own country. For God's sake, stop this nonsense. Ask Khaled to bring his wife and come home. I want to see my son and meet his wife. At least give us a chance to get to know her."

Father did not even interrupt her or say a single word. But he did not like it at all. He left the house and did not come back until after two in the morning.

On the morning of September 15, 1963, Elizabeth and Khaled celebrated the birth of their first child, Ramsey, born at the University of Michigan Hospital. A healthy seven pounds and six ounces with brown hair, light skin, and green eyes.

"He looks like a mixture of both of us," said Elizabeth when their child was a week old. "He is so beautiful."

"He is. What's more important is that he's a healthy baby."

"Yes, he is."

~

Khaled sent a telegram to his mother, followed by a letter with pictures of the baby, as well as one of the three of them.

Within a few days, Khaled received a telegram from his father.

> Congratulations, Son. I hope to see you and your family soon.

Khaled was totally dumbfounded to read his father's words. He couldn't believe his own eyes and read the telegram over and over again. Then he wrote back.

> Thank you, Yaba. I miss you all so much. Inshallah, next summer, I will be able to come home with Elizabeth and Ramsey.

Knowing how stubborn his father could be, Khaled was puzzled by this change of heart. Until he received a letter from Layali.

> *Mother started crying the moment she saw the pictures. She called all of us, "Come... come and see what we got from Khaled. Thank you, God. Now I am a grandmother, and all of you are uncles and aunts. Look... look how beautiful this baby is, she said. Look at Khaled and his wife. They all look so great." She kissed Ramsey's picture and started to cry. I cried too. When father came home, he saw the pictures that Mother left out on the living room table next to his chair. He looked at them for a long time. Without saying a word, he placed them*

back on the coffee table and walked to the big guest room. Mother followed him and closed the door.

Of course, I had to know. I waited for a few minutes, then stood outside the door listening. Guess what? I heard Mother really talking to him. Really saying things to him. She said she loves him and that he's always been a good husband and father, and she's always done what he's asked of her. But now she needed to ask something of him. To send a congratulations telegram to you and Elizabeth and ask you to come home along with your child. She misses you so much. What he's doing is breaking her heart. It's bad for her and for our family. That a mother should never be separated from her children or grandchildren. And that your siblings miss you too. The younger ones have even forgotten what you look like. She said to him, Abu Khaled, make peace with your son. Trust me, you would feel much better. So would all of us.

And Father actually just listened. Can you believe it?

Well, I have one more big, good news for you. I am getting engaged to Farouq Al-Taher. Remember him? Their house was on the road to Ramallah, not far from the bakery shop. His sister Najwa was my schoolmate and used to come to our house. Farouq went to school in London maybe three years before you left. He studied medicine and now has his own clinic. He is smart and very kind and funny. He is also very handsome, like you. Once we decide on the wedding date, I will let you know. You better plan on being here. I'm not getting married without having my dear brother at my side."

Elizabeth had already decided to take a semester off from school to stay home with Ramsey. She felt happy for her husband, but she also felt sad and even a bit jealous. Her two letters—one addressed to her parents, the other to her sister Mary Ann—with the same pictures Khaled sent to his family came back unopened. Elizabeth's fading hope of support from her family or serious help from her friends who were either going to school or working only added to her resentment and feeling of isolation.

Once Ramsey was born, Khaled and Elizabeth settled into a routine. Khaled was gone all day long while she stayed home, taking care of the baby and doing all the housekeeping chores.

"What's wrong, Elizabeth?" Khaled would ask as he came home finding his wife in a sour mood.

"What do you mean what's wrong? You're gone all day long. Then you come home bragging about how much you love your job, and all the new friends you are making, and who you went out to lunch with, while I'm stuck at home all day alone with Ramsey."

"Trust me, Elizabeth, once Ramsey gets a little older, we'll find a dependable babysitter."

"When? Remember, I was supposed to stay home for one semester? Now it's turned into two. This is not the life I wanted for myself. I'd hate to prove that my father is right, that a woman's place is at home, cooking, cleaning, and raising kids."

"That's not going to happen. Honestly, I want to see you going back to school, to graduate and find a nice job that you like."

"That's easy for you to say."

"What do you want me to say? We have a baby, and I'm glad we do. I have a good job that can provide for our family. You should be happy for us."

"Look, I love my child, and I love being a mother. What I don't like is not going to school, not seeing or hanging out with my friends, and being stuck at home. Why can't you understand that?"

"You don't have to stay home. You have your own car, take Ramsey and go out. He is a quiet baby; he hardly cries unless he is hungry or needs a change. Take him and go have lunch or coffee with your friends. Some evenings and weekends, we go out together, don't we?"

"You know what? I'm tired of having this conversation. I don't want to talk about it anymore."

She walked away, holding her tears.

"Elizabeth, come here."

He followed her and hugged her warmly.

"Please, habibti, don't cry. I know it's hard for you, especially with your family not wanting to talk to us or see the baby. I love you, Elizabeth, and I wish I could do something about it. Give them time, and I'm sure they will come around. Enjoy Ramsey. He needs you. I need you. You can always go back to university, and you will."

"It's just not fair," she said, her voice full of anger. "You have a job you love, and you're meeting new people all the time."

"Sometimes I feel I can't win. Would you rather I have a job I don't like? Or even not have a job at all?"

"I told you, I don't want to talk about it anymore."

Elizabeth snatched her purse hurriedly and rushed into the street, slamming the door behind her.

17
NEW JOB, NEW LIFE?

Elizabeth was right. Khaled did like his new job. Working at Ford Motor Company opened up a whole new world for him that he did not know existed. He never expected to find so many Arabs working at Ford. Some were recent immigrants; others were second and third generation. They could be found in every department, from top executives to workers on the assembly line. His supervisor, Mr. Shaheen, was the son of Lebanese immigrants whose family had homesteaded in North Dakota in the 1880s.

Khaled was also taken by the size of the Arab community in East Dearborn, mostly Lebanese, Palestinians and Yemenis. They had their own businesses—grocery stores, bakeries, restaurants, doctors' offices, law firms, and even a mosque. Arabic signs filled Dix and Wyoming Streets. It delighted him to hear Arabic spoken everywhere, to taste familiar food once again at Arabic restaurants and take fresh breads and other groceries home. Khaled would bring some to his friend Richard, who had also stayed in Ann Arbor after graduation.

"Here, have some falafel and Za'atar bread," Khaled offered.

"You really like Dearborn, don't you?" Richard asked with a soft smile on his face.

"I love it. Let's go there together sometime. I'll take you on a tour. Have you ever seen the Rouge Plant and the assembly line where cars are made? It's like magic. I think you'd love the neighborhood. We can have lunch there, the food is amazing! Can you believe it, some Arab families have been in Dearborn since the 1920s."

"Of all the places in the US, why would they settle in Dearborn?"

Khaled wondered about that himself, until he learned that many of his collogues' parents and grandparents were drawn to the area because there were always job openings at the Rouge Plant. Workers disliked the assembly line grind so much that turnover was always high. So, in 1914, Ford started offering five-dollars for an eight-hour shift, over twice its previous rate at the time. Khaled was also surprised to learn that since the 1920s, Ford recruited workers from so many countries, including Yemen.

"Can you believe it?" Khaled said to Richard. "Now, many of the children and grandchildren of these workers are active organizers in the labor union, as well as the Civil Rights Movement. Now, Malcolm X and Mohammad Ali are two of their heroes."

"Are you serious?"

"You should write an article about them and the South End neighborhood. So many other immigrants live there. It's hard to believe that people came from all over the world to work at Ford."

"Including you, my friend Khaled. How about taking me on a tour? Then I can ask my boss if the newspaper would be interested in me writing an article about it," Richard said with a smile that fed onto Khaled's excitement.

"It's hard to believe that I never knew about this huge Arab community before. It's as if Ann Arbor and Dearborn are worlds apart."

"From what you're telling me, it sure sounds like it."

Khaled found it a bit amusing that all through his time in Ann Arbor, he was avoiding Arab students at the university, only to be surrounded by them in Dearborn? At work, most of his friends were Arabs, and he loved going out with them to lunch. Once in a while, he would go out for a drink after work. Sometimes, he was tempted to go with them to dinner, or to the Arabic night club.

Khaled thought about the joy that invaded his heart when he got to spend time with new friends and people who understood him. But with that joy also came guilt, and the thought of Elizabeth being stuck at home all day by herself disturbed him.

In mid-August of 1964, Khaled took a three-week vacation and boarded a plane to be with his sister Layali at her wedding. He was hoping that his wife and child would join him, but Elizabeth did not want to go.

"Ramsey is too young to take such a long trip, and I want to get ready for school," said Elizabeth when he suggested the three of them travel together.

"That boy loves to sleep. He'll sleep most of the way and won't feel a thing. And we can come back before classes start. I'd really love for you to come with me. My mother is dying to meet you and Ramsey."

"You haven't seen your family in so long. It will be good for you to go alone."

"My family wants to spend time with you and Ramsey," Khaled explained again. "My mother will be disappointed. I don't think she'll be happy to see me alone."

"Of course she will," Elizabeth said more reassuringly.

Khaled was eager to have his family and friends meet Elizabeth and Ramsey, but deep inside he was relieved to go alone. After five years in the States, he wanted to travel home unconfined and without worrying if Elizabeth was having a good time or not. Not knowing what to expect from his father was already causing him enough anxiety. Even so, he was not going to miss Layali's wedding. With five younger siblings, a lot of weddings would follow. He would probably miss some, but definitely not this one.

After twenty-six hours of flying, he arrived at Jerusalem airport, exhausted. A flood of emotions took over him the minute he stepped out of the plane. After he picked up his three large suitcases filled with gifts, he found an army of family members waiting—his father and siblings, and two of his uncles and their sons. The only female among the welcoming crowd was Yasmine, After all the hugs and kisses that showered him, he asked, about his mother and Layali. Their absence unnerved him.

"They are getting dinner ready," said his father.

"Ah," he sighed. "I should have known."

Khaled looked at his five siblings, "My God, you've grown so much. I hardly recognize you." Then he hugged his sister Yasmine, who was only six when he left. "You are almost a young lady. I won't be able to carry you on my shoulders anymore. Will I?

"I guess not."

"Look at you, blushing."

"Time to go," his father interrupted. "They are waiting for us. If we don't get home soon, your mother will start worrying. You know how she is."

Khaled was happy that there were enough people to fill the three cars. He wasn't ready yet to be alone with his father. *I wonder if he's going to scold me about not coming back . . . or about not wanting to work with him . . . and definitely for marrying an American . . . He is not the accepting kind . . . It goes against his nature.*

~

Khaled's mother and Layali, along with a few aunts and female cousins, were at the door to greet him. His mother got to him first. She hugged him and soon started crying. "Thank you, God . . . Thank you, God . . . " She wouldn't let go of him.

"Enough Mama," Layali said. "Why all these tears? This is a time to celebrate." She put her hand gently on her mother's shoulder. "It's my turn to hug my brother."

Sister and brother embraced for a long time. When they separated, both were laughing as they wiped their tears with the backs of their hands.

"Thank you for coming. I guess it took getting married to make you come home."

"You're more than welcome. Although you didn't come to *my* wedding."

"Shut up Khaled. Don't let Baba hear you. We would never hear the end of it."

"Is he still mad?" Khaled asked trying to mask his worries best he could.

"You don't have to worry about him. He hasn't said much about it lately."

"With Baba, you never know."

"You're right Khaled. But who knows. He might decide to behave," Layali said, resting a hand on his shoulder.

"*Inshallah.*"

~

For the three weeks Khaled was at home, the house was always filled with people. The first week, people came to welcome him. The second was the preparation for Layali's wedding, and the third, people came to say their goodbyes. The only chance he had to be alone with his mother was early morning, and with Layali, late at night. Thanks to the Mediterranean nap culture, he was able to catch up on sleep.

"You know, Layali," Khaled told his sister as they sat alone in the living room. "I came two weeks before the wedding to spend time with you, and of course to get to know your husband Farouq. I really like him. I just wish you wouldn't be leaving right after the wedding. I miss being with you."

"I would love to stay, but we've already bought our plane tickets and booked our hotel in Rome."

"Look at you, fancy Sister, having your honeymoon in Italy. Not bad," he said with a teasing smile.

"I've always fantasized about going there. I had to find a husband to do that," she said, laughing.

Khaled was eager to know about Wafa. He took advantage of the intimate conversation with his sister to ask about her. He was surprised by the sadness he felt when he learned that Wafa had gotten married and moved to Jerusalem. Layali read his face.

"What did you expect? You got married yourself."

"I'm just curious. I assume she knows I got married. Does she?"

"Khaled, this is Al-Bireh, news travels fast. Anyway, she and I haven't seen much of each other lately."

"It's because of me, right?" he asked, feeling guilty to have pushed his sister away from Wafa.

"Whatever," Layali said shrugging. "She is happily married. You should be happy for her."

"I am, I am. I'm just curious about her news."

"Your long, sad face tells a different story. I hope you're not still in love with her."

"Of course not. I love my wife."

"Guess what," Elizabeth said to Emily as they sat sipping coffee and watching Ramsey in his playpen.

"*Guess what?*" Emily echoed with a chuckle. "You never cease to surprise me."

"I'm pregnant."

"Again?" She said, then immediately added, "I'm sorry. I didn't mean it like that. Did you want to have another child now?"

Elizabeth didn't respond.

"I thought you wanted to go back to school."

"I am going back school," Elizabeth said firmly. "And I plan to stay in school until I get my degree. I only need three semesters to graduate. This one and two more."

"I know being pregnant won't stop you," Emily said, encouraging her friend. "You did it with Ramsey."

"Nothing is going to stop me, especially now that we finally found a good babysitter. I'm hoping she will stay after I have the baby."

"I'm sure she will stay. Especially if you have another child like Ramsey," She added, smiling at the little boy. "Happy and easygoing. Does Khaled know that you're pregnant?"

"No, not yet. I just found out."

"So you'll have a Spring baby. Khaled is going to be thrilled. When is he coming back?"

"September fifth. He wanted to be here for Ramsey's first birthday."

Elizabeth and Emily were all smiles.

"I assume I'm invited."

"Don't be silly, of course you are."

But to her own disappointment, Elizabeth went to school for only the fall semester. Going to school while pregnant and then caring for a one-year-old was too much. She felt tired all the time.

On a sunny spring day in May of 1965, their second child was born. Khaled would always say that day was one of the happiest days of his life. To him, she was the most beautiful child ever born, with her dark eyes, olive skin and rosy cheeks, and full head of dark brown curly hair that framed her face. Her curious, hazel eyes looked at the world around her the moment she departed her mother's womb.

Throughout Elizabeth's difficult pregnancy, she would say, "I don't care if I have a boy or a girl, or if the baby looks like me or my husband. All I care about is that I have a healthy child.

But when she held this baby in her arms and laid her on her breast, she forgot all the labor pain. Joy, pride, and a big smile spread over her face. She looked at her husband and said, "I carried this baby for a long nine months and had a painful labor. But it was all worth it. It's a girl. Thank you, God, it's a girl."

They named her after Khaled's mother, *Jamila*—beautiful.

18
THE HOLY LAND

Summer 1966

Khaled came home from work looking forward to sharing some exciting news with Elizabeth. He had asked his boss, Mr. Shaheen, if he could take a month off to take Elizabeth and the kids to visit his family in Al-Bireh. Mr. Shaheen said yes.

"But before talking with you more about our travel plans, I have some other exciting news I'm dying to share with you. You won't believe this." Elizabeth said with a smile on her face.

"Go ahead and tell me. I'm not good at guessing."

"My sister Mary Ann called me today."

"For real?"

"Yes, for real. She just got married and moved to Flint! Her husband works there. We talked and laughed for a long time. She promised to come see us soon. But she doesn't want my parents to know that she called or plans to visit."

"I'm so happy for you," Khaled said, admiring Elizabeth's beaming face. "Did she say when she might be coming?"

"No. She said she needs a little time to settle into her new home. She gave me her phone number. I'll be able to talk with her every day. I missed her so much. I miss the rest of my family too..."

The soft smile on her face began to fade, and soon, Elizabeth couldn't say much else. and started to cry.

"I hope these are happy tears," Khaled said to try to comfort her. "This is really good news—enjoy it!"

"I know. But I miss all my family."

"Trust me, your brothers and sisters will gradually come around. I am sure of it."

The following day, Khaled brought up again the idea of visiting his family in Al-Bireh.

"It's time for you to meet my family and see where I come from. It's time for my family to meet you and the kids. Everyone, especially my mother and Layali, keep asking me when we are going to visit."

"Don't you think Ramsey and Jamila are still too young to take such a long trip?" Elizabeth asked, just as doubtful as she'd sounded the first time the trip was brought up.

"I think they'll enjoy it, especially Ramsey. And I'm sure you and I are going to have a great time. We can take side trips to special places like Jerusalem and Bethlehem. They have so much history. You're going to love it."

Elizabeth was not sure she wanted to go. But the idea of being in Jerusalem and Bethlehem was so exciting it overrode her worries about not knowing the language or the culture, or not being welcome, especially by Khaled's father. When she shared her reluctance with Emily, her friend said to her, "Elizabeth, do you have any idea how many people would love to go to the Holy Land? Trust me, it's a once-in-a-lifetime experience. Also, I am sure Khaled's family will love seeing you and the kids. Otherwise, Khaled wouldn't have insisted that you and the kids go with him."

With two young children, Khaled told his wife that it might be easier on all of them if they spent one night in a hotel at London

Airport, then flew the following day to Jerusalem with one stop over in Cairo.

By the time they arrived forty hours later, they were totally exhausted. Elizabeth could hardly recall any of the faces in the crowd that met them at the airport, except for Khaled's parents and his siter Layali. Once they arrived at their home, she had a quick bite to eat out of politeness and collected her two children, who had been hugged and kissed by at least a dozen people, and the three of them collapsed into deep sleep.

Elizabeth was glad she'd listened to Emily and Khaled's advice. As they both had assured her, everyone in Khaled's family was welcoming and kind, including Khaled's father, who spoke with her in fluent English. Many of Khaled's siblings and friends also spoke English, some better than others. They all made a point to include her in their conversations, especially Layali, who had a baby girl, Muna, only a few months older than Jamila.

During the first days of their trip, Khaled translated most of the Arabic conversations for Elizabeth. But with his mother speaking only Arabic and the large number of guests coming over to welcome them, his ability to keep up wound down. Even so, he and Layali made a special effort to introduce Elizabeth to their mother's friend, Mrs. El Khatib, a German woman who spoke fluent English, and to two of Layali's friends who taught English in Al-Bireh public high school. However, the real stars who captured everyone's attention were Ramsey and Jamila. The two were showered with gifts, hugs, and kisses while being moved from one lap to another.

Once the visitors had left, Khaled and Elizabeth escaped to their bedroom to enjoy the afternoon nap, a luxury they never got in the US.

While they were resting in each other's arms, Khaled asked,

"Elizabeth, remember when I told you I would love to take you to Jerusalem and Bethlehem? How about if we went next week for two or three days? Just the two of us." Kissing her forehead, he said, "We can leave Ramsey and Jamila with my mother. There's a lot to see here. God knows when we will have another chance to come back to Palestine . . . "

"We can't just leave the kids and go."

"Of course we can. Between my mother, Layali, and the rest of my siblings, we have the best babysitters we could ever hope for."

"Layali has her own family to take care of. She doesn't need two more kids to look after."

"She loves spending time with our kids. Didn't you notice how excited her daughter and our kids get when they are together?"

"Honestly, Khaled, I'd love to go to Jerusalem and Bethlehem and see all the holy sites. But I'd feel awkward leaving the children behind," she explained, heaving out a sigh. "I don't mind leaving Ramsey. He is older and quieter, but Jamila can't stay still for a minute. She gets into everything and needs someone to watch her all the time. Why can't we take both of them with us? I would feel much better."

"Because I want to be just with you. The only time we've been alone on this trip was when we went to Ramallah for half a day. Also, the places I want to take you to are not for kids. We'll be walking a lot. They are too young to enjoy it. You and I could use a break."

Khaled borrowed a car from his father, and he and Elizabeth headed to Jerusalem. After settling in at the National Hotel, they walked to the Old City to have breakfast at Zalatimo Bakery, which opened in 1860 in a narrow alley not far from the Church of Sepulcher. Zalatimo was famous throughout the city and the surrounding towns for its *mutabaq*, a filo dough stuffed with sweet white cheese and sprinkled with honey.

Elizabeth couldn't eat enough of it. She watched with fascination the baker as he pulled the pastry from a wood stove carved into the stone wall and brought it immediately to their table.

"Are you sure you want to keep eating more?" Khaled gently asked her. "I don't want you to get sick at the first stop of our trip."

"Don't worry about me. I'm fine. Can we come back tomorrow?" She asked still chewing the last bit of *mutabaq*.

"We can do anything you want. But please wait until you see other places. They're all special. I hope you don't ask to return to every one of them. We'll never get back to Ann Arbor."

As they walked the Old City's narrow streets and alleys, Elizabeth couldn't contain her excitement. There were large and small shops displaying their goods—carpets, embroidered cloths, colorful pottery; street vendors selling a variety of nuts and spices of every imaginable scent and color; and an abundance of summer fruits, some that Elizabeth had never tasted or even seen before. Combined with the sounds of music from transistors, children playing and chasing each other, the Mosques' call to prayer, and the church bells, it all dazzled her.

"This really is amazing," said Elizabeth. "There's so much to see and smell and listen to. It's intense. I can't decide what to look at, what to taste or buy."

"You can taste and smell whatever your heart desires. But please, let's not buy anything today, or we will have to carry stuff around. We'll come back tomorrow or the day after, and you can buy all you want. There are so many places I want to show you. We will come back, I promise."

"Say, *Wallah,* you swear," a term Elizabeth had learned since they arrived a week earlier.

"Wallah . . . Wallah . . . Wallah," Khaled obeyed, laughing.

After wandering from one shop to the next for two hours and looking at street vendors and historic buildings, Khaled said to Elizabeth, "Maybe it's time to rest. Let's sit in this coffee shop and have something to drink before we explore some more."

In the crowded coffee shop, Khaled ordered Arabic coffee while Elizabeth ordered a Coke. Despite the noisy street crowds, Elizabeth found the place in the middle of the old city rather amusing. She sat there quietly, watching people of all ages coming and going. She was particularly taken by a number of unaccompanied children playing in the streets.

"Shall we go? There is a very special place I want you to see."

"Every place in this country seems to be special," she said, looking around. "I can sit in here forever just watching people."

"I know. But I have a nice surprise for you."

Not far from the coffee shop, they turned into a steep, narrow street, and Khaled pointed to the blue street sign—*Via Dolorosa*. When he told her that the street they were on was the very same path, Jesus Christ was forced by Roman soldiers to walk as they took him to his crucifixion. Elizabeth was beside herself.

"And the Church at the end of the street, called the Church of the Holy Sepulcher, was where Christ was buried."

Awe struck, Elizabeth stared at him.

"You can ask anyone who lives in Jerusalem. Wait until we get to the church."

"We are actually walking where Jesus Christ walked almost two thousand years ago?"

"Yes, exactly."

Elizabeth was so moved that tears streamed down her face. She touched and kissed the walls of the narrow street.

Before entering the Church, she bought two candles and a rosary. Imitating other women who were about to enter the Church, she also bought a black scarf to cover her hair. By the entrance, she lit her candles, then walked toward the altar. She knelt, crossed herself and prayed in silence. When she was done, she got up and sat down on the nearest bench. Khaled sat few rows behind her.

He had never seen her pray before. When he noticed her shaking shoulders, he got up, went over to her and hugged her without saying a word. After a few minutes, she quieted down and looked at him.

"I'm here, standing where Jesus Christ was crucified. It's hard to believe this is real," said Elizabeth, with tears brimming her eyes. "I haven't been in church since I left my parent's home. I feel close to Jesus, to the Virgin Mary, and to God. I need to start going back to church. As I prayed, I promised God that I would do that as soon as we went back to the States. And I will."

Khaled didn't know what to say. He was moved by his wife's intense feelings but never expected this. He put his hand on her shoulder and walked beside her until they left the Church.

"I'm tired. I would like to go to the hotel," Elizabeth said.

The next morning, they woke up early and drove to the Dead Sea.

"I thought we were on vacation," said Elizabeth. "Why do we have to leave so early if it's only a forty-five-minute drive?"

"Because it's much hotter there. We should get there when it's still cool and serene."

"How could it be so much hotter if it's so close?"

"It's a deep valley. The Dead Sea and Jericho are way below sea level. They are actually the lowest spots on Earth. Did you know that the water in the Dead Sea is so salty that nothing can live in it? No fish, no seaweed, nothing. That's why it's called the Dead Sea."

"You're kidding," she said, raising a brow.

"No, I'm not. Wait till you feel the pressure in your ears. It's similar to what you feel when a plane is landing. And the water tastes so salty that it's almost bitter, and it burns your eyes and throat."

"I suppose no one would swim there."

"Actually, people do. It's therapeutic. People with all kinds of skin problems or arthritis go there to dip in it."

They arrived in Jericho before seven. Parking the car under a shady tree, they walked to a nearby bakery and sat at a small, low table on the sidewalk. The smells of freshly baked bread, *Ka'ak* with roasted sesame seeds, and falafel were so inviting that they ordered breakfast there with mint tea.

They sat and took in their surroundings. Field workers stopped at the bakery to have breakfast on their way to work.

"This is better than the fancy dinner we had last night," Elizabeth said.

"I agree," responded Khaled, while his mind drifted to the time his father brought him and the family on Fridays during the winter, recalling the warmth and the scent of lemon and orange blossoms.

After breakfast, they drove to a site on the east bank of the Jordan River where it is believed that Jesus Christ was baptized—the *Al-Maghtas*, also known as Bethany Beyond Jordan. Elizabeth took her shoes off, lifted her skirt, tucked the hem into the waistband, and walked into the shallow river until it reached above her knees. She cupped her hands and poured water on her hair and face, letting the water run down her neck and chest.

"Who would ever have guessed that I would be baptized in the same spot Jesus was baptized," she called to Khaled as he stood at the shore watching her.

When she walked out, her clothes were soaked. Elizabeth couldn't contain her emotions and started to cry again.

"This is supposed to be a happy trip," her husband said as he embraced her.

"Khaled, you have no idea how happy I am. It just brought back many memories of my family."

"I'm so sorry."

Elizabeth walked to a vendor, bought three bottles of holy water to take back to the US, and was ready to see more.

~

They drove south and stopped at the Dead Sea for a short time, then they headed on toward Bethlehem to visit the Church of Nativity, located where Jesus Christ was born.

"I will never forget this trip," said Elizabeth as they walked. "Do you understand what it means to me to visit these holy places?"

At the Church of the Nativity, Elizabeth lit candles, left a few dinars, prayed, and cried again. She wandered the plaza in front of the church and bought religious figurines, rosaries made of olive wood, mother-of-pearl boxes, and Christmas tree ornaments.

"What are you going to do with all these?"

"I'm not sure. I'll keep some and give some to my friends."

Elizabeth went silent.

"I'm thinking of sending some, along with pictures, to my family," she explained. "They would love to have some keepsakes from the Holy Land. I'm hoping they might come around once they know that you brought me to all these holy places. And that I got to pray in the same churches where Jesus Christ was born and crucified."

~

On their final day, they had their breakfast again at Zalatimo and bought some sesame and butter cookies to take back to Al-Bireh. Their next stops were at Al-Aqsa Mosque and the Dome of the Rock, the holiest sites for Muslims in Jerusalem.

"My God, Khaled. This place is so beautiful and serene. I can't believe I've never been to a mosque before. The golden

Dome of the Rock is amazing. And look at the mosque's yard. It's huge!"

"It's magnificent," Khaled agreed. "Now, let's go back to the souq to do our shopping."

Along the old, narrow streets of the walled city, they bought rugs, pottery plates, and bowls, blue Hebron blown glass, and colorful pillowcases and runners. They bought a typical peasant embroidered dress for Elizabeth, along with scarves and jewelry. And they bought Za'atar and other spices. Elizabeth was like Alice in Wonderland, not knowing what store to go to or what to buy. She bought so much that Khaled had to ask the hotel to ship most of the stuff to Ann Arbor.

~

After a late lunch, they packed and drove in silence. Khaled wondered if Elizabeth would actually start attending church when they went back to Ann Arbor. He'd never really practiced his own religion, and until this trip, he never saw Elizabeth practicing hers. He wondered how he would feel if she started now. But he said nothing.

19
THE 1967 WAR

It had been a long time since Khaled felt so happy and energized. To his own surprise, their trip to the holy sights rekindled his love for Elizabeth, and his young children seemed to be happier. He couldn't wait to share stories and pictures of their three-day side trip with his friends. He was proud to be from Palestine, proud of its history, monuments, and holy sites, even though he was not particularly religious. He was even a bit anxious about Elizabeth wanting to start going to church.

Elizabeth also felt closer to her husband and was relieved to meet his family. They welcomed her and treated her with love and hospitality, especially Khaled's mother, whose warmth put her at ease and touched her heart. Upon returning home, Elizabeth couldn't wait to send her parents a letter about their trip, along with gifts and pictures of the Holy Land. She also sent cards and gifts to each of her siblings and was relieved that none were sent back to her. So she waited. And waited and waited for their replies.

Nothing.

"I don't understand," she said, searching for answers. "How could they do this? Not a single one responded or acknowledged receiving my letters and gifts. How could they be so cruel?

They call themselves devout Christians, and they can't forgive or forget."

"I am sorry, Elizabeth," Khaled said in an attempt to comfort her. "But look at your sister, Mary Ann. In time, your brothers and sisters will find their own jobs, get married, and move out of the house, just as Mary Ann did."

"They are all afraid of my father, even my mother is," she sighed. "Mary Ann and I were very close. Still, it took years before she contacted me. I had to wait for her to get married. And now she's worried my parents will find out that she's talking to me."

"How are they going to find out if none of you says anything about it?"

"That's easy for you to say, Khaled. You don't know what it's like. All your family is on your side, including your father. He forgave you as soon as Ramsey was born."

"To be honest with you, if my sister Layali did what we did, I don't think she'd have gotten away with it. But I'm their son, and maybe it's different with boys," he said, trying to make sense out of it all. "It's a sad reality, but that's the way it is. Trust me, I would do anything for your family to be close again. But I really believe you would feel much better if you stopped worrying about it and went back to school."

"I plan on it, hopefully next year. But the kids are still young, and they need me."

"We have more than one good babysitter now. The longer you wait, the harder it will be. Also, the school might not accept all your credits if it's been too long since you took classes," he tried to reason.

"Thanks, Khaled. But I really don't need a lecture right now."

On June 6, 1967, less than a year after their return from visiting Khaled's family, the Arab-Israeli war broke out. The newscasts reported how the Israeli army occupied the Palestinian West Bank, East Jerusalem, and Gaza Strip. Almost overnight, close to one and a half million Palestinians found themselves under Israeli military rule.

The war altered the lives not only of Palestinians living in those areas but also of hundreds of thousands of their immediate relatives—sons and daughters, brothers and sisters who were living, working, or studying abroad.

Khaled was almost paralyzed by the news. He tried to call his parents, to send telegrams, but all communication with the West Bank had been cut off. He called his supervisor at work and requested a few days off. He spent his time glued to the TV and shortwave radio, often having both on at the same time. He cried, swore, hit the TV, and tore newspapers. He hardly ate or slept or even talked to his wife or children. While Elizabeth was concerned about her husband, she couldn't fully comprehend the gravity of the situation or the depth of his anguish.

"Khaled, maybe you are overreacting," she said, raising a hand to his shoulders. "Soon, the Israelis will have to withdraw. They can't stay there forever."

"They've already annexed Jerusalem and expelled thousands of Palestinians to Jordan. Who knows what they will do next."

"I understand, but you have children and a job. You need to take it easy on yourself and on us. It hurts me to see you in this condition."

"How do you expect me to feel?" He asked, tears slowly creeping in. "Just listen to what's happening. As if the disaster that hit us is not enough. All this support for Israel—politicians, the media! And then they portray us, the Palestinians, as the problem . . ."

"Then stop listening to the news, and go spend some time with your children. They miss you."

Khaled received a call from one of his father's friends in Amman. His father wanted him to come to the West Bank immediately.

"Why? Did someone get sick or die?" Khaled asked.

"Nothing like that. The Israeli government is conducting a census of the Palestinians living in the areas they just occupied. Your father wants you to come back immediately to be counted so you won't lose your rights to live there. Also, I'm not sure if you are aware of it, but all entry points to the West Bank have been closed except for the Allenby Bridge near Jericho. You have to come to Amman first and then go from there."

"How could they deny me that right? I was born and raised in the West Bank."

"Don't be naive. They did that to almost a million Palestinians in 1948. So just come."

Khaled flew to Amman and tried to enter the West Bank from Jordan, but the Israeli army, which had taken over control of who could enter, would not let him. He returned to Amman. And each day, for the next five days, he traveled back to the Allenby Bridge to try again. But with no luck.

Khaled felt humiliated and powerless. The possibility of losing his right to ever live in Palestine or even visit his family again ignited his anger. Exhausted and heartbroken, he flew back to Ann Arbor and to his family and job.

Khaled spent every break and lunch, and his time right after work talking to Arab co-workers. The war and the Israeli occupation dominated their conversations. He found strength in Dearborn's large community of Palestinians and other recent Arab immigrants, as well as many second and third-generation Arab Americans who understood and shared his grief and frustration. But the fallout at home seemed impossible to stop.

Writing in his notebook, Khaled wondered if his marriage and family were coming apart just because of who he was. What could he do to hold things together? Sometimes, to settle his thoughts he would write in Arabic, and Jamila would peek over his shoulder, smiling in wonder at the beautiful squiggles.

In Detroit and throughout the US, generations of those with roots in the Arab world were seeking a voice as a community, and Khaled found comfort and encouragement in being part of it. Toward the end of 1967, people from around the country gathered in Ann Arbor to meet about the country's unconditional support for Israel and the portrayal of Palestinians and Arab Americans in the media. A year later, in Chicago, the group launched the Arab American University Graduates. Khaled was proud to be among its first members.

Within a few years, Palestinians from the West Bank, including his hometown of Al-Bireh, started to arrive in Metro Detroit. Many settled in East Dearborn, driven there by the Occupation. Before long, they started political and social organizations to support the Palestinian people, and Khaled became even more active.

Elizabeth did not appreciate her husband's increasing political activities that took him away from her and from their children. He was often going to meetings or events after work and sometimes on weekends. His Palestinian solidarity work caused her additional fear and anxiety. She would accuse him of being a selfish husband and a selfish father who only cared about himself, confronting him the moment he stepped inside the house.

"Where have you been? Don't you work from nine to five?"

"I told you last night that I'd be going to a meeting," he said, not sparing her a glance.

"What kind of a meeting is that? A meeting that lasts until almost midnight? You have a wife and children—remember?"

"It's not even ten. The meeting lasted till nine. It takes almost an hour to get home. When I tried to tell you about it last night, you didn't seem interested."

"It's a meeting to support the PLO, right? Of course, I'm not interested," she said angered. "They're a terrorist organization."

"Please do not ever use that word again," he said raising his tone, now angry himself. "They have the right to resist military occupation. What about your support for the Anti-War Movement . . . the Civil Rights Movement?"

"They're nonviolent. It's not the same. What you're doing is dangerous. You're being so irresponsible. You have children!"

"We're not doing anything illegal. What the Israeli military is doing is illegal. It's our right and obligation to support our people."

In the midst of all this, Khaled and Elizabeth had their third and last child. Leila was born on October 9, 1973. Khaled took three weeks off from work, and when he started up again, he came home immediately after work. But within a couple of months, he was back to his political activity, which infuriated Elizabeth and caused their relationship to fall apart even worse than before.

Searching for a way to save his marriage, Khaled asked Richard and some of his activist friends for advice. They all agreed: moving to Dearborn might be a good solution to his marital problems. Khaled decided to discuss the idea with her.

"Elizabeth, how about we move to Dearborn? I think you would like it there. It's easier to make friends and to find babysitters. You can go back to school at the University of Michigan,

Dearborn Campus. I'll be close to my work, and the kids can go to schools where there are other Arab American kids."

"Why would I want to do that?" Elizabeth asked with a cold glare. "Why would I want to move to an Arab community? Also, the schools in Ann Arbor are much better. Do you know how many people would love to live here?"

"Dearborn isn't just Arabs. It has people from all over. We can live in West Dearborn. There are lots of white people living there."

"I'm not moving anywhere. If you want to move to Dearborn, go ahead. But the children and I are staying here."

Khaled gave up on his grand idea, and Elizabeth continued to complain about his absence during evenings and weekends while she was stuck at home with the kids. So Khaled started to take the older two children, Ramsey and Jamila, with him when there was a rally or a meeting on weekends, but this only added to his wife's complaints.

"They're children, Khaled. They need to have fun, not to go to political meetings. Are you out of your mind?"

"They're not the only children there. We meet at people's homes, and others bring their children, too. It's fun for the kids. It's not like they sit in a meeting," he tried to explain. "They go to a basement or a backyard, and they play. Two or three older kids watch them. They need to be with children who look like them and come from similar backgrounds. I'm also trying to give you a break. I don't understand what's wrong with that."

"Khaled, for God's sake, please leave the kids out of your crazy politics. I don't want them going to demonstrations or rallies or any Palestinian events. They come back and talk about it at home and at school, especially Jamila. I'm warning you, Khaled—*leave Jamila alone*!"

PART II
JAMILA

1986

From the time I was young, I used to watch my father write in his notebook. He would tell me he was writing in it because he was confused or sad, or because he missed our family in Palestine and wanted to remember them.

Sometimes, he'd write in Arabic instead of English. I loved the amazing shapes of the letters. When he wrote them, his face became more peaceful and he looked like the dad who made me feel safe. It was as if there was a connection between us that nothing could ever break. So as I learned to read and write, I wanted to have my own notebook, too.

People think my father is attractive, with his olive skin, dark wavy hair, deep brown eyes, and friendly smile. They mistake him for a mixed African American or Hispanic. For better or worse, I look like my dad. My mother is blonde with blue eyes, pale skin, and lots of freckles on her face and arms. The two of them are as different as night and day, not only in their looks but in many other ways, too.

Dad said that on the day I was born, the sun was bright but gentle, and the whole city of Ann Arbor was blooming. He said it was a perfect spring day, not too hot and not too cold. He even swore that when my mother's water broke at around midnight, the moon was as big as a baseball field, and the stars were dancing.

My dad wanted to name me Jamila, because in Arabic it means beautiful, and because it's his mother's name. Mom wanted to name me Janet after her younger sister, who she treated like her own daughter. But it was his turn to choose, because Mom named my brother Ramsey, while Dad wanted to name him Omar after his favorite uncle. Dad agreed to Ramsey because it's also an Arabic name.

Anyway, to accommodate my mother, he suggested they name me Jamila Janet Nasser. And Mom was okay with it because I was so beautiful, of course. And so Jamila it was.

I love my name. Dad's name, Khaled, means forever. We're quite the pair—Beautiful and Forever. But what in this messed-up world is beautiful forever?

I love both of my parents, but I was definitely my father's daughter. I love my dad a lot, and growing up, we were always close. Until it became clear I was a bit of a rebel. That was when I realized that our unconditional love for each other was in fact conditional.

20
A COMMUNITY CELEBRATION

November 1974

Nine-year-old Jamila pulled the comforter over her body and buried her head. It was a dark and cold Michigan fall day. The sun was still hiding behind thick clouds. Jamila wanted to stop the sound coming from the kitchen. It was her parents arguing, and she did not want to hear it.

"It's Sunday. It's too early to wake up and get into an argument. What could they be fighting about? Why can't they just talk?" Jamila murmured to herself as she wiped her crusty eyes. She was tired. All she wanted was to go back to sleep, but she could still hear her parents. Finally, she jumped out of bed and dashed into the kitchen.

"Why are you fighting now? It's Sunday. Why can't you let me sleep?" Jamila yelled, trying to use her voice to override her parents'.

"Sweetheart, we're sorry. Why don't you just go back to sleep now?" said her mother.

"You yell at us when we fight. But you and Dad fight all the time."

"Jamila, please go back to bed."

Khaled looked at Elizabeth. "She's right, that's enough." Turning to his daughter, he said, "Come here."

Jamila walked over to him.

He gave her a hug and kissed the top of her head. "Don't worry about it. Go back to sleep, and we will be quiet."

"Why are you always fighting?" She started to cry.

"We are not fighting. We're just discussing things. Adults do this sometimes. We didn't mean to be that loud. Why don't you go back to sleep? We'll be quiet."

Jamila went to her bedroom.

~

"We need to be more careful," Khaled told his wife. "Our arguing is affecting the children."

"Of course it is. We shouldn't have the kids hear us fight. Or even better, we need to find a way not to argue as much. Ramsey has told me more than once that he hates feeling caught between the two of us. He says it makes it hard for him to know what he really wants."

~

For a whole week, Khaled and Elizabeth had been arguing over his decision to take part in a community rally in Dearborn celebrating Chairman Arafat's invitation to address the United Nations.

Arafat's speech, which he had delivered a few days before, was all over the news. The Palestinian Arab American community was joyful and optimistic. Khaled had hoped his wife and children would accompany him, but Elizabeth was vehemently against it. Their arguments were getting more hostile by the day. He was shocked by her lack of interest or sympathy and her inability to realize the significance of that day, not only for him but for Palestinians around the globe.

For years, Elizabeth had been complaining about her husband's political involvement. She couldn't fathom why he would want to involve their young children in controversial issues surrounding Palestine, the PLO, and now Arafat. She kept cautioning him, "What if their teachers or other kids find out? Jamila is already complaining that kids at school are teasing her about her name, dark skin, and curly hair. You don't need to give them another reason to harass her."

~

Two hours later, Jamila walked into the living room. Ramsey and Leila were on the floor watching television. Her mother was at the dining room table sorting canceled checks, and her father was in the kitchen with his newspaper and a cup of coffee.

"We already had breakfast. Do you want something to eat?" Elizabeth asked.

"No, I'm not hungry," Jamila said as she went to join her brother and sister.

Khaled decided to try one more time, reminding himself to try to speak calmly.

"Elizabeth, please hear me out. I understand your concerns. But this isn't a demonstration or a protest. It's a celebration, a happy occasion for a change, and Palestinians don't have many of those. I really want the kids to be part of it. I'm sure there will be a lot of other children their age there. After the march, there's going to be a big party in the park. It's a historic day and we should all be there. I wish you would come with us."

"I already told you, I'm not coming. And don't assume the kids want to go either. You should ask them."

"I disagree with you. I'm sure they'd love to. I'll ask them."

Khaled carried his empty plate to the sink and took his coffee to join the kids.

~

"Remember last week when we watched Chairman Arafat on television addressing the United Nations? As I told you, I never thought I would live to see this day. This is a big victory for us. You're still too young to understand the significance of it. And today..."

"Baba, I'm not that young," said Jamila, interrupting her father. "I watched the whole speech with you. It was Ramsey who got bored and left. Not me."

"Of course, Jamila, you've never been young," said Khaled, teasing his daughter. "So guess what's happening today?"

"What... what? What's happening?" asked Jamila, all excited.

"There is a big celebration in Dearborn, and many families will be bringing their kids. I want to take you and Ramsey to see it. Do you want to go?"

"Yes... yes, I want to go! I want to go," said Jamila.

"How about you, Ramsey? You want to come? Jamila is coming."

"I'm not sure," he said, looking at his mother.

"You can go if you want," she replied. "But today, I'm taking Leila to the mall. If you come with us, you can get the ball you've been asking us for."

Khaled looked at his wife, opened his mouth, then decided not to say anything. He just shook his head and asked Jamila to go get something to eat and get ready. They had to leave in half an hour. Then he asked Ramsey one more time if he wanted to come.

"Is it okay if I don't go?"

"As you like, but you'll be missing a great day."

Khaled wasn't happy about Ramsey not joining him. While waiting for Jamila, his thoughts drifted to the time when he first met Elizabeth and how much they loved each other. How much they were in sync with each other, especially when it came to politics and religion. He never imagined that those two things would become the source of such contention between them. *I wonder how she could have changed so much... or is it me who has changed? Or maybe we both have... I guess, with no communication with her family, she had to find her own community in the church . . . just as I found my own.*

When he met Elizabeth, she wasn't religious at all. In fact, she resented religion and the church. But after their visit to Palestine and the Christian holy sites, she started occasionally going to church. A year or so later, she started to talk about taking the kids with her. "If you want to go to church, that's your choice. But leave the children out of it," Khaled would tell his wife every time she brought it up. After many arguments, Khaled relented and told her she could take them to only one of two churches, the Quaker Church or Unitarian.

"Those are not real churches," Elizabeth would argue. "Children should not grow up without a religion. They need it to anchor them. And what if their teachers or other kids ask them about their religion? What are they supposed to say? We don't have religion?"

Khaled himself was a nonpracticing Muslim, and he felt comfortable with that. His family was not particularly religious. He remembers his mother fasting and praying during the month of Ramadan. His father did even less; he did not fast, and he only prayed twice a year at the mosque on the first days of the main Muslim holidays, Eid Al-Fitr and Eid Al-Adha. He also did his *zakat* by distributing cash and fresh lamb meat to the poor on these two occasions, a tradition he was keen to observe. But some of his relatives prayed daily, including his grandparents and older aunts. For Khaled, Islam was a cultural heritage, and the Muslim Eids were festive occasions, especially for kids.

Elizabeth's interest in politics diminished with time. She had never been as interested as he was, but she always supported progressive issues and occasionally participated in them. At first, she didn't object to her husband's involvement in Palestinian issues, which was, to a great extent, a reaction to the 1967 Israeli Occupation, including of his own town. As anti-Palestinians sentiments in the US were getting worse, Elizabeth started to feel afraid for her husband and kids. "We live in America. I'm sorry our government and the media are so hostile to Palestinians. That's why I want you to be careful and to leave the kids out of politics."

"I want my kids to know who they are and where they came from. I want them to be proud Palestinians whose ancestors, including their father, come from the Holy Land."

"They're Americans. You need to come to terms with that," she retorted.

"They're both American and Palestinian. Israelis want to deny us our very existence. They want us to forget who we are, to forget our country and culture. They want to erase us from the face of the earth. I'm not going to help them do that . . ."

Interrupting her father's stream of thoughts, Jamila came out of her room all dressed up for the occasion: red dress, red shoes, matching gloves, and scarf in hand.

"You look beautiful," her mother told her. "But I think you might need a jacket or even a coat."

"But I want to show off my dress."

"Go get your warm jacket and leave it in the car just in case you change your mind."

Jamila ran to her room, came back with her jacket, and grabbed her father's hand.

"Let's go, Baba."

Khaled glanced at Ramsey, still watching television. He thought that Ramsey would have liked to come but didn't want to upset his mother. Khaled felt sad to have his son miss this once-in-a-lifetime event.

~

By the time they arrived at Dearborn City Hall on Michigan Avenue, a huge crowd had already gathered in front of the building. Palestinian flags, signs, and balloons filled the air. Men were wearing their keffiyehs, and women, including some young girls, were in their colorful Palestinian embroidered dresses. Children of all ages were running around chasing each other. Amid the political speeches people were chanting: "Long live the PLO! Long live Arafat! And *Thowra, thowrah hatta alnaser*—Revolution, revolution until victory!" Jamila wanted to know what that meant. Her father told her she should go play with the kids and promised to explain things to her later.

Once the speeches were done, the crowd walked about a mile to Hemlock Park, continuing their chants. Kids walked along carrying small Palestinian flags, as well as red, green, white, and black balloons, the same colors as the flag. At the park, a group of men and women were setting tables with food, desserts, and drinks. The smoke from barbequed meat and chicken filled the air, and loud music with revolutionary songs added to the festivities. It was a true celebration. People were joyful and happy, greeting each other with hugs and kisses, "*Mabrook, mabrook*, we're going back home soon, *Inshallah, Inshallah*," and "*Allah kareem*—God is generous".

Khaled watched his daughter running around and playing with other kids, laughing and enjoying herself. He wished Ramsey was with them but didn't want to dwell on it or think about his arguments with Elizabeth. This was his day, a happy day. He was among his own people, celebrating and feeling victorious.

On their way back to Ann Arbor, Khaled was relieved to see Jamila fall asleep within minutes. She had asked him many questions about Chairman Arafat and the slogans people were chanting in Arabic. He again promised to explain things to her later. He hoped that by the time they arrived home, she would forget her questions. He didn't want her to repeat in front of her mother what she had heard at the celebrations.

~

When they arrived home, Jamila woke up. She jumped out of her dad's car and ran to the house excitedly.

"It was so much fun. You should have come," she yelled when she saw her brother.

"I had fun, too," Ramsey answered back. "Mom took me shopping. We had lunch and ice cream at the mall."

"It's not the same. We can go to the mall any day. You should have seen how big the march was. So many people carrying flags. There were lots of balloons for the kids. There was music, too. We ended up in a big park with big picnic tables as big as our yard filled with lots of food and desserts. So many desserts and so many kids. We chased each other and played tag. It was so much fun."

"I'm glad you had a good time," her mother said. Go wash up and change your clothes. We'll be having dinner soon."

As they sat at the dinner table, Khaled turned to Ramsey, "Jamila and I had a great day. I hope you and Leila had a nice day."

"Of course they did. You and Jamila should have been with us. Sunday is a family day," replied Elizabeth.

Khaled decided to ignore her comment. He wanted to savor the day and a feeling of victory.

21
UNFINISHED GOODBYES

Winter 1977

Khaled and Elizabeth were spending a rare, quiet afternoon together. The three kids were at a birthday party two blocks down the street.

"She's going to be fine," Khaled said. "She's strong-willed and has her own mind. But that's not necessarily a bad thing, especially for a young girl. It will serve her well as she grows up."

"I'm worried about her not having enough friends," Elizabeth responded. "She only has three, two Black and one Latina. They are nice kids, but she needs to have more friends. She's bullied by white kids, especially boys. What if she gets hurt, or hurts someone?"

"If she feels more comfortable with kids who aren't white, that's fine," said Khaled. "But it's not fine she's bullied because of her looks, or because she sees things differently, or any other reason. I guess we should go talk to the principal one more time. This has to stop."

"I agree with you. I'll call the school first thing on Monday."

The phone rang. They let it ring but stopped and listened. It was Elizabeth's sister leaving a voicemail.

"Hi, this is Mary Ann. Please call me when you can."

"I'll call her later," Elizabeth said.

Within an hour, the phone rang again.

"Hi. Sorry to bug you, but I need to talk to you. It's urgent. I hate to be the one bringing you bad news. Dad is very sick. It doesn't look like he's going to make it. He wants to see you."

Elizabeth looked at her husband, a pause of silence hung in the air.

"Did you hear that?" Elizabeth finally said. "It's been almost fifteen years. Why is she telling me this? Why now? All of a sudden, he wants to see me? It doesn't make any sense." She looked around the room as if the answer hid itself in an unseen corner. "I don't want to ever see or talk to him again. Now that he is dying, he's afraid of facing his God. He thinks he can fix all the bad things he's done in his life, and he wants me to help him do that? Hell no, I won't do it! I don't care if he lives or dies."

She choked up and couldn't say more.

Elizabeth got up and started pacing around the house, going from the living room to the kitchen and then up the stairs to her bedroom, shaking her head, crying, then back to the living room, stopping, asking, almost screaming questions to Khaled. "Why now? What am I supposed to do? Just go see him as if nothing had happened?" Not waiting for a reply from him, she'd start moving around the house again, cursing her father and mother.

Khaled, too, was surprised by the unexpected call. But he wasn't surprised by his wife's reactions. He tried to talk to her, to console her, but that made her more agitated. So he let her be and just waited.

When she finally sat down, her whole body was shaking. Sweat mixed with tears flooded her red face and chin, and even her shirt was wet. It broke his heart to see her in such agony. As he gently started massaging her neck and shoulders, her cries became louder, sobs, an outpouring of all the pain her parents had inflicted on her. He hugged her tightly while she cried. For a moment, she quieted down.

"Elizabeth, I don't blame you for not wanting to see or talk to him. Or for feeling angry by this sudden request. What your parents did to you is awful. But after all, he is your father. Why don't you call Mary Ann and find out more about what's going on?"

"Leave me alone," she said weakly, "I don't want to. I can't."

"Elizabeth, please. You don't want to do anything you might regret later."

She started crying again.

"I told you I can't. Why can't everyone just leave me alone?"

She went to her bedroom and laid down on the bed.

Khaled followed her.

He laid down next to her and wrapped his arm around her. She let him. As she stopped crying and her breath became soft and steady, he relaxed his embrace, letting her sleep while staying there close to her.

As he watched his wife's body move with each breath, he felt an overpowering love and desire to protect her. And regretfully, he thought of all the arguments and disagreements they'd had over the years.

His mind drifted back to those early years of knowing each other and to the one and only time he visited Elizabeth's family. That was before he graduated. He tried to remember how her father looked, but he couldn't. He couldn't remember her mother either, or any of her siblings, except for Mary Ann. All he could recall was the old small house that needed lots of repair, the poorly dressed kids, and her grumpy father, who would stare at him without showing any interest in talking.

He wondered if Elizabeth would even remember how her own siblings looked, especially the four or five younger brothers who were so close in age and very much resembled each other. His thoughts went over all the times Elizabeth tried to reach out to her family, and her constant disappointment over them not responding to her letters, gifts, or Christmas cards, and when none of them called or came to see her children. He especially dwelled on the time when Elizabeth sent her parents and every single one of her siblings gifts and pictures from her trip to the Holy Land, but not a single one responded. As he remembered, he became furious, ready to tell his wife, *I agree with you. Fuck them. You don't have to go see them...*

"We're back, we're back!"

Khaled's anguished stream of thoughts was interrupted by the sound of Leila's exuberant voice, hollering.

He gently got out of bed, went out, and closed the door behind him. Leila was still yelling.

"Mom, Dad, where are you? We had so much fun..."

"Leila, please lower your voice. You don't need to be so loud. Your mom is sleeping. She isn't feeling well."

He looked at the other children and asked them all to be quiet, to wash up, and if hungry, to have something to eat. He also reminded them to do their homework and take care of Leila.

"Mama never sleeps in the afternoon. What's wrong with her?" Jamila asked.

"Nothing's wrong with her. She's just tired and wants to have a nap."

"But..."

"Jamila, I told you. Mom is tired."

Khaled went back to the bedroom to check on Elizabeth. He was thankful that the kids hadn't been home when Mary Ann left the message, and he wanted to be sure that she wouldn't call again. He didn't want them to hear what was going on. Definitely not now.

He waited, and Elizabeth finally woke up. Reluctantly, he asked her to call her sister. But she refused and instead kept saying, "I just can't."

So Khaled decided to call to find out what was going on with her father. He also asked Mary Ann to give Elizabeth some time and promised that she would call the next day.

~

The following morning, Elizabeth did call.

"Dad is very sick," said Mary Ann. "He has a serious diagnosis of lung cancer. He wants to see you. He begged me to bring you with me. He even cried, saying he should have never done what he did to you. He wants to ask for your forgiveness."

"That's bullshit. He would never say anything like that."

"Yes, he did! I was as shocked as you are. But I'm telling you, he did. The doctors say he doesn't have much time. And he really wants to see you. You know how hard it is for him to apologize or acknowledge wrongdoing. Please come."

As she listened to her sister, Elizabeth twirled the telephone cord between her fingers, attempting to stay calm.

"You think it was easy for me to deal with what he and Mom did? Do you expect me to go see him as if nothing had happened?"

"I know, Elizabeth. Of course, it's hasn't been easy for you," Mary Ann sighed through the line. "It hasn't been easy for any of us."

"What about Mom? She told me to give my child up for adoption. Does she want to see me or talk to me? Or is she going to scold me again that I brought shame to the family? I don't want to see her. Actually, I don't want to see either one of them, ever."

~

A couple of hours later, Elizabeth's mother called, begging Elizabeth to come home. She told her that her dad wanted to see her before he passed.

"Now he wants to see me? After both of you haven't talked to me for all these years? After you forbade my siblings from talking to me? After you never even wanted to meet your first grandchildren. Now you remember you have a daughter, and you want her to come and see you and your husband. How dare you?" she asked, her voice filled with hurt.

"Elizabeth, we are both sorry. Please, believe me, we are. Your dad cries all the time, asking himself why he did that. Ever since you went to the Holy Land and sent us pictures, he and I have been asking ourselves if we were in the wrong. He was moved by the pictures, especially the one of you in the Jordan River being baptized in the same place as Jesus. He showed the picture to our priest and asked him if he thought you washed away your sins by doing that, and the priest believes you did. Your father even told me, 'Maybe her husband is not as bad as we thought. He took her all the way to the Holy Land and had her visit these holy sites and got her baptized.'"

"I sent you those pictures years ago. It's taken this long to reach out?"

"I know, I know. We are sorry."

Elizabeth hung up the phone.

~

Khaled stayed home that day to be with her. He called Mary Ann and got the name of the hospital and her father's room number. He said that if she decided she wanted to go, he would drive her. When Elizabeth refused to call her dad, Khaled dialed the hospital number, and once he got her father on the line, he handed it to her.

"Hello . . . "

Elizabeth couldn't say more.

Her father's weak voice was trembling,

"Elizabeth, I'm so sorry for what I did . . . I don't have much time left . . . Please come . . . I have a lot I want to tell you . . . come alone. Just you and I."

"I am not sure I can come." She hung up the phone and started to cry again.

"Now he remembers I'm his daughter? He wants to see me. He's given me nothing but grief. I don't know what he wants from me. Why now? Why?" she said quietly, hiding her face in the crook of her arm.

"There's never a good time for anything like this," Khaled explained, brushing her hair with his fingers. "It's good that you talked to him and to your mother. It's going to make seeing them a bit easier. Why don't you go have a shower while I call work and ask for a few days off? After breakfast, you can decide what you want to do."

Once Elizabeth was in the shower, Khaled called the hospital and spoke to one of the nurses, who told him that her father was not doing well at all.

After she finished her shower and had calmed down a little, Khaled was finally able to convince her. Reluctantly, she agreed to go after the kids got home.

"What are we going to tell them? They know that my family and I don't talk. They'll start asking all kinds of questions, especially Jamila."

"We tell them the truth. Your father is sick, and you need to go see him. We don't have to say more. Now let me call Jenny, Leila's babysitter. Hopefully, she can come to stay with the kids."

~

By the time all the kids came home from school, Elizabeth and Khaled were packed and ready to go.

"Ramsey, your mom and I have to leave for a few days. You're an adult now. Can we depend on you to take care of yourself and your sisters? Jenny will come and stay with you. We should be home in a couple of days."

"Where are you going?" Ramsey asked. "You never leave us alone. What happened?"

"Yes . . . yes, what happened? I want to know," Jamila insisted.

"Your mom and I need to go to Grand Rapids to visit your grandparents."

"But I thought mom was mad at her family. What is happening?" Jamila asked.

"Jamila, this is an adult conversation. We want you and Ramsey to take care of Leila."

"You can't just tell me this is an adult conversation every time I ask. I want to know," Jamila said while crossing her arms.

"Can I come . . . ?" cried Leila. "Please, Mama, I want to come."

"Sweetheart, you can't. Not this time. Jenny is coming to spend time with you. You love Jenny, don't you?"

Khaled and Elizabeth also asked their neighbors on both sides to keep an eye on the kids.

Before leaving, Jamila went to her dad.

"Baba, what is going on? Why is mom crying so hard?"

"Her dad is very sick."

"But she never cared about her dad. He has never visited us. No one from her family has ever visited. Why? What happened?"

"Jamila, I just told you. Her dad is sick, and we have to go visit him."

"But they never visit us and we never visit them, and they live only three hours away. Teta and Jido live in Palestine, and we go visit them, and they call and send us gifts and pictures. I want to know why Mom's parents don't talk to her. It's not fair."

Khaled could only sigh.

"Habibti, we have to go now."

After their parents left, Jamila stayed up thinking about her mother. After an hour or so of pondering, she decided to talk to her brother. Maybe he knew something. She went to his room.

"Hey, Ramsey," she called from the doorway. "Why do you think Mom and her family don't talk? She has so many brothers and sisters, and we don't know any of them except Aunt Mary Ann. They never visit, call, or even send us Christmas cards. It's strange, don't you think? Mom must have done something really bad to piss them off, or else they did something bad to her. She never wants to talk to them. What could it be? Maybe they are mad because she married Dad?"

"Why would they be? Dad is a good guy."

"Just because he's Palestinian and Muslim and kind of dark. White people don't like dark ones. You look like Mom, so people leave you alone," she tried to explain. "I look like Dad and look how the kids harass me in school."

"I think it might be something else."

"Like what? What?" she said, approaching his bed.

"Well, I can't tell you. You're still young, and also you don't know how to keep a secret."

"Ramsey, please tell me. I won't say anything, I promise," she pleaded, leaning over his bed.

"Okay. I'm not sure, but maybe, I'm just saying, could it be that Mom got pregnant before she married Dad, and that made her parents real mad?"

Jamila was quiet for a moment as if running the numbers through a calculator.

"For real? Could they have done that? And how do you know?"

"I figured it out last year. When they celebrated their anniversary. Mom said it was their fourteenth. When I asked her how that could be, she insisted she made a mistake."

22
TOO LITTLE, TOO LATE

Elizabeth and Khaled walked into the gray dim hospital after seven PM. They'd been directed to the second floor: Room 219. As they entered the elevator, Elizabeth started to shake. Khaled moved closer to her, wrapping his arm around her shoulder. When they got off the elevator, they walked together toward her father's room. Despite the end of visiting hours, a sizable group was gathered in the rest area. Mary Ann called her sister's name, and Elizabeth stopped in her tracks.

She stared at all the people, her eyes moving from one to another as if wondering who was who. Everyone stared at her, while staying in their seats. Suddenly, a young woman jumped up from her chair and dashed toward Elizabeth. The two of them locked in a tight embrace, weeping silently, their bodies shaking. It was her younger sister Janet, who was only five when Elizabeth had last seen her. Her other siblings followed suit, except the two oldest brothers who just shook her hand and ignored Khaled.

Khaled walked Elizabeth to her father's room and nudged her to go in.

"It's going to be all right. Just go in. Take your time, I'll be waiting for you right here."

She took two steps into the room and stopped. Her heart was beating loud, but her tears were nowhere to be found. She looked around.

Her father's small body was wrapped in a white sheet and hooked up to a few tubes and a beeping monitor. He didn't seem to have seen or recognized her. Her mother was also there. She got up from her seat, walked over to her daughter, and embraced her.

"Elizabeth, you're here. You came. Thank you, God, she is here."

Elizabeth couldn't make her arms move to hug her mom back. Suddenly, she heard her father's weak call. She moved closer to him.

"Dad."

"Elizabeth."

He stared at his daughter and struggled to move his hand.

"Forgive me, my daughter. I should never have done what I did."

His voice gave way, and he slowly lost a fight against deep sleep. Elizabeth's heart skipped a beat. She stepped back and stood looking at him.

"Don't be scared," her mom reassured her. "He will wake up again soon. They gave him lots of drugs to ease the pain. Come sit here," she said, pointing to the empty chair next to her.

But Elizabeth stood still, silently gazing at her dad for long minutes as if wondering if he would wake up again.

"I'm tired," she said, breaking the spell of silence. "I'll come back tomorrow morning," she explained, leaving the room.

Khaled was standing by the door, waiting. He held her hand, and they walked away, feeling the many eyes staring at them.

Elizabeth was back the following day. A few of her siblings came, some accompanied by their spouses or children, most of them ranging from toddlers to teens. After a short visit with her father, she sat in the waiting room, which was packed with mostly family members. Some said hello, others nodded their heads in acknowledgment, and a few said nothing. A priest arrived and headed directly to her father's room.

That morning, Elizabeth went to her father's room twice: once when she arrived and once before she left. She spent the three hours she was there sitting for a few minutes in the waiting area, then leaving for a walk in the hallways or going to a rest area on other floors. She was happy to meet Khaled at noon at the entrance of the hospital as they had arranged. After having lunch, Elizabeth told her husband to take her to the hotel. She was exhausted.

In their hotel room, they pondered what to do next. *Should they go back home or wait?* Suddenly, the phone rang. Her father had passed away.

They rushed back to the hospital. Her mom and all of the kids, including Elizabeth, bid him farewell.

Everyone went to the family home, but Elizabeth couldn't. She begged Khaled to drive her to their home. She wanted to be with her kids.

Khaled managed to avoid answering their questions, except for telling them that their grandfather had died and they should leave their mother alone.

Two days later, they drove back for the viewing and the funeral. During these days, Elizabeth and Khaled warmed up to her two sisters and a couple of her younger brothers. Elizabeth couldn't say much to her mother, and Khaled kept a polite distance.

When it was time to leave, they said their goodbyes and promised to come back.

~

On their way home, they went back and forth about what to say to the children.

"I don't know what to tell them," Elizabeth said, looking out her window. "They had asked me before about my parents and family, especially Jamila. I've avoided giving them a straight answer. All they know is that we don't talk to each other, but I never told them why."

"Jamila was asking me about it before we left. Maybe it's time to tell them the truth," Khaled suggested. "They're old enough, especially Ramsey and Jamila."

"So you want me to tell Ramsey that my mother wanted me to give him up for adoption?" she asked, exasperated. "Then say to him, 'Hey Ramsey, let's go see your grandma?' And do you really think you can tell Jamila half the truth? She's way too smart for that. She'll keep coming after us until we tell her the whole story."

"Maybe we could tell them that your parents disapproved that you married me. That was part of why your family was unhappy. Wasn't it?"

"But . . . " Elizabeth stopped and couldn't say more. During the one-week ordeal, she had fought through enough tears for a lifetime.

"Go ahead and have a nap. Let me figure out how much we're going to tell the kids," Khaled said to her, unaware that Ramsey and Jamila had already done their math.

When they arrived at home, Elizabeth went to the bedroom and slept for sixteen hours.

23
TALKING WITH MOM

A few years later, Ann Arbor, 1984

Elizabeth had spent her afternoon looking forward, though with anticipation, to her daughters visit. She took her time setting the table on the backyard patio and getting dresses. After hugging and welcoming her daughter, they walked to the patio to enjoy the unusually warm March afternoon sunshine.

"I'm glad your dad and Leila aren't coming home till later. And Ramsey won't be here till Sunday morning. It's nice having you to myself, just the two of us."

Jamila had come home from college to spend the weekend with her family. It was her first year at Michigan State University in East Lansing. This time, to her surprise, her mother was wearing a beautiful casual dress, her hair was freshly washed, and she'd even applied a hint of makeup. She had also prepared an elaborate spread to welcome her daughter: plates of nuts and fruit, a variety of cheeses, olives and crackers, and an expensive bottle of wine. All of this, along with the family's best plates and wine glasses, were resting on an orange and yellow tablecloth with matching napkins.

"Wow! Thanks, Mom," she said, mesmerized by the full table. "You look beautiful, by the way. And all this food and drink!

What's the occasion?"

"You haven't been home for almost a month. I miss you. That's all."

"I miss you too, Mom."

Growing up, Jamila was never as close to her mother as she was to her father. She'd had a special relationship with him since she was a child. When her brother or sister complained about their father loving her more, he would tell them, "How could you say that? A parent can never love one child more than another." Elizabeth also complained about Khaled's relationship with Jamila. "You spoil her. She's hot-headed, argumentative, and difficult. She doesn't even listen to me."

"Try giving her more attention, and you'll be surprised," her dad used to explain. "She thinks you don't love her. I often have to tell her, 'Jamila, stop this nonsense. Of course, your mother loves you. There is no love in the world like a mother's love.' I always thought there was a special bond between a mother and her daughters, but somehow, I don't see it between the two of you."

"Don't you think I would love to have a closer relationship with Jamila? Do you know how guilty I feel about not having one?" Elizabeth said, frustrated, "But her attitude doesn't help."

"Elizabeth, you're the adult here. Maybe you ought to try a different approach."

Jamila sipped her wine slowly, trying to relish her mother's attention and company, as well as the soft sun caressing her face. After the two of them talked about the weather, they exchanged news about the family: Khaled's work, his continued involvement in Palestinian politics, Leila doing so well in school, Ramsey, who now was in his third year at the University of Michigan and not coming home as much, and Jamila's school and what she was planning to major in, their conversation came to a halt. Neither seemed to have anything more to say.

After a few uncomfortable minutes, Elizabeth broke the silence.

"So, Jamila," she began, her voice soft but a little shaky. "I hear that you and Ali are seeing each other. Is that true?"

Jamila shifted in her chair, swallowed hard, and looked away, avoiding her mother's gaze.

"Jamila, I just asked you a question."

Jamila, did not respond. She reached for her wine glass and took a big gulp, trying to figure out what to say. True, she was not that close to her mother. But in the past, especially during her last two years of high school, Elizbeth did ask her more than once if she liked any of the boys at her school, or if she had met someone she would like to date. But this time her mother's question seemed to be loaded. She was obviously anxious and reluctant to ask.

Elizabeth's patience was running out.

"Jamila, I am waiting. Did you not hear me? Are you going to talk or just sit there and totally ignore me."

"Yes, Mom, I did hear you," she answered, a bit frustrated. "I'm not sure what you are hinting at or who told you what. I've always liked Ali. I've known him since I was in middle school. Now we are both at the same university, of course, I see him."

"Come on, Jamila. Please don't play dumb with me. You know what I mean."

"No, Mom. I don't know what you mean. I'm just wondering if this is your version of mother-daughter relaxation or if all this playing dress-up and food and wine is just a cover-up for an interrogation. Is that it?"

Jamila's voice was louder and harsher than she intended.

"I'm sorry, I didn't mean to upset you. I'm just curious."

"Curious about what?"

"Well, I'm curious if you are dating Ali. Isn't it normal for a mother to want to know if her daughter is dating someone? What's so upsetting about that?"

"Well, if you insist on knowing, yes, I am. But I want to know who told you."

Silence returned to invade their space, with Jamila waiting for her mother's reaction and Elizabeth at a loss for words.

"So now you know. Are you going to say something? Or are you going to just sit there with your neck and face turning red?"

"I don't know what to say."

"If you don't know what to say, why bother asking?"

"How long have you been dating him? I hope it's not serious."

"And what if it is?"

"You know, Jamila . . . he is, he's . . . "

"He is what?" Jamila yelled, sensing where her mother was going with this.

"I hate to say it, but he is Black."

"I can't believe this. I cannot believe what I am hearing." Jamila's voice was getting louder and angrier. "Really, Mom? Did you just realize that? He's been Black all his life, since the day he was born and the whole time you've known him. He's been my brother's best friend since they were in middle school. He's been to our home a million times. He has slept, eaten, and played here. You want to tell me you never noticed he's Black?"

"Don't be silly. Of course I noticed, but . . . "

"But what, Mom?" Jamila waited, receiving nothing but silence. "Actually, I don't want to hear any of your 'buts.'"

Jamila got up and pushed the chair away so hard it fell behind her. She slammed her wine glass on the table, spilling it over the freshly washed and ironed tablecloth, and stormed off the deck and into the house.

~

Elizabeth sat there, staring at her shaky hands. After a few minutes, she took two slow sips of her wine, got up, lifted the chair, and used her napkin to wipe the tablecloth. She sat back down and poured herself another glass of wine, but soon she changed her mind and went into the house.

In the kitchen, Elizabeth paced back and forth, opening and closing the fridge, looking in the food pantry, trying to start dinner, but unable to accomplish anything. Then she walked up the stairs to Jamila's room, only to come back down before reaching the top of the stairs. After a few ups and downs and up again, she mustered her courage and knocked on her daughter's bedroom door. No answer. She knocked again.

"Jamila, please open the door," she pleaded. "I'm sorry if I said something to upset you. I'm worried about you. I just don't want to see you get hurt."

Jamila sat on her bed, bawling and mumbling, *"I can't believe this... I can't believe this... What did I come home for?"* stopping only to wipe her tears and dripping nose with the sleeves of her blouse. Coming home, she had not expected this confrontation.

She hadn't told any of her family about Ali yet, not because she thought any of them would object, but because she hadn't been dating him for long. Her mother's reaction threw her off guard and infuriated her, to say the least. Jamila was also sad about not being close enough to her mother to confide in her about Ali and other issues.

Jamila thought of the many times she had tried to get closer to her mother, but she didn't know how. Elizabeth had tried, too. But the two seemed to be locked in a confrontational pattern neither one knew how to remedy. Jamila often envied her girlfriends for having close relationships with their mothers. She yearned for moments like the one she just had, but her mother had to spoil it.

Elizabeth continued to tap on Jamila's bedroom door.

"Please open the door, I am sorry. I did not mean to hurt you."

Jamila finally opened the door. Her eyes and nose were red and puffy.

"I'm already hurt," she said, wiping her tears. "You just can't help yourself. You had to say something hurtful, didn't you?"

"I'm just trying to protect you and keep our family together," Elizabeth explained, trying to sound reasonable.

Jamila lost it. She got angrier and almost screamed at her mom.

"You're saying all this because I'm dating Ali, who we've known and loved for years! Aren't you the one who couldn't stop praising him? 'Oh, Ali, he is so handsome, he's so kind, so smart, and so good in school,'" Jamila mimicked. "You were so enamored with him to the point that Ramsey would get jealous. Aren't you the one who always said Ali was a good influence on him? Or is Ali only good when he helps your son? You are such a hypocrite and a phony. You're being racist."

"Jamila, I'm not racist. And don't you ever dare call me that again. I love Ali, and I know that he is a good man. And yes, he did have a positive influence on your brother. But that does not mean I'd be happy to see you marry him. Trust me, his family won't be happy to see him marry you, either. They'll want him to marry a Black girl," Elizabeth said, exasperated. "Jamila, my dear, you are both too young and naïve to understand. This is the United States of America we live in. Race matters."

"How ironic. Isn't that what *your* mother told *you* when she found out you were dating Dad? Wasn't she mad because you were dating a Palestinian or, even worse, a Muslim? Didn't she want you to date a good Catholic boy? Now you want to tell me I cannot date Ali because he is Black? For real?"

"Yes, that's what my mother told me, and sometimes I wish I had listened to her. Not because your father is Palestinian or Muslim. That's not the issue. It's just that mixed marriages often don't work. Can't you see how hard it's been for me and your dad to get along?"

"I never heard you before saying mix marriages don't work. Now that I'm dating Ali, you want to blame your problems with Dad on your mixed marriage? How convenient. Besides, who said I was going to marry him or marry any other man? I'm not thinking of marriage. I can't believe we are having this conversation."

"When I started dating your dad, I wasn't planning to get married either. But look where we are now."

Jamila knew that her mother had gotten pregnant before she was married and often wondered if that was why she ended up marrying her dad. She was also curious if that was the reason her grandparents refused to talk to her mother for so long. Khaled and Elizabeth never mentioned these things to their children, and Jamila never asked. She was tempted to confront her mother about this now. But she resisted the urge, instead she said, "Bottom line, you married who you loved, despite your parents' objection."

"Jamila, do you realize what it would mean for your future, or for our family, especially your father if you were to marry a Black man? Besides— "

"Leave Dad out of this," Jamila screamed. "Don't use him to cover up your own prejudice!"

"I'm not prejudiced, nor is your father. But neither of us could approve of this. Go ahead and tell him if you want. Let's see if he reacts differently."

Elizabeth covered her face as tears started coming down her cheeks.

"Mom, why are you being so dramatic? You always cry when things don't go your way."

"That is not true. I love you, Jamila, and I don't want to see you get hurt and end up like me. That's what makes me cry!"

24
FALLING FOR ALI

Jamila stayed in her bedroom, wishing she'd never come home. She kept going over her conversation with her mom, and the more she thought about it, the more furious she became.

At dinner time, she heard a soft knock on her door. She ignored it. *Here she comes again, with her pretentious apologies and phony care*, she fumed. She ignored the second and third knocks until she heard Leila.

"Jamila, it's me. Please open the door."

"Sorry, Leila, I thought it was Mom," she replied in a croaky voice as she peered through the door.

"Oh my God, Jamila, you look awful. What's wrong? You've been crying? What happened?"

"Nothing happened, habibti, I just don't feel good," she said trudging back into the room.

"What do you mean nothing happened? You're not sick. You're mad. Did you have another fight with Mom?" she asked, letting herself in. "You two argue and fight all the time. Mom is very nice, and so are you. I don't understand it. And I don't like it."

"I'm sorry, Leila. You don't have to worry about it. Sometimes Mom and I don't see eye to eye. That's all."

Leila started to cry, as she often did when her parents or

Jamila and their mom were at each other's throats. Whenever she complained about it or asked what was happening, everyone would tell her she was too young to understand, or "Don't worry about it."

Seeing her eleven-year-old sister sad only added to Jamila's misery. She hugged her, and the two of them laid in bed, nestling in each other's arms.

"Mom sent me to tell you dinner's ready."

"I'm not hungry. Maybe I'll come down later."

"Please, Jamila," Leila said as she faced her sister, "tell me what's wrong. Why are you and Mom fighting now? I'm not that young anymore. You can tell me."

"I promise I will, but not now. I'm really tired."

"Can I get you something to eat or drink? How about water or a cup of tea with chocolate chip cookies? The ones you like. Mom bought them, especially for you. Can I get you some?"

"Thank you. You are very sweet. Maybe later. Right now, I want to sleep."

~

Elizabeth came back, trying to convince her daughter to come to dinner, but Jamila wouldn't open the door. She tried again Saturday morning and then at noon.

"Jamila, I said I'm sorry. How many times do I have to tell you? I didn't mean to upset you. You're being unreasonable."

But no matter what Elizabeth said, Jamila refused to open the door. Her mother's words, *but he's Black*, played over and over again in her head. And the more she thought about it, the angrier she got.

Jamila had planned to spend the weekend at home. She was actually looking forward to it, especially Sunday morning brunch, when Ramsey was supposed to come. She knew that her mother would cook them a special meal with all their favorites. But staying home after their conversation was uncomfortable. She was so mad at her mother that she didn't want to see or talk to her. Definitely not then, and maybe never. Even when her father came twice to check on her, she refused to leave her room or tell him what happened. Jamila only allowed Leila to come to sit with her and bring her little things to eat and drink.

~

On Sunday morning, Jamila woke up wondering how her mother knew about Ali. Who could have told her? None of her friends in East Lansing knew her mother. Could she have left something in her room? She searched her desk, closet, drawers, and bookshelves but found nothing. She went through her diary that she kept for years. She remembered writing something about liking and maybe even loving Ali when she was still in high school. She frantically looked at that but found nothing incriminating. She was frustrated but relieved. She did, however, find a pair of old jeans and a worn-out sweatshirt that she decided to wear.

She took a shower, got dressed, and came down carrying her duffel bag and backpack. Ramsey was already there sitting with their father, who was still in his pajamas, chatting and drinking coffee. Elizabeth was in the kitchen making breakfast.

"Look who's here, sleeping till almost noon," Ramsey said, getting up to hug her.

Jamila embraced her brother for a long time, her eyes getting watery.

"What's going on, Sis? I hear you're sick. Are you okay?"

"Yes. I just have a lot on my mind."

"She hasn't been feeling well since Friday," Elizabeth interrupted, then she turned to her daughter, looking at the bags on the floor.

"How are you feeling this morning? Much better, I hope. I see you're all packed. You're not leaving now, are you?"

"She can't leave now. I came to see her. She wouldn't do that," Ramsey said.

"Sorry, Ramsey. I am leaving. I have an exam this week. I need to study."

"You're not feeling well, and you've hardly eaten in two days," said her mom. "Why don't you stay and leave tomorrow? You can study here."

"I have to— "

"Jamila, listen to your mother," Khaled interrupted.

"I'm okay, Dad. I study much better in my room or at the library. Also, I don't have my books or notes with me."

"At least have breakfast before you leave. We will be eating soon," Elizabeth said.

"I'm not hungry."

"But . . . "

As Elizabeth tried to respond to her daughter, Khaled raised his palm, gesturing to her to stop. He looked at his daughter.

"All right, Jamila. If you want to go back to school right now, you can go,"

Then he asked Ramsey if he would drive his sister to the bus station.

"But I don't want her to go," Leila chimed in. "Jamila, please stay."

"Sweetheart, I'll be back soon. I promise."

The minute Jamila and Ramsey left, Elizabeth turned to Khaled.

"When I tell you she is spoiled and stubborn, you defend her. You tell me I don't know how to handle her."

"Elizabeth, it's too early to get into a discussion about Jamila. Can we just have a quiet breakfast?"

Exhausted from crying and lack of sleep, Jamila sat in the car, staring out the window.

"Hello, Sis. You're so quiet. What's going on?"

Jamila ignored her brother. She kept going over her conversation with her mother and the words Elizabeth used when she apologized to her: "I am sorry I upset you," "I didn't mean to hurt you." But she never apologized for what she had said about Ali, Ramsey's best friend.

"Come on, it can't be that bad. Are you just going to sit there pouting?"

"Yes, it was bad. You wouldn't believe it if I told you."

"Try me."

Jamila didn't respond. She loved her brother. The two of them had always been close. Less than two years apart, they had done a lot together and shared stories and secrets. But she was drained and didn't feel like talking about her mother or anything else. Knowing his sister well, Ramsey decided to let it go.

On the bus, Jamila thought about Ali. She had always liked him and found him affectionate and kind. She recalled the many times she came back from school angry because some kids teased her about her name or long curly hair. Ali would tell her those kids were jealous of her because she was very smart and beautiful. Sometimes she would cry out of frustration, and he would hug her and say, "Jamila, you shouldn't waste your precious tears on stupid boys."

When she had arguments with her mother, he would reassure her that her mother loved her. During her middle and high school years, she often played with Ali and Ramsey, and accompanied them to get ice cream or see a movie. She recalled how, during Ali's last school year, they flirted behind her brother's back and kissed a few times. They also went on a couple of dates without telling anyone. But that was two years ago, and most high schoolers did that and more. So, when she first went to East Lansing, she didn't think of Ali as a potential boyfriend, but only as a good friend she could count on to call whenever she needed help or had a question about school, or whenever she felt lonely or homesick. It didn't take much to rekindle the feelings she once felt for him.

Jamila remembered the time when Ali first told her he loved her. She enjoyed his affection, but did she really love him? Was he like a brother or a friend or a lover? When did she first feel attracted to him? Why did they stop? Was it Ali who stopped or was it her? Tired of trying to figure everything out, she drifted away, dreaming about him.

~

She arrived at her dorm room to find a telephone message.

"Hello, Jamila, I guess you're not back yet. Call me once you settle in. I miss you."

She was not ready to talk to or see Ali. Not yet.

"Hi, Jamila, you're scaring me by not answering. What's going on? I just called Ramsey, and he told me you've been sick all weekend and that you're still not feeling well. If I don't hear from you soon, I'll just stop by."

Jamila called.

"Hi, Ali. I'm sorry for not calling you back earlier. I'm not feeling well and won't be able to see you soon. I need to save the little energy I have to go to my classes and study."

It wasn't that she did not want to see him. In fact, she was missing him more than ever. But she wasn't sure how to explain her unsettled state of mind.

She wished she could talk to someone about what happened,

but she definitely couldn't tell Ali. She had befriended a couple of Arab students: Rola, a Palestinian American from Livonia, and Huda, a daughter of Lebanese immigrants who had recently fled the Civil War back home and settled in Dearborn. Like her, they had joined the Palestinian student organization and shared similar interests in politics. They both knew Ali and liked him a lot. They were happy when Jamila told them she started dating him. Another possibility was Pauline, who was Black and a good friend of Ali's. But Jamila couldn't bring herself to share what was on her mind with any of them. She was not only livid with what her mother said, but she was also ashamed.

~

When Jamila was finally ready to see Ali, she suggested they go to the cinema, where she could be with him, but not a place for serious conversation. After the movie, Ali asked her if she wanted to get something to eat. She apologized, saying she needed to go home.

When he tried to find out what was going on with her, Jamila insisted that it was nothing and that she was just tired.

Her shaky voice betrayed her.

"Don't tell me it's nothing. You've been avoiding me since you came back. It makes me sad to see you hurting. Jamila, please talk to me."

Jamila was silent for a while.

"I had a fight with my mom."

"What kind of fight would make you upset for this long? Everybody argues with their parents. And you and your mom often don't get along."

"This time was different."

"How? Are you going to tell me?"

"Well... she asked me if I am dating you. When I said yes, she wasn't happy about it. She got upset... Ali, my mom loves you, but she thinks I should be focusing on my studies and not on dating. That's all."

"That doesn't make sense."

"Nothing about my mother makes sense. I really don't want to talk about her right now. I shouldn't have brought it up."

Ali did not respond. He was silent for a while, avoiding looking at Jamila. He scratched his head, then rested his palm on his cheek with his little finger on his lips. He walked two steps ahead of her, totally lost in his own thoughts.

Jamila panicked.

"Ali, where are you going? Talk to me."

"I am not sure what to say, and I'm reluctant to ask. I hope . . . I hope . . . "Ali did not say more.

"You are reluctant to ask? I don't understand."

"It's not because I'm Black, is it?"

"Of course not. How could you even think that?" Jamila said. "You know that everyone in my family loves you, including my mother."

"This is really confusing to me," he finally said, "If you don't want us to date, just say it. We can stay friends."

"No Ali, no, please don't say that. I just need some time."

"Whatever you like. But I'm not sure what you need time for."

Jamila wasn't sure either.

~

Jamila's conversation with her mother had opened a floodgate of questions—about her distant relationship with her mother, her remarks about Ali, and most importantly, what she'd said about her father: *Do you realize what it could mean for our family—especially your father—if you marry a Black man?*

Jamila didn't even want to go there.

25
BIRTHDAY GIFTS

As if her fight with her mom wasn't bad enough, Jamila felt even worse after seeing Ali. She regretted telling him she needed time to think. She panicked. What if he didn't want to see her anymore? Jamila yearned for the time before her last visit home.

She was definitely falling in love. Things were moving smoothly. They went to their classes, saw each other two or three times a week, and spent more time together during the weekend with their friends or at Ali's apartment, especially when his two roommates were not around.

Ali, not knowing what to make of his encounter with Jamila, decided to talk to his friend Pauline.

"All Jamila has asked for is some time. So give it to her. Be patient."

Ali waited a few days. When he didn't hear from her, he decided to call.

"I've been worried about you," he told her. "If you need anything, I'm here for you, as a friend if you prefer, although I'd rather it be as your boyfriend. I love you. I'd never judge you by what your mother says."

When Jamila saw him that evening, she threw her arms around him.

"I am so sorry, Ali. Maybe my mom is right. I'm such a bonehead."

To her own surprise, Jamila found herself defending her mother.

"Maybe my mother isn't really racist. You know how she and Dad don't see eye to eye on so many things, and she believes it's because they come from different backgrounds. I tried to tell her that times have changed. I reminded her that you and I were born and raised in the same town. We both went to Ann Arbor public schools and now we are at the same university, and we have known each other forever. But she's not convinced. She just keeps saying, 'Mixed marriages don't work.'"

"Oh, we're getting married now? How come nobody told me?" he teased.

"Shut up, Ali. Who said I want to marry you?"

They both laughed.

~

One week before Jamila's nineteenth birthday, Ali told her he had some birthday presents for her, including dinner at a nice restaurant on the day of her birthday, May 4th, followed by a weekend getaway.

"I like the dinner idea," Jamila said, "but let me think about the weekend."

Before Jamila had a chance to think, Elizabeth called to tell her she was planning a birthday party for her.

~

When Jamila first started school at MSU, she would come home often, sometimes every—or at least, every other—weekend. Her first few months were particularly hard. She felt lonely and homesick, missing her family, especially her dad. But as the year went by, she became more comfortable and didn't visit as often.

Still, she came home for all the holidays, including Christmas, Easter, and the Muslim Eids. She also came home on Mother's Day and birthdays. But after her last visit, she didn't feel like coming home at all.

When her mother called, she said, "I am planning a nice birthday for you. I know it's on Wednesday, but we can celebrate it over the weekend. We're looking forward to seeing you."

"I can't come."

"You haven't been home for almost six weeks. We want to celebrate as a family. I miss you. So do your father and siblings."

"Mom, I told you. I can't come."

"Why? What keeps you from coming home and seeing your family?"

"Because . . ."

"Jamila, you're not still upset, are you? Sometimes, children and parents don't agree on everything. You're old enough to understand that."

"Mom, how many times do I have to tell you I can't come?"

"You can't, or you don't want to?"

"Whatever."

"This is not like Jamila," Khaled said to Elizabeth. "I don't understand. She doesn't want to come home or talk much to any of us. She's even short with me. Since her last visit, she hasn't been herself. I'm worried about her. If she doesn't come this weekend, I'm going to East Lansing. I need to find out what's going on with her."

"Jamila and I had a fight," Elizabeth sighed. "I didn't want to tell you because I didn't think it was a big deal, but you know your daughter. No one can tell her what she can or can't do. She is making a big fuss out of nothing. I'm her mother, after all. I should be able to talk to her without all this dramas."

"I don't understand. What could you have said that made her that upset? What did you argue about?"

"Well, I found out that she's dating Ali, Ramsey's friend. When I told her she should focus on her studies, she got mad and accused me of being racist. I've tried to reason with her, but she won't listen. I'm giving up on her. She doesn't want to come home or see any of us. That's fine with me."

Khaled thought for a moment, and then decided it was better to stay silent.

~

After his conversation with Elizabeth, Khaled became confused and angry. He didn't think Jamila was old enough to date, and growing up in a conservative town, dating was not acceptable. But deep in his heart, he knew that was not the real reason. Before coming to the US, he and Wafa had flirted, exchanged notes, and touched when no one was looking. They declared their commitment to each other and exchanged letters for almost three years. He wouldn't be surprised if his sister Layali would have done the same.

He couldn't understand why he was so angry. Was it because Ali was Black? But he and Elizabeth always liked Ali and thought he was a great kid. Or maybe it was because Jamila started dating? But he knew that, sooner or later, Jamila was bound to date and fall in love. *Would I feel the same,* he wondered, *if she was dating an Arab?* And then Khaled's thoughts seemed to fall perfectly in place... *Yes, that's it... I'm upset because I wanted her to marry an Arab—a Palestinian...*

~

On Jamila's birthday, Khaled drove to East Lansing to see his daughter. He needed to hear directly from his daughter. Since he'd learned about her dating Ali, his thoughts had begun to torment him. Khaled had always been close to his daughter. He loved and encouraged her passion and fighting spirit. He knew that she always felt more at home in the company of Black, Latino, and other minority kids. When Jamila decided to go to Michigan State, he was glad Ali was already there. But it never crossed his mind that the two of them would end up together.

As he drove, Khaled reflected on his conversation with Elizabeth. Jamila had argued and fought a lot with her mother since she was a child. It saddened him that his wife and daughter were not close. As Khaled thought about his own relationship with Jamila, it suddenly dawned on him: despite their closeness, he'd never had an intimate conversation with her. The realization caught him off guard.

~

To celebrate her birthday, Khaled and Jamila went to Robert's French Restaurant. Once they were seated, he immediately confided what was on his mind.

"Listen, Jamila. You know I love you dearly and want to see you happy. So does your mom. But you're still too young to get into a committed relationship, with Ali or anyone else."

"Dad, why are you and Mom making such a big deal about this? I'm not too young to be dating. Also, you both like Ali, so why are you giving me a hard time for going out with him?"

"No one is giving you a hard time. You're right. I do like Ali. He's a great kid, a good friend to you and to our family," Khaled said, wringing his hands in search of words."But we just don't think you need to get into a serious relationship or . . . or think about marriage now."

"It's you and Mom who are talking about marriage. Not me. Who knows how I will feel about him or anyone else in a few months or a few years?"

Jamila went silent, sorting out how to actually say what was on her mind.

"But what I really want to know, is how would you feel if, after I graduate, I find myself still in love with Ali and want to marry him? Would you object to that?"

Khaled laughed nervously.

"We'll cross that bridge when we get there. You're fortunate that you can attend a college like this. Take advantage of it and focus on your studies. You're a beautiful, smart, capable young woman. You've hardly finished your freshman year. I hope you won't think about marriage before getting at least your master's degree, maybe even your doctorate. You always told me your dream is to work for the United Nations. Habibti, focus on your education and achieving your dreams before we talk about— "

"Mom said she does not want me to date Ali because he's Black," Jamila said, cutting her father off. "As much as I hate her for saying that, at least she was honest. She also said, 'You don't know what marrying a Black man would do to your father.' What did she mean by that? I want to hear from you, Dad. Be honest with me."

By then, Jamila's voice was shaking and her eyes filled with tears.

"I don't know what your mom said or why she said it. But if you want me to be honest with you, I would love to see you marry a Palestinian."

"Since when? I've never heard you say this before."

"Because you're still young, I didn't think it was time to discuss dating or marriage. And you are the only one among my kids who's interested in Palestine. I'd love for at least one of you give me Palestinian grandchildren—to keep our people's identity alive rather than having it erased after I die, which is what the Israelis want. That's why."

"So now it's my personal responsibility to save our people's identity?" Jamila asked, sinking a little deeper into her chair. "Isn't that a bit much to ask?"

"Yes, it is. But it's my right to hope, isn't it?"

Khaled looked at his watch.

"I suppose we could talk about this all night long. It's getting late, and I have a long drive ahead of me. But before I leave, I have a nice surprise for you. Consider it your birthday gift."

"What surprise?"

"We are all going to Palestine this summer."

"How come?" Jamila asked, now leaning forward and confused by the news. "What happened? How come you didn't tell me about it before now?"

"Nothing happened. I just miss my family. My father is getting old. God only knows how long he's going to be with us."

"I don't understand. I'm planning to take summer classes."

"Why don't you do that next summer? This summer you can practice your Arabic. Taking university courses in languages isn't enough," Khaled suggested, as he dropped his napkin on the table ready to leave. "Also, I promised my mother that we would all come this summer."

"That's funny. And you never thought of mentioning it to me?"

"Jamila, please stop arguing. I wanted to surprise you on your birthday. You always loved going to Palestine. Don't you remember? Last summer, I was planning to take you there as a graduation gift, but we couldn't go. So this trip will be both your birthday and graduation gift."

"I really don't feel like going. You can go without me."

"Seriously? My mother and your Aunt Layali would send me back to get you."

Khaled stood up, making it clear he was done talking.

Jamila didn't know what to make of her father's visit and his evasiveness about Ali. She loved and idealized him and hated to think that he wasn't being honest with her. She wondered if this sudden family trip to Palestine was intended to get her away from Ali. She decided not to think about it. *Actually*, she thought, *maybe it'd be better not to know*. At least not now.

The moment Khaled left, Jamila rushed to meet Ali who was in his apartment, anxiously waiting for her. She plopped down on the other end of the couch from him and sat there silently. He moved closer to her and put his hand on her shoulder.

"Please don't be upset, Jamila. He's your dad, and he loves you. Don't obsess about what he and your mother want. The important thing is how you and I feel about each other. That's what really matters."

Jamila did not respond. She was thinking about her father's plan to take her to Palestine. Finally, she said, "Can you believe this. My dad already made plans to take the whole family to Palestine this summer. He did not even bother to ask me if I want to go. But no matter what he thinks or wants, I'm not going."

"What do you mean you're not going? Are you crazy? I wish someone would take me on a trip overseas like that. You've always loved it there. You should definitely go."

"I do love it there. But not with them . . . "

26
BIRZEIT UNIVERSITY

West Bank, Summer 1984

Jamila had been to Palestine several times with her family. When she was younger, she couldn't wait to go again. Her favorite part was spending time with her grandmother, her Aunt Layali, and her cousin Muna. And there were so many other things Jamila loved about being there.

There were the Fridays when her aunts, uncles, and their families came to spend the day at her grandparents' home; the adults spoiling her with endless gifts and cash; and there were all the cousins and their friends with whom she played, went to the movies, and went on long walks to explore the city or to get ice cream, shawarma or falafel sandwiches. She especially cherished the feeling of freedom of not having to tell her parents where she was every minute of the day.

But her absolute favorite was when her father would rent a car to take her and her siblings to explore different parts of Palestine. Sometimes, one of her uncles would drive them to Jerusalem, where they could rent a car with a yellow Israeli license plate and visit Arab cities and towns inside Israel, like Jafa, Haifa, Aka, and Nazareth.

Curious Jamila asked her father, "Why do we have to come

to Jerusalem to rent a car? Can't we rent one in Al-Bireh or use Amo's car?"

"Because we need a car with a yellow license plate in order to go to Yafa or Aka."

"How many different colors are there?"

"Two—yellow for the Israelis and blue for the Palestinians."

"How come? Which is better?"

"It's hard to explain. Maybe we can talk about it later."

Jamila was saddened by stories her father told them about the 1948 Nakba, and by the fact that none of her cousins could join them on these trips because, unlike them, her cousins did not have American passports.

"It's not fair," she would protest.

"I agree with you, Jamila. Unfortunately, there is far too much that is unfair in this holy land."

~

Despite the heavy weight of the Occupation, Jamila always felt more at home in Palestine. This time, however, going there was different. Jamila wasn't excited about being with her parents for a whole month. But with Ali's encouragement and her desire not to escalate tension with her parents, especially her father, she decided to go.

~

When they arrived, the whole extended family and some of the neighbors were at her grandparents' house. Seeing the festive welcome lifted Jamila's spirits. What made her feel even better were all the comments as people welcomed her: "My God, you've grown so tall and elegant"... "Look at these big eyes and dark lashes"... "Your hair is so thick, and what beautiful curls—she looks like her grandmother!" Jamila soaked it all in, and when she looked in the mirror, she swore she could see a better-looking version of herself.

Meanwhile, Khaled, who hadn't been there for four years, was shocked by how much his father had aged. He was fragile and had lost a lot of weight. At the same time, he was surprised by how loving and affectionate his father seemed, especially toward him and his family.

"I guess old age suits my father," Khaled said to his mother. "He is much nicer and more loving than he ever was."

"Khaled, that is not a nice thing to say about your father. He has worked very hard and sacrificed a lot so that all of his children, especially you, could have a good education and be successful. Just look at you and your siblings. Where would you all be without him?"

"That's because of you, Yamma."

"Stop it, Khaled. Don't you ever forget how much he has done for you! Also look how nice he treats Elizabeth, and how much he cherish your children."

But Khaled couldn't escape comparing the way he was talking about his father with the way his daughter often talked about her mother. He wondered how much he may have had to do with that... *What goes around, comes around?* he asked himself.

Having always been close to his sister Layali, Khaled went over to her house needing to talk. The weight of his relationship with his wife, and now with Jamila, was weighing heavily on him.

"What's wrong, Khaled?" Layali asked. "You don't seem to be yourself. Neither do Elizabeth and Jamila."

Khaled was quiet for a long time, his hands resting on his lap, his fingers intertwined, and his eyes fixated on the floor.

"Sister Layali, I don't know where to start. Maybe Yaba was right to be upset that I married Elizabeth. Maybe I should never have gone to the US. Elizabeth and I haven't been getting along lately. We argue a lot, and it has affected the children, especially Jamila. Don't get me wrong, Elizabeth is a good woman, and America is a great country. But it's a lonely place, especially for immigrants and their children. We're often made to feel that we don't belong. Poor Jamila was bullied all throughout her school years and has had a hard time making friends. Even now, at the university, she only has a few close friends. It's hard to believe, but Jamila is much happier when she is here. She loves your daughter. She and Muna are like sisters. It might be good for her to stay here for a year.

"She could go to Birzeit University. If you wouldn't mind, I'd love it if you'd suggest it to her, convince her to stay. She'd be more receptive to the idea if it came from you or from Muna rather than from me or her mother."

Layali listened intently to her brother, observing his hunched shoulders and sad face.

"I'm so sorry, Khaled. I can tell that you and Elizabeth aren't getting along well. I also noticed that Jamila has been subdued and hardly speaks to her mother. Is there something else you're not telling me?"

Khaled insisted that there wasn't. He just wanted some help convincing Jamila to stay.

"I thought you and Jamila were very close. Are you sure you want her to be away from you for a whole year?"

"Yes, we're close. Jamila is a beautiful and smart young woman, although sometimes she can be very stubborn. She's the only one of the children who has a strong sense of her Palestinian identity, and shares my interest in politics," Khaled sighed. "I want her to spend time here because I love her. I want to see her happy. Who knows, maybe she'll fall in love with a young Palestinian and decide to stay."

"Look at you, brother, becoming a real American, talking about your own daughter falling in love."

"I just hope you wouldn't mind having another young woman to look after," Khaled said, half kidding, trying to lighten his dim mood.

Jamila was intrigued by the idea of studying and spending a year in Palestine. She loved being there, especially without her parents. Going to Birzeit University with Muna sounded appealing, but she wasn't sure if she wanted to be away from Ali for a whole year, or if her university would accept the credits she would earn from Birzeit University. When she shared her dilemma with Muna, her cousin told her, "If you really love each other, staying here for a year will only cement your relationship. As far as transfer of credits, we can go ask the registrar office; there are many Palestinians students from the US who come here for a one-year study abroad. I know some of them, we can ask them too."

When Jamila told her father about her concern about credit transfer, he promised that he or Ramsey would talk to her advisor at Michigan State as soon as they got back to the US. Khaled's eagerness to help made her wonder if the idea of her going to Birzeit university was in fact his. So she turned to her cousin, searching for an answer.

"Muna, I want you to be honest with me. Did my dad ask you to convince me to stay?"

"No, no. It was my idea, I swear," Muna insisted. "I want to have a chance to spend time with my favorite cousin. Seeing you once every three or four years is not enough."

"Swear by it. Say Wallah."

"Wallah, Wallah, Wallah."

When Jamila called Ali to find out how he would feel about her staying, he told her, "I'm really going to miss you. But this is an amazing opportunity. I think you should do it, just as long as you don't fall in love with some Palestinian guy."

Relieved to say goodbye to her family, who left four weeks before her school year started, Jamila spent her time between her grandparents and her Aunt Layali. The two young cousins would stay up all night talking and laughing. Jamila insisted on speaking in her broken Arabic, and Muna would correct her. They talked about family gossip, fashion, school, and what they wanted to study. And, of course, they talked about boys, lust, and love.

"Wait until you see all the handsome boys at Birzeit. I'm sure you will soon forget about your Ali."

"No, I won't. No man can be more handsome or kind."

"Poor Jamila, love sure is blind."

Meanwhile, staying without the rest of her family at her grandparents' allowed Jamila to get closer to her grandfather, who, as Khaled noticed, had mellowed a lot in his old age. He would teach Jamila new Arabic words, or play card games with her. He confided to her, "You are smarter than your dad, and much more fun. But don't you ever tell him I said that."

Ramsey talked to Jamila's advisor in East Lansing, and connected her to the registrar office at Birzeit University. With his help, Jamila was able to pick up a few classes taught in English and an Arabic language class with the approval of her university.

Jamila was excited to start the school year with Muna. The two decided to share a room in the dorm. Before long, Jamila met all of Muna's friends and made some of her own, too. In her Arabic class, she met other Palestinian Americans who, like her, were there for a year or more.

Jamila enjoyed her classes and talking to other students, many of whom were interested in meeting her and learning about life in America. She was also amazed by the variety of student activities, many of which centered around Palestinian history and culture. There were poetry and book readings, theater performances, films, and exhibits—all of this, in addition to numerous guest speakers who came from around the globe to express solidarity with the Palestinian people. Jamila was in heaven soaking it all in. She tried to learn as much as she could about Palestine. Once in a while, Muna had to remind her that she also needed to study.

Unlike at home at MSU, on Birzeit's campus there were always student demonstrations protesting the Occupation and its oppressive policies. The first time Jamila saw the Israeli army enter the campus with its heavy machine guns and military vehicles, she was so scared she started to cry. As time went by, she got used to seeing these confrontations. Soon, her fear was replaced by anger. In no time, she started to join the student protests, many of which ended in violent confrontations with the Israeli military. Her grandmother became worried about her increasing political activity and begged her to stop.

"Sometimes students get arrested and injured. But they also get killed by the Israel army. The last thing I want is to see you hurt. Your father would never forgive us if anything happened to you."

"Yamma, let her be, let her be," Layali would say, reminding her mother about Khaled's youth and the price he had paid for defying his father.

"I hate to remember that time," the older woman sighed dejectedly. "But I guess you are right."

It did not take long for Jamila to understand her father's pain and anger about what was going on in his country. As she told Ali in one of her letters,

> *In just these few months, I learned about and experienced the real meaning of words like settlers, ethnic cleansing,*

collective punishment. It gives me more sense of what it's been like for so long for Black people in the States. I guess it's hard to feel what a situation is really like without experiencing it firsthand. Life under the Israeli military occupation is hard and depressing. But I'm totally inspired by the resilience and determination of people here. How much I wish you could be with me.

~

Early one December morning, Muna was lying in bed, warm and cozy under her wool blanket, while her cousin was deep in sleep. The dorm was still quiet, and not many students were up yet. The soft knock at the door startled her.

She got out of bed, threw a robe over her shoulders, and quietly opened the door, trying not to wake Jamila up. Her eyes grew bigger when she saw Ms. Dalia, the dorm supervisor, standing there.

"Ms. Dalia. Why are you here? Did something happen?"

"Good morning, Muna. I'm sorry. Did I wake you up?"

"It doesn't matter. Tell me, what's going on?"

"I'm so sorry, Muna. I hate to bring you bad news. Your mother called. She asked me to tell you. Your grandfather died early this morning. She wants you and Jamila to come home."

"Oh my God. No, no . . . " Muna covered her face with her hands and started to sob.

Ms. Dalia hugged her, and a few students gathered around, wondering what was going on. Ms. Dalia explained, and they all hugged their grieving friend, asking if they could do anything to help.

Muna shook her head. "How am I going to tell Jamila?"

She started to cry again.

Sitting on the bed, the two cousins embraced and cried for a while.

"I cannot believe he is gone. Why now? Just as I started to know him better and love him more. Why now? Why?" Jamila started to cry again.

"I love him too." said Muna. "We should go."

Jamila opened her closet and pulled out a light green sweater.

"You can't wear that for the *Azza,*" Muna said.

"Why?"

"Because we have to dress in black. That's the way it is. Take some clothes with you. Only black. We're going to be there for a few days."

"What should I do? I don't have many black clothes," Jamila said as she leafed through her closet.

"Take what you have, and I'll take all my black clothes. We can share."

The girls hadn't known that their grandfather had been sick, and then he deteriorated rapidly. He died peacefully early that morning, which turned into a sunny, warm December day.

By the time Muna and Jamila arrived home, the burial, often a male-only ceremony, which includes washing and taking the body to the cemetery, had already been completed. As a Muslim tradition dictates, "the dignity of the dead is in their fast burial."

Layali met her daughter and niece as they entered the house. After exchanging tearful hugs, she handed them two white scarves to cover their hair. "Go first and see your grandmother. She is in the family room. Then find a couple of seats and just sit."

Jamila, who was not familiar with Palestinian mourning rituals, was shocked by the number of people at her grandparents' home. Dozens of women, all dressed in black, with white scarves, sat on chairs placed next to each other. Her grandmother sat on a larger, more comfortable chair facing the room's entrance. Both granddaughters rushed to her, hugged her, and wept, exchanging unintelligible words. Two women got up, walked over to the grandmother, expressed their sorrow over her loss, and quietly left.

Muna and Jamila sat in the two empty chairs, separated from their grandmother and from each other. The women sat in silence except for words of comfort—"May Allah give you strength, *Allah yerhamo*, may Allah have mercy on him"—expressed now and then. A recital of the Quran could be heard from the salon where the men were seated, as a woman relative passed around a plate of fresh dates and small cups of bitter coffee.

~

The big formal salon was packed with men in dark suits and black ties, including an elder sheik and Khaled's three brothers. Unlike the women, the men were engaged in conversation, mostly about politics and business. Most of the non-immediate relatives stayed only a short time in order to make room for the stream of people who were coming to pay their respects.

In the kitchen, a few women were attending to the large amounts of food that arrived every hour from relatives, neighbors, and business associates. At lunch and dinner time, all visitors who were there were asked to join for a *rahmeh*—mercy—meal. The crowd subsided after three days, only to return on the one week and fortieth-day observances—called *osbooh* and *arbaeen*—with more reciting of the Quran, more food, and more men and women, each knowing which room to go to and when to make room for more mourners.

People were pleasantly surprised when Khaled appeared suddenly in the afternoon of the third day of the *Azza*. He immediately went to see his mother, who was shocked to see her son enter the living room. She cried her heart out as she hugged him. Khaled cried, too.

He greeted the women guests and walked to the salon.

Jamila was delighted to see her father there. She didn't realize how much she had missed him. They both shed tears as they embraced, not knowing if the tears were over the old man's death or their own broken closeness.

With his jet lag and the continuous daily visitors, including his six siblings and their families, Khaled was totally exhausted. But he was not ready to leave without spending time alone with his mother and with his daughter.

"Yamma, I miss you. With so many people coming and going, we haven't had a chance to talk. Could we, please, before you go to sleep?"

"Of course we can. I miss you, too."

Khaled sat at the foot of his mother's bed.

"I can send you money each month," he assured her.

"Your father mellowed a lot in his old age. He even told me once, 'Um Khaled, you have put up with me a lot. After I die, I want to be sure you continue to live comfortably. I made arrangements that the house will be totally yours, and you will have a monthly income.'"

Khaled sat in regretful silence.

"Despite my conflict with Dad, he was a generous man."

"Yes, he was."

They hugged.

"I want to ask you about Jamila. How do you like having her here? How is she doing? Do you think she's happy?"

"Habibti, she is such a sweet girl. I believe she is very happy here. Everyone loves her. You should have seen her with your dad. *Allah yerhamo,* his face was all smiles when he saw her. How much he adored her. He was extremely happy to have her here. And she and Muna love each other, they are like sisters. But when it comes to politics, she's just like you. Sometimes, I worry about her going to demonstrations at the university. It's not the same as when you were active. The Israeli army can be vicious."

"You don't have to worry about her. But she can be stubborn. She does what she wants to do."

"She is definitely your daughter."

27
BACK IN THE USA

When Jamila first arrived, she'd had mixed feelings about accompanying her parents to Palestine. Now, she found herself having a harder time leaving.

She had fallen in love with the country's warmth and hospitality. She relished being with her family and friends, and with other people who looked like her and embraced and loved her. Never before had Jamila been surrounded by so many aunts, uncles, cousins, and friends. The endless goodbyes filled with gifts, hugs, and kisses overwhelmed her and brought a flood of tears every time she said farewell to a friend or a relative.

Before leaving, Jamila bought the largest card she could find and left it under Muna's pillow.

> *Habibti Muna. I feel funny writing this card to you, but there is no other way I can tell you how I feel without crying. I never knew that saying goodbye could be so hard and painful, especially to you, to Sitti, the sweetest woman on earth, and to your mama, Khalto Layali, who's treated me like her own daughter. I really don't know how to thank you for all you've done for me. You are only a few months older, but you treated me so kindly and cared for me as if I were your baby sister. You took me*

under your wing and taught me a lot. Most importantly, you listened to me. I can tell you anything without worrying about how you might react or if you are going to judge me. You have no idea how much I'm going to miss you and our time together, especially when we stayed up all night talking. I have never had such a close relationship with anyone before. Wallah, if it weren't for Ali, I would stay forever. I do belong here. But I left my heart in East Lansing, and so I have to go back. I hope it won't be too long before we see each other again. I've found in you a genuine friend and a loving sister. I know I will be back soon, Inshallah. Please do write to me. I love you so, so much.

~

Sad and tired, Jamila arrived at Detroit Metro Airport after twenty hours of traveling. She was also upset; she'd needed to ask Ali not to come to the airport because she wasn't ready for a confrontation with her parents.

Her father, Ramsey, and Leila were there at the airport to meet her. When she asked about her mother, Khaled told her, "Your mom would have loved to come, but she decided to stay home to get dinner ready. She spent her day in the kitchen cooking and baking."

~

The moment she heard the door open, Elizabeth ran to her daughter, wiping her hands on her flowery apron. "Welcome home, my love, I missed you so much. I'm so glad you're finally here."

Jamila tried to meet her mother with the same warmth and enthusiasm. But despite her sincerest efforts, she could not succeed. Although she was still troubled by her dad's ambiguous response to her relationship with Ali, she was happy to see him. When it came to her mother, she was tormented by her mixed feelings: anger at what she said about Ali, and guilt for not being able to warm up to her, even after being away for ten months. She longed to have with her mother even a small fraction of what Muna had with hers.

~

When dinner was ready, the dining table, which was usually stacked with magazines, newspapers, and unsorted mail, was filled with Jamila's favorite dishes: chicken with carrots and potatoes, lasagna, freshly baked cheesecake, and chocolate chip cookies. Her mother had set the table with china dishes, crystal glasses, expensive silverware, and a tablecloth Jamila had never seen before. The elaborate setting reminded her of the one her mom prepared for her when she wanted to find out if she was dating Ali.

Tension tightened her neck and hunched her shoulders. Suddenly she wasn't hungry anymore. She wished she had stayed in Palestine. Jamila forced herself to eat a little and respond to the endless questions: her father asking about his family and her school, Elizabeth wanting to know what kind of friends she made, Ramsey wanting to know about her experience studying abroad, and Leila wondering what gifts her sister had brought her. After briefly answering all of their questions, she told them, "I'm sorry. I'm tired and jet-lagged. Can I go to bed?"

~

The day after her arrival, the two young lovers had made plans to meet that afternoon at the arboretum in Ann Arbor.

When they spotted each other, they ran to one another, hugged and kissed, cried, and laughed. After a short walk, Jamila said, "I'm tired. I guess my jet lag is catching up with me."

They found a bench in an area that provided some privacy. She laid on the bench with her head resting on his lap. He softly caressed her face.

"My God, I never believed you could die from missing somebody so much, but I almost did," Ali told her.

A gentle relaxation swept her body. She put her hand over his, wanting to savor the sensation of his touch again.

"You know, Ali, if it weren't for you, I would've stayed in Palestine."

"I'm glad you didn't. I'm not ready to chase you all over the world."

Silence prevailed except when they giggled as someone passed by, wondering if they were caught.

"I'm hungry and sleepy," Jamila said after almost an hour.

"You want to go for some food?"

"No, I'd rather stay here. Your lap is comfy. I can eat and sleep when I get home."

"Did your parents say something about us? Do they know you are here with me?"

"Are you crazy? You want me to get in a fight with them the day after I arrive? Be patient. I'm sure I will, sooner or later."

"That might not be a bad thing, especially if it'll make you come to Lansing sooner."

"I don't think I'm ready for a fight, and definitely not now. Anyway, I'm coming in a few days to bring some stuff to my new apartment. Ramsey will come with me. We can go out to eat then."

"I was hoping you'd stay until your classes started."

"Nope. I'll go back to Ann Arbor for two more weeks. Then I'll be back in time for my classes."

~

Elizabeth and Khaled were not happy to learn that Jamila had registered for summer classes and made arrangements with her two girlfriends, Rola and Huda, to share an apartment. When her father protested, telling her that they had missed her and wanted to have her spend the summer with them, she said, "Remember, Dad, I was planning to take classes last summer, but you insisted I go with you to Palestine. You told me I could take them this summer, right?"

During her two-week stay in Ann Arbor, she avoided spending time with her parents just in case they decided to ask about Ali. Two days before Jamila was planning to leave for Lansing, Elizabeth complained bitterly to her husband, "I believe she stayed in touch with Ali while she was away. She might have seen him the day after she got back. She told me she was going for a walk, but she was gone for a long time. I was reluctant to ask."

"Better not to mention it now. Let's keep watching, hoping her year in Palestine made her forget about him. Even better, hopefully Ali has found another girl. You know how young people are now. They can't live without dating someone."

Just then, Ramsey walked into the house for a quick visit. The loud voices of his parents stopped him in his tracks. Hesitantly, he walked closer to the living room as if he wasn't sure he wanted to hear what was going on. His ears perked up when he heard Ali and Jamila's names, and he paused briefly to listen. Then he dashed into the living room, startling both of his parents.

"What's the problem? What are you two arguing about now?"

"You're not eavesdropping, are you?" Elizabeth snapped.

"I didn't have to," he explained calmly. "You were talking so loud the neighbors could hear you. I hope my sisters aren't home."

There was a beat of silence.

"I never knew Jamila was dating Ali. Are you sure she is? For how long?" he asked, wanting to know more.

"Of course, she is. We've known about it since March of last year." Elizabeth said.

"That long? How come no one told me? And why are you so

upset about it? Ali is my best friend. I don't understand the fuss."

No one answered, and as Ramsey began to remember his sister's disappointments with their parents, the dots began to connect.

"I hope him being Black has nothing to do with it."

"Of course not," Khaled raced to explain himself. "We know Ali is a good kid, and we love him. But that doesn't mean Jamila should be dating him... or anyone else. She's still young and needs to focus on her studies."

"For real? Sorry to say it, Dad, but you're not being honest. I think you're lying to me and maybe lying to yourself. Jamila's twenty. When I heard the way you two were talking about it, I couldn't believe my ears. My parents, especially my father, conspiring against his own daughter to end her relationship with someone we've known for years? Someone who's part of our family and who you and Mom claim to love? Really? That's not right. We only love Black people as long as they don't come too close to us? As long as—"

"Ramsey!" screamed Elizabeth. "You're being rude. Stop talking to us this way."

"As long— "

"I said stop!" Elizabeth screamed even louder. "Just... shut... up!"

Ramsey nodded in disappointment and left the room, trying to loosen the tightness in his chest.

~

As he drove his sister and her belongings to Lansing, Ramsey was unusually silent. But his face revealed the anger and sense of betrayal brewing inside him. Jamila, who had always been close to her brother could tell that something bad had happened.

"What's wrong, Brother? You look sad. What's going on?"

"You've been dating Ali for almost a year and a half, and

neither one of you has had the courtesy to tell me? I had to hear it from our parents? You told them, but not me? I'm not only sad, I'm mad. Why would you and Ali hide this from me? Why?"

Jamila didn't see this coming and did not know how to respond. Like a short silent movie, her mind traveled to March the year before, to the time she and her mother had their confrontation about Ali, to her dad driving to Lansing all dressed up to take her to a fancy dinner, and later, all the way to Palestine as a "birthday gift"—all of that to get her away from Ali. She intentionally did not want to tell her brother and had begged Ali not to tell him. She dreaded the slim possibility that Ramsey would react the way Khaled did. She felt she had already lost her father and that their relationship would never be the same. She wasn't ready to now lose Ramsey, a brother she'd been close to since she was born, a brother who always helped her and loved her and who always protected her. But after her father's reaction, she wasn't sure what to expect from Ramsey.

"Jamila, I asked you a question. Why did you hide this from me?" he said turning his head away from the road to look at her.

With no filters or restrictions, Jamila shared all her thoughts and fears with her brother. But when she finally said, "Because I was terrified I would lose you too," the pain gripped her throat, and she could say no more.

As soon as he could find a safe place to park, Ramsey pulled off the road. He hugged his sister and let her cry until she had no more tears left to spill.

"Do you want me to keep going, or shall we stop to get you something to drink?"

They decided to keep going and resumed their drive.

"I don't understand how you could think I would be upset if you dated Ali," he told his sister.

"I am so sorry, Ramsey. I should've known better." She placed a quick kiss on his cheek.

"It's okay," he said. But don't do anything stupid like that again. I'm your brother, and I'll always have your back."

~

In Lansing, Jamila felt happy and free. She loved living in her third-floor, sunny, and freshly painted apartment. Her roommates were kind enough to give her the medium-sized room with a big window overlooking a small yard, a much nicer room than the one she'd had in the dorm. The kitchen, dining area, and living room were all furnished by her roommates.

Unlike what her parents had hoped for, Jamila and Ali's love not only survived the distance but blossomed. They couldn't wait to be back together in the same city. Jamila reflected again on what her cousin Muna had said, "If you really love each other, being physically apart will only cement your relationship." And it did.

During Jamila's year in Palestine, they had exchanged letters and cards almost weekly and had called each other on special occasions. "I wish I could call you more often, but calling long distance is so expensive," Ali would tell her. "But I'm going to make it up to you when you get back. I'm going to call you every day, as many times as you like. Even better, I can talk to you in person. I can hold you, kiss you, and so much more!"

~

Jamila called Ali as soon as she arrived in Lansing. In less than half an hour, he was there in his raggedy khaki shorts and t-shirt, with a large, beautiful flower bouquet in hand. They embraced and laughed so hard while he swept her up and carried her, asking which room was hers. She pointed with the flowers and they entered and closed the door.

They laid on the bed hugging and kissing. They had done this before, but never with such intensity and pleasure. As they started to touch more intimately, Jamila said,

"As much as I want to make love to you, I don't think we should. I'm sorry, I don't think I'm ready."

"It's okay. All I care about right now is having you back. And knowing that you love me."

"Of course I do. Silly Ali. *Inta habibi,*" she said, brushing her fingers over his cheek.

"What did you say?"

Jamila laughed.

"I said, *inta habibi*—You are my love. And you should tell me *inti habibti.*

Ali gazed at her for a moment, sounding it out in his head.

"*Inti habibti,*" he replied.

28
TURNING TWENTY-ONE

1986

Ever since Khaled and Elizabeth found out about their daughter's relationship with Ali, they had become united by one mission: to separate the young lovers.

Khaled never seriously thought about who his daughter would fall in love with or whom she would marry. He had just assumed, or more accurately, had hoped, that Jamila would marry a Palestinian, or at least an Arab. The only consolation Khaled had was his own confidence that he was going to find a way to convince Jamila to leave Ali. Though he was not certain how.

Elizabeth was not as optimistic. She knew her daughter: determined, stubborn, and with a mind of her own. She wanted to get Jamila away from East Lansing and enrolled at a different university; the farther away, the better. The West Coast, Europe, even back to Palestine—all could be options. "If you can convince her, that would be fine with me," Khaled said.

Elizabeth tried to sell her grandiose idea to her daughter by talking endlessly about the envy of other students and the glamour and excitement of the other places she could enjoy. But Jamila wouldn't fall for it. She wasn't even impressed. Elizabeth became so frustrated that she actually thought of cutting off her daughter financially, but Khaled refused.

"Threatening Jamila won't work. Leave it to me. I can convince her."

"Honestly, Khaled, I'm not sure where your soft approach is going to get us. She's been dating him since her first year, and now she's almost twenty-one. The older she gets, the harder it will be to get her to change her mind."

In fact, Khaled wasn't at all sure how to deal with his daughter's "problem." So he wrote in his diary, his trusted companion, whenever he found himself at a loss. Only one thing was clear to him: no matter what happened, he needed to keep communicating with his daughter.

Khaled's trips to East Lansing became more frequent, and so did his requests to Jamila to come home more often for her brother's or sister's birthdays, for holidays, to go to the movies with him, or to join him for a political event, lecture, or conference. With Ali's encouragement, Jamila did respond to most of her father's appeals and tried to be on her best behavior. While father and daughter both avoided talking about Ali, Khaled managed to tell Jamila more than once, "All your mother and I want from you is a promise that you won't make any serious commitment to, or plans for, marriage—until you get your master's degree."

"Inshallah," or "I'll think about it" were the best replies he could get.

For Jamila's twenty-first birthday, Khaled wanted to have a special family dinner at Weber's Restaurant in Ann Arbor. Elizabeth protested.

"You're going to have a nice birthday dinner for her? What kind of conflicting messages are we sending?"

"What other options do we have? You know your daughter. She has a big heart and can be loving, gentle, and rational. But when pushed, she can be hardheaded, and it's frustrating. I don't want to alienate her any further."

Jamila was not that excited about her dad's birthday idea either. She complained to Ali, "This is my third birthday since we've been together, and I've never had the chance to spend any of them with you. I thought we were going to Chicago."

"We are, but it doesn't have to be this Saturday," he said quietly. "You should go ahead and celebrate it with your family and try to really enjoy it. You and I can celebrate on Monday, your actual birthday. Then we'll go to Chicago the following weekend. I've been waiting for this special birthday for two years."

"Me too. Chicago here we come."

~

When Jamila told her three close girlfriends—Pauline, Huda, and Rola—about her plans with Ali, they decided to throw a mini-birthday party for her. They spent the day decorating the apartment, cooking, baking, shopping, and wrapping gifts. The four of them ate and shared a bottle of champagne and lots of wine. They teased Jamila about the anticipated "real sex" while unwrapping gifts of panties, bras, and a nightgown and laughing themselves to tears.

"Thank you, guys. I've been crying from all the grief my parents have been giving me. I'm glad to finally have some happy tears."

"Wait until you experience tears of pleasure. He better be worthy of all the waiting."

At Weber's, the family of five sat at a round table, with Jamila between Leila and Ramsey. All dressed up in a new red dress that accentuated her glowing olive skin, Jamila's hair was pulled back, highlighting her big bright green eyes, thick eyebrows, and cheekbones. Everyone commented on how beautiful she looked.

"You should dress like this all the time," Leila told her.

"No," her father said, "she'll have all the boys chasing her."

Little did they know that this was her dress rehearsal for the real celebration of her birthday with Ali.

"You gave her a nice birthday," Elizabeth told Khaled afterward. "That's not going to make her leave him."

"I am working on it. Just give me some time."

"Khaled, I am giving you only a few more months. If she doesn't leave him by the end of summer, I'm going to handle this myself," Elizabeth said and walked away.

While her parents kept searching for answers and hoping she and Ali would ultimately break up, the young couple were planning not only to go to Chicago to celebrate Jamila's twenty-first birthday, but also to move in together after the school year ended. Ali was about to graduate and had been accepted to Cooley Law School at Michigan State with a full scholarship. They had a lot to celebrate.

Jamila decided not to tell her parents until she had already moved. She wanted to present it to them as a done deal rather than get into fruitless arguments. And she wanted Ali to do the same. She wasn't ready to deal with reactions from two sets of parents.

"My parents have known for a long time that we've been dating," Ali told Jamila. "And we've been to their house so many times. I can't see them being that surprised. But that doesn't mean they're going to like it. Sooner or later, they have to know. And besides, I want you and Ramsey to be with me on my graduation day and join our small family dinner," he said as he brushed her hair away from her face. "I'm going home this weekend, and I prefer just to tell them. I'm sure they're going to ask me about my plans, *what am I doing this summer, am I spending the summer with them,* or *where am I going to live?* I'd rather get it over with now. We know they're not going to like it. I'm their only child, and they have big dreams for me. They'll say living with a White girl is not one of them."

Jamila frowned and stopped him.

"What are you talking about? I'm not a *White girl*. I'm Palestinian. They know that."

"Jamila, please. For them, you're a White girl. Just about any girl who isn't Black is a White girl. But I don't think they're going to be mean about it. Don't worry."

~

But she couldn't help but worry. Anxiously awaiting Ali's return. Jamila could not sit still, study, or have a restful night. *Did he tell them? Were they mad? What happens if they said no*? Her roommate kept telling her to relax and be patient, but she couldn't. When Ali finally came back, Huda and Rana said their hellos and goodbyes. The minute they closed the door behind them, Jamila started to pepper Ali with questions.

"I promise to tell you all about it. How about a hug and something to drink first?"

He pulled up a chair and sat at the kitchen table sipping a beer. Jamila sat facing him, pulling on her curls.

"How long am I supposed to wait before you spit it out? How bad was it?"

"It wasn't too bad."

"What is that supposed to mean?"

"I don't understand you getting so upset about it before you hear me out."

"Please, go ahead and tell me."

Ali was quiet for a while, his face resting between his palms, looking at Jamila. She got up and gave him a kiss on top of his head and went back to her seat.

"Sorry, Ali, I'm just anxious."

"I know . . . Well, just as we expected, they were not thrilled. My father remined me that he'd warned me early on that dating you was not a good idea. How could I expect him to bless living together and with a White girl? He told me 'Soon, you'll be telling me you're with child, and have to get married. You haven't even graduated yet.' He wants me to go to law school and to see me practicing law to help our people. And not screwing up my life."

Ali stopped to take a sip of his beer. Jamila stood up abruptly and started to walk away again.

"I thought you wanted to know how my parents felt."

"I do. But this is making me too nervous."

She sat down again.

"Okay, what did your mother say?" she asked, picking at her nails.

"My mom was also disappointed, but was more accepting than my dad. Just like your parents, she insisted that racially mixed relationships don't work. But when my dad said, 'White people will always be racists, no matter what they pretend to be,' my mother was not okay with that. She said, 'Jamila comes from a good family. Her parents were always fond of Ali.'

"Even so, my mother thinks I should only date Black girls. When I told her that the world has changed, she said, 'Don't be a fool, this country has a long way to go before it changes. Sometimes I wonder if it ever will.' But when I left, she hugged me and said that all she wanted was to see me happy because she loved me."

Jamila was quiet for a few minutes, trying to digest everything she'd just heard. Lines appeared on her forehead, and her dark, thick eyebrows furrowed, almost touching.

"What's the matter? It wasn't all bad," he said, looking up at her.

"I'm just tired of it. Why is everyone giving us a hard time?" Jamila said, getting up again. Ali reached for her hand.

"Come here, *habib... habib...*"

"Ti... habibti," she coached firmly.

He pulled her toward him, sat her on his lap, and they embraced.

"I'm sure our parents will come around. Most people don't like mixed marriages. They just don't," he said with a sigh.

After Ali left, Jamila decided she needed a shower to calm down. She couldn't stop thinking about Ali's parents' reaction. *What if they're not kind to me? Or if they say something mean? I'll be so upset that I might say something stupid that I regret later. I don't want to spoil Ali's graduation.*

When she later shared her thoughts with Ali, he hugged her and reassured her.

"Come on, Jamila, my parents have always been welcoming and kind to you. So why would they change now?"

"Because now we're planning to move in together. That's why."

29
MOVING IN WITH ALI

Khaled was surprised to see his wife still up. She was sitting on the brown leather sofa staring out the window with a glass of wine resting in her hand. She turned her head and glanced at him for a quick second, then looked away. The dim light did not allow him to see the expression on her face. When Khaled asked her if everything was okay she started sobbing. Khaled hurried over to her.

"What's wrong, Elizabeth? Why are you crying now? Did anything happen to the kids? Did someone get hurt?"

Without replying, she started to cry more intensely.

"Elizabeth, tell me what happened."

"She moved in with Ali."

Khaled stood there, almost frozen.

"I cannot believe this." Elizabeth continued in a low voice shaking her head. "She is going to do exactly what I did. End up marrying him. I cannot let her repeat my mistake."

She got up and went to the kitchen.

Khaled was unsettled by his wife's sadness and disturbed by hearing her refer to their marriage as a mistake. He followed her into the kitchen, stood behind her, and hugged her.

"Our marriage was not a mistake," he whispered to her.

Then he poured himself a generous glass of whiskey, and together they walked back to the living room.

"This is where your understanding approach has gotten us . . ."

"Please, Elizabeth, not now."

They sat quietly, sipping their drinks, as if not knowing what more to say. Once done with her wine, Elizabeth stood up.

"I'm tired. I'm going to bed," she said and walked away.

How could Jamila do this to us? Khaled wondered. *Why would she move in with him? Is it possible that she's pregnant? Is that what Elizabeth meant by saying she can't repeat our mistake? Could she be planning to marry Ali without telling us?*

Khaled thought back to the time when Elizabeth got pregnant, and how they didn't dare live together until they were married. He knew the world had changed, not only in the States but even back home. Even so, having his daughter date Ali was bad enough, but now she'd moved in with him. He wondered what he or Elizabeth might have done to make her challenge them in such a cruel way. Could they have handled the situation differently? He had raised her to be independent and expected her to start dating in college. But moving in with someone?

~

For about a week, Khaled kept pretty much to himself. He went to work, ate dinner with Elizabeth and Leila, chatted briefly with them, then took refuge in his study and in his diary, exploring his options.

Finally, he decided to talk to his daughter. He called to tell her he wanted to come to East Lansing to take her out to dinner.

"You know that Ali and I moved in together, don't you?" Jamila asked.

"Yes, I do."

That was all Khaled said. He didn't want to talk about this more over the phone.

"So, you're okay with that? You still want to see me?"

"If by okay, you mean I like what you are doing, the answer is no, I don't. You and I need to sit down and discuss this."

"It depends on what you mean by discussing. If you want to ask me to stop seeing Ali or to move out, please don't come. I love him and I want to be with him. You sent me all the way to Palestine for a whole year hoping I'd forget him. Well, that didn't happen. Are you about to send me back for a few more years, or even better, send me to the moon so I stop loving him? I'm sorry, Dad, that won't work either. I'm not interested in arguing with you or Mom. I love you both, but you have to respect my choices."

She sounded firm, but by the time she spoke her mind, her hands were shaking and her mouth was so dry it almost hurt.

"Jamila," Khaled yelled. "You want us to listen to you, to respect your choices, while you don't think you have to listen to your parents?!"

He slammed the phone down so hard that he almost broke it.

I don't want her to live with any man without being married. What's with this generation? What am I going to tell my family, my friends—that my single daughter is living with a man?

~

Despite his best efforts, things were getting worse. Khaled had to find a way to at least get Jamila to move back to the apartment she shared with her girlfriends, or to anyplace other than with Ali. After pages of ideas and plots, he finally thought he figured it out.

"Hello, Ali. I hope I'm not disturbing you. Do you have a minute?"

Jamila could hear him.

"Is that my dad? What does he want now?"

Ali covered the phone with his hand.

"Please, wait, Jamila."

"Ali, are you there?"

"Yes . . . yes, Mr. Nasser. I do have time. Is everything okay?"

"No. You know it's not . . . Listen to me, Ali, I want to talk to you as I would talk to my own son. I hope you know how much Elizabeth and I love you. So do Ramsey and Leila."

"I love you too. You are like a second family to me. I will always cherish that."

Ali looked at Jamila, puzzled.

"I'm calling to ask you for a favor. Frankly, I don't like you and Jamila living together. This is not the way I raised my daughter or your parents raised you. If you really love Jamila, you need to end this relationship. This is not good for either one of you. You're a decent man and I trust you will do the right thing. Let it come from you."

"Excuse me, Mr. Nasser, I'm a bit confused. You know I love Jamila, and she loves me, too. Are you asking me to end my relationship with her? Don't you think you are asking too much?"

Jamila jumped up from her chair.

"Am I hearing this right?"

Ali raised his hand, gesturing for her to be quiet. But she ignored him and came to grab the phone.

"Excuse me, Mr. Nasser. Give me a minute, please."

"Jamila, stop it." Then he returned to Khaled. "I am sorry for the interruption."

"Yes, Ali, this is exactly what I'm asking you to do. To end this relationship now. This will be good for both of you. And yes, I do believe it's better if it comes from you."

"Seriously? Better for whom?" Ali asked, while gesturing to Jamila to keep quiet.

"Trust me, Ali, this relationship is not going to work. I'm talking to you from experience. I'm sure your parents feel the same and that they would rather see you marry a Black girl. Same for me. I want Jamila to marry a Palestinian. Ali, I'm asking you to do the right thing."

"Jamila is living with me because she wants to. If she chooses to leave, I will respect whatever decision she makes. But you can't expect me to tell her to leave or to end my relationship with her just because you asked me to."

"I am sorry to hear you say that. You and Jamila are destroying your future. I love you like a son and this is how you treat me and my family?"

"Mr. Nasser, I've always treated you and your family with love and respect. But right now, I am deeply hurt. I know you don't want me to date Jamila because I'm Black. I know you've always been supportive of Black people. But we actually don't need it. I'm sorry, Mr. Nasser, I don't have anything else to say."

~

When Ali told Jamila more about what her father said, she lost it. She called her father and the minute he said hello, she went on a rant.

"How dare you? How dare you call Ali and ask him to leave me? You have no right. I'm sure you would not do that if I were in love with an Arab, or for that matter with a redneck White man. How come you didn't marry a Palestinian or an Arab or a Muslim woman? Mom didn't marry a White Catholic either. She was pregnant before you two got married. Just because you never talked to us about it doesn't mean Ramsey and I couldn't figure that out. But when it comes to me, I can't love or marry someone I choose, no matter how good he is or how much you claim to love him? How ironic. You're just acting like a hypocrite. Don't talk to me about what's right. I don't believe you anymore. I've been listening to you all my life. I can't believe how stupid I've been. I would appreciate it if you just left me alone."

It was Jamila's turn to slam down the phone.

30
A LETTER FROM MOM

Jamila waited for Ali to leave the apartment. With shaky hands, she stared at the letter for a few minutes, dreading to open it. Reluctantly, she started to read,

August 10, 1986

Dear Jamila,

I never thought I would sit down to write this letter. But I feel I have to. I am hoping you can put our differences aside and read it with an open mind and open heart.

First, I want you to know that I love you more than you could imagine. Having our conflicts and disagreements would never affect my love for you. I'm just terrified that you—my Jamila, my beautiful and smart Jamila—are taking the same path I did and could end up as resentful and sad as I am. You think I don't want you to date or marry Ali because he is Black. Trust me, that is not true. I'm just a mother who knows, deep in my heart, that your relationship with Ali won't work.

When your dad and I started dating neither of us was thinking about marriage. But after two and a half years, I got

pregnant—a fact your father and I decided not to tell you, but I'm sure you've figured it out. Back then, I was not a practicing Christian, but I refused to have an abortion. I just couldn't. It was against the values my parents and my church instilled in me since I was a child. Abortion was not only a sin but also a crime. A murder. Your father, being the caring person he is, insisted that we get married. Looking back, I'm glad I did not have an abortion. I cannot imagine our lives without Ramsey.

When I told my mother about my pregnancy and my plan to marry your dad she became infuriated. She wanted me to go someplace where nobody knew me, to stay there until I delivered, and then give my baby up for adoption. When I refused, she told my father, and he and my mother disowned me and forbade all my siblings to contact or talk to me. You have no idea how hard that was. It broke my heart to be totally disconnected from my family, especially from my sister Mary Ann, and my other younger siblings.

As much as I resented the way my parents treated me, what I resented even more was having my own children grow up without knowing my family. Only God knows how sad I felt when one of you would ask me about my parents or when I saw all the grandparents coming to watch their grandkids at school games or field trips. My heart sank every time one of your friends mentioned spending time with an aunt or an uncle or playing with some cousins. I hated every single holiday that brought families together, Christmas, Thanksgivings and Mother's Day.

While I resented my parents and their cruelty, truth be told, I missed them terribly. I often wondered if I could have saved myself and my family all that pain and loss by listening to my parents. The only thing I don't regret is having you and Ramsey and Leila.

As I said, when I fell in love with your dad, I had no plans to marry him. But love—or maybe it was lust—has no logic. By the time I realized the extent to which our different backgrounds affected our relationship, it was too late. I became a stay-at-home mom with three kids. I never finished college and had no family to rely on. Honestly, Jamila, when I look at myself now, I don't like what I see. I often wonder what happened to the happy, smart, and ambitious Elizabeth I once was. What happened to my plans to be independent, to finish school, and to find a job I liked? How did I allow my life to become centered only around my husband, children, and housework without realizing that I'd turned into a totally different person? One that I don't even like? And now I don't know how to get back to being the person I once was.

Adding to all of this is the fact that no matter how warm and loving your father's family has been, I know that I'm not the wife they had hoped for their son. To them, I'm the reason their son never came back home. I will always be the ajnabiye, *the "foreigner" who doesn't share their culture, language, or religion. And to be honest, they will always be the same to me. I have no doubt that this is going to happen to you and Ali if you stay together. You'll always be aware that his parents would rather he had dated and married a Black girl. For Ali, he'll always be aware that despite our love for him, we did not want him to be our son-in-law. And if you think it was hard for you to be bullied in school because you looked a little different, imagine how bad it's going to be for your racially mixed kids. Ask yourself, is this the life you want for yourself or your children?*

My dear Jamila, I know we are not as close as a mother and daughter should be. Trust me, I've tried many times to change that, and I know you did try too. But I'm your mother. I should have been more caring and attentive, but I did not know how. Please hear me, Jamila. I love you, and I will always love you. I will never ever do to you what my parents did to me. You are my daughter, and this is your home, and you will always be welcome. But I also want you to understand where I'm coming from. I'm a loving mother who is tormented by the idea that my own daughter could end up following the same path I took. How do you expect me to watch you moving in that direction and say nothing? Please don't make the same mistake I did. You have a life ahead of you, don't give it away. It kills me to think that you might do that. Please, Jamila, I am begging you. I've already had enough heartache.

Your loving mother

By the time Jamila read just the first page, a stream of warm tears had found its way down her face. As she read on, she stopped every few moments to clear her vision, sniff her dripping nose, or wipe it with the tail of her shirt. A loud sob would escape her chest.

When she finished, she read and re-read it. Exhausted, she lied down on her bed breathing heavily, only to soon get up to look at the letter, then lie back down again. Finally, she hid the letter and went for a very long walk.

A week later she sent her mother a card.

Dear Mom,

As I read and re-read your letter, a flood of emotions and love toward you came over me. I cried my heart out and felt so sad about all the pain you had to endure. Trust me, Mom, I hear you.

But Ali and I live in different times. No disrespect intended, but it's not the same. I am not you, and Ali isn't Dad. Just because that was your experience doesn't mean it has to be mine.

I love Ali, and I'm not going to leave him. I hope you and Dad can somehow come to understand and accept that.

Love you always,
Jamila

31
STAYING THE COURSE

Summer- Fall 1986

After her phone confrontation with her dad about living with Ali and her short reply to her mother's long, pained letter, Jamila's relationship with her parents deteriorated even further. Khaled and Elizabeth both felt humiliated and defeated by their daughter. Not knowing what more they could do or say, they kept their distance from Jamila and from each other.

Ramsey tried to reason with them, begging them to reach out to Jamila and give up their unreasonable expectations.

"She's a great daughter and sister. Do you really want to lose her?"

"What else do you want me to do?" his mom replied. "I sent her a long letter explaining why it's so hard for us to have her date or, even worse, move in with Ali. Writing that letter was very hard for me. But I wanted her to understand why I think her relationship with Ali won't work. What was her answer? 'Sorry for your pain, but I don't plan to leave him.'"

"For God's sake, Mom, isn't she old enough to love and marry whomever she wants? Isn't that what you and Dad did? Just look at how Leila feels. She shouldn't be dealing with all this fighting."

"I warned Jamila early on. I told her that what she was doing was bad for her and for our whole family. But she's selfish. Look at us all now."

"Mom, I'm tired of arguing," Ramsey sighed. "If you and Dad really love Jamila, you ought to fix this. Go visit her. Tell her she's old enough to make her own decisions and that you respect her choices. Go talk to Dad. And then, talk to Ali. You owe them both an apology."

"You go talk to your father."

~

Anticipating that her parents might cut her off financially. Jamila found a job and got a student loan. Her father sent her a message through Ramsey, telling her he would pay for her tuition, but nothing else; definitely not for an apartment she'd be sharing with Ali.

"Tell him thanks. I don't need his money," Jamila said.

Ramsey tried to make up for things by calling and visiting his sister more often and by assuring her that their parents would come around. He also encouraged her to step up and try to mend her relationship with them.

"You know Dad. He has a lot of pride. You can't expect him to act normal after you yelled at him and told him to leave you alone. You could at least apologize for that."

"I'm not reaching out to him either," Jamila said, feigning disinterest. "I have pride, too."

~

Leila's thirteenth birthday was coming up. To Elizabeth, birthdays, especially her children's, were extra important, more so than holidays. She wanted to have a nice party for her youngest child entering her teenage years.

But Leila, who often begged her parents to stop being mad at Jamila, felt torn about it. She told them, "She is my sister. I love her. I miss her. And I don't want a birthday party unless Jamila comes."

Feeling bad for Leila, Khaled said to her, "You can invite her to your birthday. Your mom and I don't mind her coming."

"No, Dad. You call her."

When Khaled ignored Leila's request, Elizabeth called.

"Not if Dad won't talk to me," Jamila said.

With pressure from his wife and kids, Khaled finally called.

"Hi Jamila. We're having a birthday party for Leila. She'll be happy to see you. I hope you can make it."

There was an uneasy silence.

"Thanks for calling," Jamila finally said. "I will try my best."

But it was an odd welcome. Her parents gave her stiff, cold hugs, and the conversation between them was forced, none of them knowing what to say to each other. Jamila stayed close to Ramsey and Leila, as if seeking their love and protection. She spent the night and left early in the next morning.

The holidays that followed were not much different.

With Ali, things felt more like home. They settled into a routine. Both went to school full time and worked part-time. Ali, who had earned a full scholarship, didn't want her to be the only one working. He also liked having some extra income so Jamila wouldn't feel the pinch of not having her dad's support. They ate dinner together, studied together, and split up the household chores. They also continued to be active politically, Ali with a juvenile defender's office and Jamila with the Palestine student organization.

On weekends they made a point to go out with friends on Saturday nights and take half days on Sunday for themselves. Their conversations often veered toward what they were discovering: about themselves, one another, their multiple worlds—Palestine, the war in Lebanon, Black youth, the Jessie Jackson presidential campaign.

So despite their full schedules, things between Ali and Jamila went smoothly, except for the deep resentment and sadness Jamila felt toward her family. Ali usually sensed what was troubling her on any given day. He'd assure her that her parents loved her and that they would get over their pride soon. Sometimes he would join her in letting off steam about them. They'd improvise names for them and break out laughing, impressed by their own verbal ingenuity.

~

With Jamila's graduation approaching, her parents were not sure how to handle it. Deep down, they were happy that she had completed her studies and not gotten pregnant or married. They were even more delighted when Ramsey told them that Jamila would be graduating with honors and a scholarship to get her master's in education. But their hopes that she would leave Ali were fading, and they could not overcome the humiliation they felt from their daughter's defiance. Happy to be pressured by his wife and kids, Khaled suggested that they all go to the graduation ceremony and have lunch afterward. Ramsey suggested his father invite Ali.

"There is a limit to what I'm willing to do. She should be happy we're still talking to her."

When Ramsey told Ali about his father's attitude and his fear that Jamila wouldn't come if Ali was not invited, Ali said, "Don't worry about it. I will convince her to go. We're having our own party on Saturday. I'm counting on you to join us. Jamila would love it if you brought Leila with you."

Staying on course, almost three years passed in a blink. Jamila finished her master's and immediately landed a teaching job. Ali passed his bar exam and was hired by a community law firm specializing in civil rights. Once settled in their careers, they began to talk about marriage. Jamila wanted to elope and get married in Hawaii.

It's less expensive and less headache," she said. "I can't handle getting caught up in another round of arguments with my parents. When we come back, I will tell them. By then it'll be too late for them to try to convince me not to do it. To be honest with you, at this point, I don't really care. If they bless our marriage, that would be wonderful. If they don't, I'm not going to let them spoil more years of our lives."

"All the more power to you, Jamila. But I'm going to tell my family beforehand."

"I have been dreaming about this day for years," said Ali's mom. "How can you deprive me of it? It's not like I have other kids' weddings to celebrate."

"Jamila doesn't want to tell her parents ahead of time about us getting married. She wants to present it as a done deal. I believe we should respect that."

"What about respect for your parents? I don't get it," said Ali's father, Jerome.

As a compromise, Jamila and Ali agreed to let his parents have a modest reception after they come back, and after Jamila told her parents.

"Jamila, I know that you and your parents don't get along," Ali's mom, Patricia, said, resting a hand on Jamila's shoulder. "But I want to invite them to the reception."

"You can do that, but don't be upset if they don't show up."

When Patricia told her husband that she was going to call Elizabeth to discuss the reception, he said, "Why discuss it? Just tell her this is what we are doing. If they come, that's fine. If not, that's their choice. As long as they don't come with gloomy faces and spoil things for everyone."

"This is not about us. It's about our son. Let's face it, we did not like Ali marrying Jamila either."

~

Ali's mom called Elizabeth. After exchanging pleasantries, she said, "I know that you and your husband are not happy that our children got married. We aren't happy either. But they've been dating for more than six years now, and they clearly love each other. Ali is our only son, and we plan to have a wedding reception for them. Jerome and I would love to have you join us."

"Thank you for the invitation. Let me discuss it with Khaled. I will get back to you soon."

Khaled refused to go, no matter what Elizabeth and Ramsey told him or how many tears Leila shed.

"Our daughter did not even have the courtesy to tell us she was getting married. She and her Ali can go to hell."

Elizabeth called Patricia, thanked her for the invitation, and told her that she, Ramsey, and Leila would be there. She didn't explain why Khaled wasn't going. Patricia didn't ask.

A few weeks later, Ramsey called Jamila.

"Sorry to tell you this, but Dad talked to his mom today. He told her you married a Syrian doctor. He wants to be sure that you don't say otherwise to Grandma or anyone else in his family."

"Tell him to stop giving me orders about what I can do or say."

When Jamila started to fume, Ali hugged her and said, "I thought you weren't going to let him spoil one more day of our lives."

"I did. I guess talk is cheap. Let's go to a movie."

Unlike what their parents predicted, Jamila and Ali built a happy, easygoing marriage. She very much enjoyed elementary school teaching and being with her students, who came from diverse backgrounds. Ali's work on civil rights took him into the heartbeat of different communities. Then, in November 1991, sixteen months after they got married, they had their first child. A boy they named Kareem, who very much resembled his mother, and who they nicknamed Kareem Falasteen.

A year and a half later came Nura, who looked like her father, and who they called their African Queen. Jamila's little sister Leila, who also decided to go to Michigan State, became their built-in babysitter.

Even so, the badly frayed relationship with her parents—especially her dad—never stopped gnawing at her. In spite of all the heartache he had inflicted on her, she missed him, missed the closeness she had once shared with him. It made her yearn to return to Palestine to see her family, her aunt Layali and cousin Muna, and especially her dad's mother, her *Sitti.*

Ali would console her, "I'm not sure when, but one day soon, you will go back to Palestine."

"But I want to go while Sitti is still with us. She is getting old."

"You will. Trust me, you will."

32
BACK TO THE WEST BANK

Summer 2000

Jamila tucked her two kids—Kareem, age eight and Nura, who was seven—in their beds. She kissed them, turned off the lights, and closed their bedroom doors behind her. Slowly and quietly, she walked into the living room.

"I'm conflicted about my decision to go on this trip. I feel guilty leaving them," she told her husband as she sat on the couch next to him, resting her hand on his knee.

"No worries. They're going to be fine," Ali said.

"I know you'll take good care of them. You always do. But I've never left them before."

"You'll only be gone for two weeks. I took time off to be with them for most of the time you're gone. My parents are coming over for one weekend, and Leila is coming the second one. I think the kids will have a great time with all the love and attention. Why are you so concerned?"

"I'm a mother. I can't help it."

"You've been wanting to go to Palestine for so long. It sounds like a great trip. The program seems very exciting, and Nadia will help you if you need anything. It's a perfect opportunity to see your family, especially your grandmother. I know how much you miss her. I'm sure she'll be overjoyed to see you."

Jamila did not respond. She sat there next to her husband, staring at nothing in particular.

"What is it?" he asked.

"Nothing."

"It's not *nothing*."

"I'm just trying to sort out all these conflicting emotions. It's not anything I haven't told you a dozen times before. I'm happy to be taking this trip and I do want to see my family. But I'm also anxious about being with relatives I haven't seen since my second year of college. So much has happened since then, and I'm not sure what I should share with them. I don't want my dad to be mad at me."

"Your dad will be mad no matter what you do. So, what if they don't like you taking this trip or visiting family? They're your family, too. Do what you want. You're strong."

"I'm tired of trying to be strong."

"Jamila, I'm sure you will figure things out. It's getting late. You must be tired. You have a long trip ahead of you. Let's go to bed."

Nadia, settling into her hotel room in Jerusalem, was started by a soft knock on her door. Leading a Witness for Peace delegation of a dozen people from the US, she was deep into writing her notes about their trip so far and had lost track of time. She searched for her watch—it was past eleven PM. Her damp hair was wrapped with an old, thin, striped towel, and her long white cotton nightdress was wrinkled. She didn't feel like she was in a condition to see anyone this time of night.

Putting her notebook down on her bed, Nadia took off her reading glasses, but kept them in her hand as she cautiously walked to the door.

"Who is it?" she asked, almost whispering as if fearing to wake up other hotel guests.

"It's me, Jamila. Can I come in?"

Nadia slowly opened the door.

"Of course, come in."

Seeing Jamila's red face and puffy eyes, Nadia wrapped one arm around her shoulder as she closed the door. Jamila wished Nadia would embrace her and hold her tight.

"What's wrong? Are you sick?" Nadia asked, gently placing her palm on Jamila's forehead.

"No, Nadia. I'm not sick. Maybe I'm just too worried. Can I sit down for a few minutes?"

"Of course."

She removed a bunch of clothes from one of the two chairs in the barren room.

"Would you like something to drink? How about some yansoon tea? It's calming. It will help you sleep. I can call the kitchen."

~

The two women sipped their tea in silence except for the occasional sound of a passing car. Jamila looked out the large window staring at the beautiful lit Dome of the Rock, not knowing exactly how to ask Nadia for what she came for.

Jamila had met her only once when Nadia, who lived in San Francisco, visited East Lansing to give a talk about the work of Witness for Peace. Jamila was so impressed that she invited Nadia for dinner and became a member. With two young kids and a full-time job, Jamila had not been involved the way she'd been during her university years. Meeting Nadia renewed her energy and her desire to be active again. Now, a year later, Jamila found herself part of this delegation. The longer the silence lasted, the more embarrassed she felt.

"I came to ask a big favor," she finally said. "I hope you can help me."

"Of course, I'll help you. What is it? What happened?" Nadia asked.

"I'm going to Al-Bireh tomorrow to visit my grandmother. I haven't seen her or any of my father's family for over fourteen years. I'm scared to go alone and nervous about getting there. I know I'm asking for too much, but I would really appreciate it if you would come with me."

Jamila felt relieved, as she had been thinking of asking Nadia this since they arrived in Jerusalem a week before.

"Is that it?" Nadia asked, squinting her eyes and hiding a smile. "There's nothing scary about going to Al-Bireh. At the most, it's fifteen miles away. Abu Kamal can secure a taxi and a reliable driver to take you and bring you back. If that's too expensive, I'm sure there is public transportation. It might not be direct, and it'll probably take much longer."

Abu Kamal, the owner of the Mount of Olives Hotel, where the delegation was staying, was a very kind man. He had American citizenship and used to like with his wife and four children in Michigan. When Israel occupied and annexed East Jerusalem after the 1967 war, he immediately returned to Jerusalem. He was afraid that the Israeli government would use his absence as an excuse to confiscate his hotel and other properties.

"What about the checkpoint outside Jerusalem?" Jamila asked. "I was told the soldiers there are really mean."

"Don't worry about it. I doubt they'll bother you. You have an American passport."

"We'll take a taxi. I don't care how much it costs. We'll come back the same day. Please, Nadia... please come with me. I can't do this alone."

"But we have two free days. After all these years, don't you want to be alone with your family and maybe spend the night?"

"No, no... I don't want to sleep there. I don't know how else to explain it to you. I'm afraid I won't be able to do it alone."

Nadia got up from her chair and gave Jamila a long hug.

"Are you all right? What's going on? Is all this really fear about going to Al-Bireh to see your family?"

"I don't know where to start. I'm caught in a lie my father told his family. I feel damned if I keep his lie going and damned if I tell the truth."

"What do you mean?"

"Well, my parents and I hardly speak to each other. They both were upset because I married an African American man. My dad lied to his family, telling them I was married to a Syrian doctor. I'm not sure how to handle this without creating more drama. I'm proud of my husband, and I love him dearly. It's my father I'm ashamed of, and I refuse to go along with his lie. But if I tell the truth, my grandmother will be hurt that her son has been lying to her all these years, and my dad will be mad at me for talking about it. And I'm not sure how my grandmother might react to the fact that I am married to an African American. I'm hoping if you come with me, the conversation will not be as personal, and I can be saved from having to lie or tell my grandmother the truth."

"I am sorry, Jamila. That's a lot for you to deal with."

"It is a lot. I would be forever grateful if you would come with me. I know I'm asking for too much, but please at least consider it."

"I promise I will. You go ahead and have a good night's sleep. We'll talk tomorrow. It's getting late. Both of us need to go to bed."

Jamila walked the dark, narrow hallway to her room, exhausted but relieved that she had finally asked. Feeling the calming effect of the yansoon tea, she went immediately to bed, clinging to Nadia's promise.

At breakfast, Jamila sat next to Nadia and whispered in her ear, "Are you coming with me? Please."

"Yes, I will."

Nadia, who had led many delegations to the area before, was familiar with life under Occupation there. She had asked Abu Kamal to arrange for a taxi with a yellow license plate so they wouldn't be delayed at the two Israeli checkpoints, but they were. The fifteen-mile trip from East Jerusalem to Al-Bireh took them almost two hours. With their Arabic names and looks, neither the Israeli yellow license plates nor their American passports were of much help.

The longer they had to wait at the checkpoints, the more anxious Jamila became. She had not been to the West Bank for many years, and being surrounded by Israeli soldiers with huge machine guns added to her fears. She kept asking Nadia, "Do you think they will let us go through? Why is it taking so long?" They watched as soldiers made Palestinian men get out of their cars and stand facing the wall.

"They want to make people's lives absolutely miserable so they will leave, or in our case, never come back, even for a visit."

"My grandmother is waiting. She's going to be worried. I told her we'd be arriving around 10 PM. It never took us this long before."

"You can spend the night if you want, and I can go back to Jerusalem by myself."

"I know, but I prefer to go back with you."

Other than at the checkpoints, Jamila was silent for the rest of the way, gazing out of the window while biting her nails or pulling on the curls of her hair.

"Are you okay?" asked Nadia.

"I guess I'm as okay as I can be."

"You seem so quiet."

"I'm just thinking. I miss this land. I miss my family."

33
A GENEROUS WELCOME

Jamila and Nadia arrived at her grandmother's home around eleven-thirty in the morning. The large front yard was packed with people—men, women, children, including toddlers—to welcome Jamila, who couldn't recognize most of them. Then, scanning the crowd, she spotted her Aunt Layali dashing from the house, yelling, "She's here, she's here!" Aunt and niece locked in a long embrace.

"Habibti Jamila, how much did I miss you!"

Uncle Majed also walked hurriedly toward Jamila and hugged her tightly, kissing the top of her head.

"Welcome home. My God, you've grown to be a beautiful young woman. It's about time you visited us."

"You're right, Uncle, it's been too long," Jamila said, hugging him back. "I'm so happy to finally be here. I missed you, too. This is Nadia, my friend from the US. We are traveling together."

After Nadia was given a warm welcome, Jamila asked her Aunt Layali, "Where is my cousin Muna?"

"She went to Turkey for a vacation. She is going to be so upset that she missed you. Had she known you were coming, she would have stayed," Layali said.

"I'm so sorry to miss her. And where is my Sitti?"

"She is inside waiting for you. She's been waiting since dawn."

"We were delayed at the checkpoints. I didn't realize it was going to take us that long."

"Those bastards. They can't help themselves but make our lives more miserable. Come on, let us go see your grandmother," Layali said, grabbing her niece's hand and leading the way.

~

Jamila entered the large living room. Her grandmother, like an ancient queen who had witnessed a century of turbulence, sat on a couch facing the entrance. Her long braids rested on her large bosom. A red silk shawl was placed next to her knees. The bright light penetrated the widows, illuminating the old woman's silvery hair, blurry eyes, and deep facial lines.

"*Mashallah . . . mashallah*. Look at you. You have grown so much. You are so beautiful," said her grandmother as she struggled to get to her feet.

"Sitti, please don't get up," Jamila ran toward her and sat down next to her on the couch. "Sitti, Sitti. I missed you so much."

Her grandmother cupped Jamila's face in her two hands.

"Jamila, habibti, I missed you, too. Every day, I pray to Allah to keep me on this earth a bit longer . . . I beg Him, 'Please don't take me until I see her.' I ask him every time I kneel to pray."

"Sitti, please don't say this."

"*Ya binti ya habibti,* no one lives forever. Now tell me your news. I want to hear it all. How are you? Your dad tells me you got your university degree before you got married, and you already have two children. *Mabrook, ya binti, mabrook*. Your parents have been here a few times—twice with Leila and once with Ramsey. I was glad to see them, but it's not the same without you. How come you don't visit us anymore?"

"I'm sorry, Sitti. I should visit you more often. But with a job and young children, it's hard to travel."

"What kind of a job do you have? Your husband is a doctor. You don't have to work, do you?"

"No, I don't. But I went to the university for six years, and I have a master's degree in education. I should work, don't you think?"

"So, what kind of a job do you have?"

"I'm a school teacher. I love teaching kids, and I love my students. And with a teaching job, my kids and I have the same schedule. So I spend a lot of time with them."

"I guess you're right. The world has changed. Not like when I was young," her grandmother said with a soft smile. "As long as you're happy, that's what matters."

"Yes, Sitti, I am. I have a wonderful husband and kids and work I like."

"I'm so glad to hear it. But before you were married, you used to send me letters and pictures. You would call me on the *Eids*, all the holidays. Since you got married, I hardly hear from you. It's as if you forgot you have a family here. I wish you had brought your husband and kids with you now. I want to meet them. I'm getting old, and I want to see them before I meet my *rabbi.*"

"Sitti, you know how much I love you and how much I wanted to come. Inshallah, we will all come visit soon."

Not wanting this conversation to go any deeper, Jamila looked over at Nadia.

"I'm so sorry. I haven't seen my grandmother for a long time. Come sit closer with us. Sitti, my friend Nadia, is also from America. We are traveling together. With all the checkpoints and Israeli soldiers, I was afraid to come here by myself. She was kind enough to come with me."

"*Ahlan wa Sahlan*. Come here, sit closer. Glad to meet you. Thank you for coming with Jamila. *Inti Falastinia? Sah? Enti bint meen?*"

"Yes, I'm Palestinian, from Al-Lod. My family left in '48.

I grew up in Jordan, and now I live in California."

"May Allah never forgive the ones who disrupted our lives, stole our country, and scattered us all over the world," said her grandmother. Then she turned her attention back to Jamila.

"You never even sent me pictures of your husband and children. How old are the young ones now?"

"Kareem is eight, and Nura is seven."

"Arabic names, good for you, Jamila! How come you never sent us pictures? I hope you brought us some."

"I did, I did."

Jamila went through her purse and then her wallet but could find only one picture.

"I am sorry, Sitti, I can't find the pictures. I must have left them at the hotel. I just have this one of Kareem."

Jamila gave the small picture to her grandmother.

"*Mashallah... mashallah,* he is so handsome, just like Khaled."

The picture was passed from one hand to the next.

"*Ism Allah,* in God's name he is so beautiful, so handsome."

"He looks like his grandfather."

"No, not really, he looks like his mother."

"Too bad you did not bring a picture of your daughter. Does she look like her brother? Who does she look like?"

"It's time to eat," interrupted Layali. "It's almost two o'clock."

~

Relieved that the conversation about her family had come to an end, Jamila helped her grandmother to the dining room, where she took her seat at the head of the table. She insisted that Jamila and Nadia sit on each side of her.

About fifteen people managed to squeeze around the long table, which seemed to be packed with every dish the Arabs had ever invented. There was enough to feed the thirty-some people who were there for a whole week. Two additional tables were set up in the other parts of the house to accommodate the rest of the guests.

Pushing food on Jamila and Nadia, Um Khaled asked her son Majed to look after the rest of the people around the table, making sure everyone was well-fed. She also asked her daughter Layali to be sure that people at the other two tables had enough to eat. Once everyone was stuffed, Um Khaled suggested they have dessert and tea in the living room where she could be more comfortable.

~

After the freshly baked *knafeh* dessert and a variety of summer fruits—along with coffee and tea—were served, many guests said their goodbyes. Once the room quieted, her grandmother turned to Jamila.

"Habibti, I haven't seen you in so many years. Only God knows how long I'm going to live or if I will see you again. Please call the taxi driver and ask him not to come. It doesn't make sense that you came all the way from America to spend only a few hours with your family, with your grandmother. With all of these people around, I haven't had a chance to talk to you."

Then she turned to Nadia.

"Habibti, this is your home. You can stay with us tonight. We have plenty of room."

"Thank you, but I have to go back. Jamila can stay if she wants."

"Sitti, we really can't. Nadia is leading our delegation, and she needs to go back, and I shouldn't let her go by herself. Not after she took the time to come with me."

"If you can't stay now, why don't you come back for a few days before you leave for the States?"

"I promise you, I'll try my best. Let me call my husband to see if he can take care of the kids for a few more days."

"Now that's settled, let's call your father."

"We don't need to call him now. Sitti, I'm here to see you. I can call him from the hotel."

"But I miss him. I'm sure he will be happy to hear from both of us."

Jamila panicked.

"Sitti, please don't. With the time difference, he will be at work. I will call him tomorrow."

Not paying attention to what Jamila was telling her, she dialed her son's number.

"Guess who's here? Jamila, I'm so happy to see her. Yes, yes, she is here. She came with her friend Nadia . . . no, she does not want to spend the night . . . here, you can talk to her."

She handed the phone to her granddaughter.

Silence.

Jamila's face reddened.

"What's wrong, Jamila?"

"Nothing. I think we got disconnected."

Um Khaled pointed to Layali to come closer, then whispered in her ear.

"I need to talk to Jamila alone. Take everyone and go sit in the guest room."

Then she turned to Nadia.

"Habibti, I need to talk to Jamila alone before she leaves. I hope you don't mind. It won't be long. Our home is yours—you can have a nap if you like or a cup of coffee with Layali."

Nadia looked at Jamila as if asking her what to do.

"I guess my Sitti wants to talk to me in private."

"That's fine. After all the food I ate, I think a long walk would do me some good. I'll be back before the taxi comes."

34
TALKING WITH SITTI

As the commotion of the day came to its end, an uneasy silence hovered over the emptied room. The quietness stirred Jamila with dread, wondering what would come next in her never-ending family drama. Although deep down she knew no harm could come from this gentle old soul, her grandmother, she was still afraid of the unknown.

When Um Khaled finally spoke, her voice was soft and pleading.

"*Ya binti, ya habibti,* talk to me. What's going on, tell me? Is your father sick? Your mother? How are Ramsey and Leila?"

With a wobbly voice, and without looking at her grandmother, Jamila insisted that nothing was going on. It was just that the phone was disconnected. Everyone was fine.

"Please stop saying everything's fine," Um Khaled replied. "You and your father are keeping something from me. Something happened a few years ago, but no one wants to talk about it. I could tell from the first time your parents and brother and sister visited without you. I shouldn't die not knowing the truth."

Um Khaled's voice gave out on her.

Jamila stared at her grandmother. It pained her to see her sniffling and wiping away tears with her hands. Jamila reached out to the coffee table, grabbed a few tissues, handed her one, and wiped her own tears with the other.

"I'm so sorry, Sitti. Please don't cry. I'll do anything you want."

"All I want is to know the truth. Is that too much to ask?"

"Okay. If you want to know, I'll tell you. But you'll wish you never asked."

"The truth can't hurt more than not knowing. So whatever it is, let it out. I want to know everything."

Jamila started talking, but then choked on her words. They wouldn't come out. She teared up.

"*Ya binti*, go ahead and cry."

As if she'd needed permission from her, the years of bottled-up pain came pouring out. Sitti remained silent, letting her cry until she quieted down.

"I want to hear it all, no matter what it is."

Jamila paused.

"My dad has been lying to you and to his whole family. Even to Aunt Layali."

"Lying about what?"

Sensing the disappointment in her grandmother's face and voice, Jamila did not respond.

"About what? Lying about what?"

"About his life, his marriage," Jamila said quietly. "Lying about me."

"What are you saying? I'm not understanding."

"Honestly, I'm not sure where to start. It's been years now. I don't want to hurt you. I don't want you to be mad at me or my father. You are too kind. You don't deserve this."

"Spell it out. I need to hear it. All of it," she insisted firmly. Clearly, Sitti was not going to let go until she got an answer.

"My parents are not... happy together. They argue all the time. Mom's parents wouldn't talk to her for almost thirteen years because she married a Palestinian, a Muslim. My dad lied to you about me. I'm not married to a Syrian doctor. That's why I haven't been coming to visit you. That's why I don't call or write. Because I couldn't lie to you."

"Are you married or not? Why would Khaled tell us you are? Did you get a divorce? What you're saying doesn't make sense."

"Yes, I am married. But not to an Arab. Or a doctor."

Jamila started to cry again.

"Why are you crying? Who are you married to?"

"I'm married to a man named Ali. My parents are so upset. We hardly speak or see each other."

Um Khaled was silent for a long while. She stared at her hands resting on her lap. Lost in thought, she whispered to herself, "Khaled, *Allah Yesamhak,* may God forgive you. I can't believe this."

"I can't hear you, Sitti. What are you saying?"

Finally, Um Khaled looked up at Jamila.

"Tell me more about your husband. You said his name is Ali?"

"Yes, Ali."

"It's a nice name. It's the name of Prophet Mohammad's cousin. He must be a Muslim." Um Khaled said gently.

"Yes, he is."

"Then what makes your parents so upset about him? There must be a good reason.

"Your father loves you so much, you were always his favorite. Why would he lie to us and tell us you married someone else?"

"*Wallah,* I swear I'm telling you the truth. I was as surprised as you are," Jamila said with a weak laugh. "Ali is my brother Ramsey's best friend. My parents have known him for years. They always loved him and thought he was a great influence on my brother. But they didn't want me to marry him."

"Why? They must have their reasons."

"I think it's because he's Black, although they deny it. They insisted that mixed marriages don't work. That I shouldn't make the same mistakes they did. But I don't believe them. Why else would my dad lie to you? Why didn't he tell you that I'm married to Ali?" Jamila looked at her grandmother and started crying again.

"Come here, Jamila," Um Khaled said, patting the spot beside her on the couch.

Jamila stared at her grandmother, bewildered, as if not knowing how to respond. Um Khaled waited until Jamila slowly got up from her chair, came over, and sat down on the edge of the couch.

"Come closer. Move here."

Once Jamila's body was almost touching hers, the old woman wrapped her arm around her granddaughter and hugged her close. Jamila rested her head on Sitti's chest and started to cry even harder.

"No more tears."

"My dad is going to be so mad at me because I told you the truth."

"I'm the one who should be mad. How could my own son lie to me about who you are married to? How could he tell me that you're married to a Syrian doctor? As if all doctors are good men or good husbands! Did he forget how disappointed and surprised we were when he married your mother? We didn't see it coming, not even Layali, who's very close to him. Khaled never mentioned anything about it until he was already married, and expecting a child. Was I upset? Of course I was. But what was I supposed to do? He is my son, my own flesh and blood, and I love him. But your grandfather was livid. He sent Khaled a telegram telling him he was no longer his son and that he never wanted to see him or talk to him again. But I kept after my husband until he finally gave in and made peace with Khaled . . . I never expected your father would treat his own children the way his father treated him."

"To be honest, Sitti, I was totally surprised by my parents' reaction. They always treated Ali with affection, like one of the family. And all their lives, they seemed to support Black people. But it was different when it came to their daughter marrying one."

"Habibti, I never thought that Khaled would do something like this... But are you happy with your husband? Do you love him? Does he love you and treat you well? Is he a good father?"

"Yes, Sitti, he loves me and loves the kids—he's taking care of them right now. He's the one who pushed me to come and visit you."

"Does he have an education and a good job? How about his family? Are they good people? Are they nice to you?"

"He's an attorney. A hardworking and honest one who cares about people," Jamila said with a soft smile as she thought of her husband. "He comes from a good family. Ali and Ramsey have been best friends since they were in middle school."

"For God's sake, did Khaled forget that Bilal, a close companion and a friend of Prophet Mohammad, and the first muezzin, calling Muslims to prayer, was Black? His name was Bilal. A slave who converted to Islam. 'Bilal the Unbreakable,' he was called, so strong was his faith. *Ya binti ya Jamila, kul al-nas kheer oh baraka,* all people are good and a blessing. I've lived long enough to know that the most important thing in this life is to have a good husband who listens to you and respects you, who is kind to you and to your children."

Um Khaled took a deep breath while her eyes scanned the room, and her voice became so soft, almost whispering, as if she was afraid someone else will hear her.

"Between you and me, if I'd had a choice, I would never have married your grandfather. He was so much older than me. But that was the way it was. Thankfully, it's different nowadays. What does it matter if your husband is Black? Then she recited a verse from the Quran, "We had created you different nations and different peoples so you can live together peacefully. The best among you are the most pious."

Jamila was dumbfounded by her grandmother's response.

All these years she'd been afraid to visit or even contact her. She felt she had to live her father's lie.

"Sitti, how did you become so understanding? You are so loving, so much more open-minded than my own dad, who went to one of the best schools in America."

"No one can deny education is important for everyone, *ya binti.* But sometimes, there's no better school than life. That is the truth," Um Khaled said, with a loving soft voice. "I never went to school beyond sixth grade. But you don't have to go to school to know right from wrong, to want for others what you want for yourself, to be kind. When I married your grandfather, he was forty, and I was only sixteen. I could have been his daughter. He went to America for almost twenty years. After making money there, he came back and started his own business. My parents thought he would give me a good life. That was the way things were then. There were so many rules and traditions that don't make sense to me anymore. Don't get me wrong, Abu Khaled was a hardworking man, a good provider, and generous, and he wanted the best for his children. Though we shouldn't speak ill of the dead, *Allah yerhamo,* he was not a very kind man. He was stubborn and things always had to be his way. And women were supposed to listen to their husbands. It took me years before I could stand up to him and say no. It started when Khaled was a teenager, and his father and he did not see eye to eye. I wanted to protect my son from his father's rage. My husband was hard on all the kids, especially the boys. But as he aged, he softened a bit. That's why I'm so disappointed by Khaled. He should know better."

Jamila felt that the heavy weight she had been carrying since her first year of college had finally been lifted. She hugged her grandmother and showered her face with kisses, then started to cry again.

"Too much, too much sadness. Too many tears," said Sitti, embracing her. "Life is too precious to waste."

35
SITTI'S WAY

Layali, who was eavesdropping behind the door, bolted into the room.

"What's going on? What are all the tears for?"

"It's all my fault," said Um Khaled. "I should have insisted that Khaled go to Beirut or Cairo, to a nearby university where we could visit him, and he could come home on holidays."

Jamila stopped crying and hugged her grandmother.

"Sitti, don't be upset. We will try to come next summer."

"Who knows if I'll still be alive by then."

But Layali persisted.

"I don't understand. Khaled is married. He has a nice wife and beautiful children and grandchildren. Shouldn't you be happy Jamila is here now?"

"I'm mad because Khaled is not happy. His wife and children are not happy," said Um Khaled. "Don't get me wrong, Elizabeth is a good woman, and I love her. Yes, we were upset when Khaled got married, not only because she is not Palestinian or Arab, but also because we knew that once he got married to an American woman, he wouldn't be coming back. I'm still mad at my husband, *Allah yerhamo,* for forcing him to go to America. I'm mad at myself for not being strong enough to defy him and to insist that Khaled go to a nearby University. And I'm upset because I knew he liked this nice girl but . . . "

Jamila's ears perked up.

"What girl, Sitti? What girl?"

"She is married now and has kids and grandkids. *Allah yusturha*, she is beautiful, kind, smart. Comes from a good family. What more could I have asked for in a daughter-in-law? I should have listened to Khaled when he tried to tell me about her.

"But those were different times. We thought no boy or girl should talk to each other, let alone fall in love before marriage. When his father insisted he go to America, we could have let them get engaged, or even get married and go to America together. We had enough money to support them. If we had done that, they would have come back and lived here. Looking back, I'm so sorry. How ignorant I was. Guilt eats me alive every day and night."

"Sitti, how can you say this?" Jamila objected. "If that happened, I wouldn't be here."

"Of course you would. I would also have your parents and your siblings living here. I would know your husband and kids. I don't even know what they look like. What a pity."

Layali came closer and hugged her mother.

"Please, Yamma, stop blaming yourself. We are all here, six of us with our husbands, wives, and children. And we all love you. That's the way God wants it."

"God never wants a mother to be separated from her children."

~

When the moment of leaving arrived Um Khaled, looked at Jamila.

"Promise me you will come back to stay with us for a few days, before going back to America."

"I will . . . I promise I will."

~

A dreadful silence accompanied Jamila and Nadia as they returned to their hotel. The ride back was even longer and more stressful than when they came. Their taxi stood idle for over an hour and a half at the checkpoint, waiting to enter Jerusalem. It was past nine at night when they arrived. Abu Kamal was waiting for them.

"I'm glad you are back. We kept your dinner warm for you."

"Thank you," said Nadia. "Let's wash up first. We'll be back in a few minutes."

The two women climbed up the stairway to the second floor without saying much until they arrived at Nadia's door.

"I'm not hungry, you go ahead and eat," said Jamila. Not wanting to hear her friend's response, she kept walking down the hallway to her room.

The moment Jamila entered her room, she took some painkillers. She crashed on her bed and stared at the ceiling for a long while. Her eyes were burning, and her head felt like it was about to explode. The painkillers were useless. At around half past ten, she heard a quiet knock on her door.

"Jamila, it's me," Nadia said through the door. "I saw that your lights were still on. Are you up? You must be hungry, I brought you a cheese sandwich and *yansoon* tea."

Jamila regretted keeping her lights on. She wanted Nadia to leave her alone. But she couldn't tell her that, not after all the time Nadia had spent with her that day. She opened the door to find her holding a large food tray.

"Oh my God, Jamila. I'm sorry to say it, but you look awful. Was the conversation with your grandmother that bad? I'm worried about you."

Nadia sat down on a chair and gazed at Jamila, waiting.

"Not really. I'm just tired."

"Don't tell me it's nothing. Look at your face."

Jamila sat on her bed hugging her knees and burying her face in her long colorful skirt, the one she'd worn all day.

"I want to be respectful of your privacy, but I'm really worried about you, Jamila. What happened? You've been quiet and even more withdrawn since your conversation with your grandmother. Do you want to talk about it?"

"My grandmother knew we were hiding something from her. She asked me to tell her the truth no matter how bad it was. And I did."

"How did she take it?"

"Of course, she didn't like that my father lied to her. But as far as me being married to an African American man, she was fine. She had no problem with it at all. She even gave me a history lesson with a quotation from the Quran. Honestly, I am so impressed and amazed by her thoughtfulness and wisdom. Believe it or not, she is much more open-minded than my own father."

"I'm not surprised. I've always been in awe of our older women like your grandmother. What she told you should make you happy, not sad."

"You're right. But telling my grandmother the truth brought back lots of sad memories about my parents, especially my dad. We had a special bond. But once he knew I was dating Ali, things between us started to fall apart. I was very disappointed by his reaction. Somehow, it was like I was betraying our own people by not marrying a Palestinian. We got into a few arguments and fights. They never accepted the fact that I love Ali, although we've been together for almost fifteen years. They refuse to see how wonderful of a husband and father he is."

"At least now your grandmother knows the truth and you don't have to worry about it anymore," Nadia said.

"Not really. My dad is going to be furious when he finds out what I told his mom. Anyway, I want to let you know that I won't be going back with you to the States. I promised my grandmother I'd spend a few days with her after our delegation leaves."

"I am glad you did. Try to eat something before you go to sleep. You'll feel better."

~

After the Witness for Peace delegation finished their stay and departed, Jamila returned to her grandmother's house. This time, the visit was more relaxed. Her favorite cousin, Muna, was there with her husband and two children, back from their vacation. Fewer people were there than during her previous visit.

When it was time for Jamila to leave, her grandmother whispered in her ear.

"Everything is going to be all right."

"What do you mean, Sitti?"

"You heard me. Everything is going to be all right. Listen, Jamila, family teaches us to love with all our heart. It teaches us there are ties that can never be broken and they are there for us longer than our lifetime. No matter what we suffer, we will always hold onto one another in our heart, through hell and fire. We can never, ever let misunderstanding or bitterness tear us apart. May God be with you, habibti."

Jamila was silent.

"Thank you, Sitti . . ." she finally said. "You are the absolute best."

~

Jamila leaned back in her seat at the airport and closed her eyes. She had a more than twenty-hour trip ahead of her: four and a half hours from Tel Aviv to Paris, a six hour layover in Charles De Gaulle, an eight-hour flight to New York, and then two more hours of layover before taking the last two-hour flight to Detroit. She felt exhausted and drained.

She missed Ali and the kids and couldn't wait to see them. But what she truly wanted was a break from everything. She wished she could go someplace where she didn't know anyone and no one knew her, a place where she could forget and be alone.

Her dad would be mad she visited his family, and madder if he found out that she told her grandmother the truth . . . the whole truth. She wondered what her Sitti meant saying everything is going to be all right. As she reflected on her trip and what awaited her, especially from her dad, a tempting thought crossed her mind: *What if I don't stay on the plane all the way to Detroit? What if I just stay in Paris, instead . . .*

~

At Detroit Metro Airport, Jamila dragged her large two suitcases behind her, filled with gifts, mostly for her children.

To her complete surprise, her parents were there waiting for her, along with Ramsey, Leila, Ali and the kids.

"What are you all doing here?"

"Welcoming you home," Khaled said, as he hugged his daughter tightly, an embrace that reminded her of times that seemed so long ago. She hung on to him, but refused to allow her tears betray her.

Before she had a chance to hug her kids, her mom rushed to hug her.

"I've missed you, Jamila. I've missed you so much."

"I've missed you too, Mom."

When it was her turn to hug her children, and then her husband, she whispered in Ali's ear, "What is going on? What happened?"

"Ramsey can tell you more. All I know is that your grandmother had a long talk with your dad. Afterward, your dad called me to say that he and your mom wanted to be at the airport to meet you."

Jamila was at a loss for words. She couldn't hold back her tears.

"No more tears, Jamila," Ali said quietly.

She brushed away a tear with her thumb.

"Yes, you are right," she agreed softly. "Like Sitti said, 'No more tears.'"

ACKNOWLEDGMENTS

It has long been a dream of mine to write this novel, a story that has been simmering in my brain and scattered notes for so many years. This is my first novel, and I have shared its themes with so many friends and received nothing but encouragement. Although it is a work of fiction, I have done a lot of research and consulted many people regarding dates, historical events, and personal experiences relevant to its themes. And just like it takes a village to raise a child, it took the support and help of a large number of my friends and colleagues to make my dream of writing it a reality.

First, I would be remiss if I didn't thank my friend, Michel Moushabeck, founder of Interlink Publishing. Thank you, Michel, for your vision, talent, and service to our community. Thank you for understanding our need for a publishing house that is welcoming, and one that provides us with a space where we can narrate our own stories with our own voices. Since Interlink was founded in 1987, you have welcomed hundreds of authors from all walks of life from around the world and provided them with an opportunity to have their voices heard and talents shared with the public. Without Interlink, many great books would never have been published, and thousands of readers would be deprived of enjoying and learning from them. And thank you, Michel, for your courageous stand against the genocidal war in Gaza.

My thanks always to the production team at Interlink: designers Pam Fontes-May and Harrison Williams, and editors Mila Massaki Gomes and Greta Morgenstern, for your insightful suggestions and skilled, dedicated attention, and to editor John Sobhieh Fiscella for advocating for this story with so much love and care, as if the family in it were your own.

~

My heartfelt gratitude goes to my husband, Noel Saleh, who has repeatedly read every single word of this book, spending endless evenings and weekends reading, editing, and brainstorming with me. His thoughtful feedback, patience, and wisdom have been extremely helpful. Many thanks to my dear friend, Evelyn Alsultany, the first person with whom I discussed this novel. Your insight and support were truly invaluable. Thanks to my writer friends, Karen Wolf and Shelley Shanfield, for their continued support throughout my journey of writing this and other books, and to my friend, Therese Jarjoura, for her help in exploring with me different tittles for the book. And thanks to the many friends from the Ann Arbor Writers Group and the Saline Writers Group, who were willing to critique my writing and provide me with invaluable advice.

I want to acknowledge my dear friend, Abdeen Jabara, for taking the time to share his knowledge and personal experience about student life at the University of Michigan, especially the activism during the late 1950s and early 1960s; and Salim Tamari and Ida Odeh who assisted me in finding resources about life in the Palestinian city of Al-Bireh during the first half of the twentieth century.

My gratitude also goes to the many people who were willing to share with me their personal experiences that are relevant to this novel, including religion, campus life, activism, and marriage outside their own culture, ethnicity, race, or religion.

This includes the parents who shared with me the feelings they had around the prospect of losing their children versus accepting their choices. Likewise, I am thankful for the perspectives of their children, who defied their parents to do what they believed to be the right choice. I am keenly aware that for many of them it was painful to recall these experiences, and for that I am forever grateful.

Last but in no way least, how can I but be indebted to my dear friend and copy editor, Greta Anderson Finn, who for over twenty some years has been reading and editing almost all of my writings, regardless of the genre. I know that without her, some of my writings would have never seen the light. Thank you, Greta, for your friendship and support.

Anan Ameri is an activist, educator, and founder of the Arab American National Museum and the Palestine Aid Society of America. Her previous books include the two-volume memoir, *The Scent of Jasmine: Coming of Age in Jerusalem and Damascus* and *The Wandering Palestinian*. She is co-author of *Arab Americans in Metro Detroit: A Pictorial History*. Anan received her doctorate in sociology from Wayne State University in Detroit and is the recipient of numerous awards, including induction into the Michigan Women's Hall of Fame in 2016 and the ACCESS Arab American of the Year Award in 2020.